Beautiful Dreamer

LIZ RYAN

Beautiful Dreamer

Hodder & Stoughton

First published in Great Britain in 2005 by Hodder and Stoughton
A division of Hodder Headline

The right of Liz Ryan to be identified as the Author of
the Work has been asserted by her in accordance with the Copyright,
Designs and Patents Act 1988.

1

A CIP catalogue record for this title is available from the British Library

Hardback ISBN 0 340 82922 2
Trade Paperback 0 340 82923 0

Typeset in Plantin Light by
Phoenix Typesetting, Auldgirth, Dumfriesshire

Printed and bound in Great Britain by
Mackays of Chatham Ltd, Chatham, Kent

Hodder Headline's policy is to use papers that are natural, renewable and recyclable
products and made from wood grown in sustainable forests. The logging and
manufacturing processes are expected to conform to the environmental regulations
of the country of origin

Hodder and Stoughton
A division of Hodder Headline
338 Euston Road
London NW1 3BH

ACKNOWLEDGEMENTS

Writing is traditionally a lonely business, which is why I am so lucky in the wonderful friends who have aided and abetted me for so long: Aidan, Annie, Eithne, Mary, Philip, Rita, Sharon and Terry. For putting up with all the panic, juggling such confusion, laughing off a crisis and seeing sense in the midst of chaos, I can never express enough love or gratitude. Your support, and your smiles, are simply invaluable.

With special thanks to Breda Purdue for her enduring vision and faith.

I

Ciara Lunny was absolutely brilliant at her job, which was being the full-time wife of James Lunny and mother of the Lunny twins, Tara and Michael. On her CV, if she'd ever had to write one, she would have put 'household management executive', resisting the temptation to add 'extremely successful'.

Like father, like son: Michael insisted on being called Mike, just as James insisted on being called Jake, even though Ciara thought 'Jake' made her husband sound more like a lumber-jack or sheep-shearer than a commercial pilot with a considerable degree of seniority. Jake wasn't a captain yet, but he'd waited so long for the promotion that it must surely come soon. All Ciara had to do, she reckoned, was steer a steady course. Just a few more games of golf on his part, a few more nice dinner parties on hers, and it would be in the bag. *Captain* Lunny. It had a reassuring ring to it, just as Jake himself had always had a reassuring ring to him, which was one of the main reasons she had married him. Steady, calm, trustworthy Jake: no surprises there, no nasty shocks or sudden turbulence. He and Ciara had been married for nine-teen years and were still very happy – as well they might be, considering the amount of work that went into the Lunny marriage. Right from the start, the first day she had been old enough to think about it, Ciara had known that marriage would be her priority. Good old-fashioned marriage: as a career option, you couldn't beat it.

She couldn't, anyway, and didn't want to. Other women might rave and rant, rail against the endless demands of the job, the 'captivity' as her neighbour Lee called it, but Ciara enjoyed being what the magazines called a 'homemaker'. And why not? Was there something wrong with making a pleasant, happy home for four people, a sanctuary from the storms that endlessly lashed the outside world? Was it a crime to devote yourself to the raising of two happy, well-balanced children, to the wellbeing of a hard-working man whose job involved a lot of stress and responsibility? Not in Ciara's opinion; on the contrary, it was her very pleasant duty to run their peaceful, attractive home, to cook delicious meals, to drive the children to their various activities in her chunky, trendy four-wheel drive. And to look good, of course, because Jake Lunny's wife had absolutely no excuse for looking anything other than wonderful. With the children ready to embark on their first year at college, there would be more time than ever for visits to the hairdresser, the manicurist, the boutiques and the gym, which was just as well when you were thirty-nine years of age, perilously close to the dreaded, unmentionable forty.

Forty! Sometimes the word tolled like a bell deep in the depths of Ciara's mind, making her flinch as she baked a quiche or plucked a scented air-freshener from Tesco's shelves. Forty was what happened to other people, a kind of dreaded disease that couldn't possibly strike anyone who weighed exactly the same fifty-four kilos as on the day of her marriage, anyone who got her California-blonde streaks done religiously every six weeks. Forty wasn't contagious, it couldn't happen to any woman who wore trendy cargo pants and tiny tank tops, baseball caps and the just-out-of-bed cut.

2

No way. If you discreetly stepped up your aerobics classes from two a week to four, invested in Lancôme's entire range and only ever bought low-cal, low-fat produce, nobody could suspect that forty was even remotely looming on your horizon.

Immobilised in traffic on this windy, annoyingly cloudy morning – was it July or wasn't it? – Ciara frowned briefly as she drove home from her dance class. And then she undid the frown, replacing it with a sunny smile as she remembered her mother's warning: frowning gives you wrinkles. Hah! That came well from a woman who had gone off to live in Marbella, where the sun gave people more wrinkles than a Fortuny curtain. Much as she loved the sun, Ciara never went out in it without a solid wall of SP40, and would sooner boil her children for breakfast than live in it. *Sun!* Mother must be mad.

And poor Dad, dragged off to Marbella as well . . . of course, it was different for men. Wrinkles didn't matter so much if you were a man. In fact one or two small ones gave Jake rather an impressive air of authority, now that he was over forty himself, a milestone he hadn't appeared to mind hitting two years ago. But Ciara wasn't going to pretend she didn't mind – not to him, anyway, since he knew her date of birth and there was nothing she could do about it.

'Are you insane?!' she'd yelped just recently, when he'd suggested she might like a party on the looming date, now only four months distant. 'Throw a party to announce to the whole world that your wife is *forty*?! Over my dead body!'

But she'd thrown a party for him, he pointed out, when it had been his turn. 'Yes! But you're a *man*! I'm a woman and I am going to be thirty-nine for *years*! Until I'm at least *fifty*!'

Laughing, he had let the matter drop, as he always did when he sensed her reluctance to discuss something. On her birthday late next October, he would take her out to a discreet, elegant restaurant, where they would sip champagne and have some oysters and say no more about it. Throw a party, and you might as well put it on the national news: Ciara Lunny is forty, folks, doesn't she look well *for her age*?

Oh, no. There would be no party, no mention of the awful event at all. Fulminating at the very thought, she slid a CD into its slot and let the music distract her – Cuban, salsa, funky. Recently, Jake had started to develop a curious taste for opera, which she refused to share because opera, for God's sake, was so ageing. Opera was for two kinds of people, gays and grannies. She would tolerate it if he wanted it, but she would never listen to it voluntarily. Once, they'd had to attend a real live opera, a corporate event sponsored by his airline, and it had been hideous, made bearable only by the chance to show off her gorgeous new John Rocha outfit. She had been, she knew, one of the chicest, most attractive women in the theatre, and he'd been proud to have her on his arm, so that was all right. But that was as far as opera went, or ever would.

Tapping her hand on the steering wheel, she hummed along to the Cuban music, wondering what to wear to her golf game after lunch. Golf was going to be even less fun than usual, in this windy weather, but you had to play: all the corporate wives did, and she knew she wasn't the only one who secretly hated it. The ones who didn't care about sport, the ones who, like herself, merely used it as a chance to catch up on local gossip, give their Lacoste shirts an airing and work off that chocolate éclair they'd sneaked with their morning coffee. Golf was part of the job definition of wives who drove Range Rovers, shopped at BT, sent their children to private schools and lived in estates like Huxley Wood.

4

Not that Huxley Wood was an *estate*, she corrected herself as she finally turned into it, in the awful suburban sense of the word. No. It was much more than that. It was what the developer had accurately described as 'an oasis of gracious living', encompassing only eighteen widely spaced homes, each one individually designed and landscaped, approached by a cobble-lock driveway, embraced by either a teak deck or a stone-flagged patio with water feature. Some of the houses were bungalow-style, others were duplex, most had conservatories and all were immaculate. All were owned by pilots, or stockbrokers, or politicians, or men who did something terribly complicated in technology. All except Lee Warner's.

Automatically, Ciara scanned Lee's house as she drove up to her own, ready to wave to the American divorcée should there be any sign of her, but there was none, and she felt an irrational twinge of disappointment. How or why she had got friendly with Lee she still didn't really know; all she could say for sure was that Lee was different. Lee was out of the loop, out of the social swim, had no husband or children or 'status' whatsoever. She lived in Huxley Wood, she said, because it was quiet and comfortable and, being near the airport motorway, suited her purpose, which was to sell vast quantities of her hand-made jewellery to as many American boutiques as she could persuade to take it. She sold a great deal of it but – rather aggravatingly – she didn't need the money, because she had got an 'absolutely huge' divorce settlement from her 'first and last' husband, the ill-fated Freddie. This money, which she gleefully called her 'fuck-off' money, enabled her to live exactly as she wished, doing what she liked and, more importantly, not doing what she didn't like. Ciara could only wonder at the impunity of it all.

Oh, well. No Lee today. No Jake, either, because he was on

5

an overnight to Los Angeles and wouldn't be back until after lunch. And no Tara, no Mike; as she got out of her car, slung her dance kitbag over her shoulder and made her way into the double-doored hall of her house, which was called Puerto Banus in memory of her lovely, lovely honeymoon, Ciara felt an unexpected sense of . . . what? Nothing definite, rather an absence of something . . . the children, of course. Like a fool she'd stopped at two, been rather taken aback when they arrived in unison, but had not succumbed to Jake's occasional murmurs about maybe having a third later on. Two were enough, as she'd pointed out, with the price of private schooling these days, and besides she'd wanted both twins to have lots of quality time, individual attention from their parents. Plus, Jake wanted her to look good, didn't he? A third child would really have been stretching it – as it was, it had taken fully six months to eradicate the stretch marks after the twins. You had to be reasonable about these things. She still remembered Jake's slightly sardonic laugh.

'But Ciara, what will you do all day, when the twins grow up? Turn shopping into an art form, a fulltime career?'

That had been a bit below the belt: after all he liked her to look good, didn't he? It was part of her job description, wasn't it? He'd loved her to shop when they'd first married, hadn't he, showing off his status on the career ladder? If she did have sixty pairs of shoes in her wardrobe, they were for his benefit, weren't they?

'Well' he'd remarked recently, 'maybe the stilettos will come in handy for stabbing my promotion rivals' leaving her with the feeling that he was not quite taking her seriously. Nor his promotion, either. But at least they never had any real rows over her spending, never let it come between them, and she had been relieved when he decently didn't pursue the

6

question of having more children. Tara and Mike were lovely, and quite enough in this day and age.

Only now . . . now, she felt it was almost a shame they'd been born so soon, barely a year after her wedding, because although their youth reflected youth on her, they were moving on so fast! It felt slightly odd, at thirty-nine, to already be coming home to an empty house, a house that had seemed so full of bikes and skates, friends and sleepovers, music and posters, only last month, last year . . . but they were eighteen now, both working in America for the summer, Tara as a camp counsellor in Florida, Mike as a waiter at a club in the Hamptons.

Of course they'd be home in September, but then gone again almost immediately to their new colleges . . . suppressing a small sigh, Ciara threw her dance kit into the laundry bin in the utility room, and extracted a lettuce from the fridge for lunch. Maybe she should have had that third child, after all? The 'bonus baby' that some of her friends had had in recent years, laughing as they insisted it had been a total accident. Laughing, looking rejuvenated as they hauled her off shopping for tiny, exquisite little Oshkosh outfits . . . but they couldn't possibly be getting much sleep, could they? On one or two of their faces, wear and tear must surely begin to show soon. It was already showing on one or two of their figures; a little slippage could definitely be detected. And after all that hard work at the gym, in the pool, on the golf course – ouch!

Chucking a handful of radishes into the lettuce, drizzling on a dressing in which lemon juice outweighed olive oil, Ciara poured a glass of mineral water and sat down to eat her salad at the breakfast bar: no point in setting the entire dining table for such a solitary snack. Hurry up Jake, come on home, I'm dying to see you! From a shelf, a photo of him smiled down at her in a way that was both affectionate and somehow protective, and she smiled back, thinking how lucky she was to have such a lovely husband. Not every man was worth endless lettuce lunches – no wonder Kate Dolan was going to pot, married to the likes of Alan Dolan – but Jake was worth whatever it took. After all, his happiness generated her happiness, because her entire life revolved around him . . . their home, their children, their social life, their money, their holidays, their joint property, their love life. Everything.

'You' Lee Warner scoffed, 'have all your eggs in one basket, honey.' And yes, maybe she had. But it was a nice, deep, sturdy basket, and Ciara had no intention of dropping it. Security mattered to her, for herself and for her family, and so she held the basket in a tight grip, was careful never to drop it on any hard surface or swing it idly high as she sauntered through life's leafy glade.

Jake provided all the eggs, and it was her job to keep them safe, a job she had been doing expertly from day one, the day she said 'I do' at the altar of St Matthew's church nineteen years ago. While other people ran themselves ragged trying to manage both families and jobs 'outside the home', she devoted herself exclusively to being in the home, at its glowing centre, and was very thankful she didn't have to get up at six, drive two hours to travel twenty miles, fill in ghastly paperwork, contend with brutal bosses or screeching clients, race back to relieve a malcontent childminder or do any of the other exhausting stuff so many of the other wives did. She had made a good bargain that day at St Matthew's, and she was keeping it religiously, with honour and with pleasure.

Plus, she loved Jake Lunny. Loved him very much and, after almost two decades of marriage, still fancied the arse off him. How could any woman not love such a calm, cheerful, hard-working husband? How could any woman not adore such a handsome, curly-haired, well-muscled man? Sometimes she wondered how, but had no basis for the slightest suspicion. Even his cabin-crew colleagues, when she met them, lamented his complete lack of interest in the shenanigans everyone else got up to in New York, Madrid, London or wherever.

'Just-married Jake' they called him, because he was as faithful to his wife as any newly-wed; it was a matter of record that he had never once veered off course. And why would he? As Paul Newman once famously asked, 'Who needs to go out for a burger when there's fillet steak at home?' It was a crude remark, but Ciara entirely endorsed it. Jake was happy, she was happy, and the Lunnys were simply that rarest of entities, a happy family. Anyone who wondered why she didn't want to get a job now the children were growing up, or why Jake didn't have more 'fun' on his travels, or why she was happily eating this rabbit's lunch, simply didn't have any imagination. Either that, or they were jealous. Or both.

Glancing at her watch, Ciara decided on her pink Ellesse shirt for this afternoon's golf game . . . unless of course Jake got home before she left for the club. If that were the case, he would be in one of two moods: either dog-tired, craving sleep, or on the high that long-haul flights sometimes induced, grabbing her the moment he arrived, hauling her off to the bed that was somehow naughty, extra-exciting when you hit it in broad daylight, the middle of the afternoon.

During her schooldays with the nuns, and his with the Jesuits, afternoons had been strictly for maths, or history, or some such supervised, stuffy activity. Whereas now – she stifled a giggle – they were for biology! Blissful biology,

9

followed by a glass of duty-free champagne and a long chat, punctuated with kisses and a lot of sympathetic nodding: Ciara was careful never to bore Jake with her domestic trivia, always to put his agenda first, his talk of airline activity and money-market movement. An astute investor, Jake had bought shares in the airline when it was still a new, risky venture, barely off the ground as he said, and now his portfolio was worth even more than his hefty pilot's salary. Ciara thought of all that money nestling in the bank with immense affection, almost as tenderly as if it were a baby nestling in its fluffy, rosy little cot. Or one of her cashmere cardis, soft, warm and colour-coordinated on its shelf. Clever Jake! And lucky, lucky Ciara. What a good investment they had made in each other.

After a glass of mint tea, she took a shower, and was just changing into her golf gear when she heard the hum of Jake's Jag on the drive. It was an old car, albeit recently acquired, and she was at a loss to understand what he saw in it. 'Vintage' he said, 'classy.' Personally she preferred her own nifty 4x4, bang up to date, this year's model. But if it kept him happy . . . gliding on some lipstick, she bounded out of the bathroom to greet him.

'Hi hon, welcome home!' Eagerly, she flew into his arms, and he lifted her off her feet, swinging her round the hall, laughing at her enthusiasm. Something in his twinkly green eyes did it for her, always had, always did; the minute she saw him she wanted to be in bed with him, remembering Lee's comment about how 'a man in uniform is sexier than a man in nothing at all.'

But no. Not today. Ciara only had to glance at Jake to see that, despite his broad smile, he was tired. Any number of things could go wrong on long flights, and one or other often did. He never bored her with technical talk of delays, of engines or mechanics or spare parts or sudden storms, but she'd long since learned to read the signs. Clearly, one or more of those things had happened in the last forty-eight hours. Instantly, she went into maternal mode.

'My poor baby! You're exhausted! Come with me . . . you need a hot bath, and a warm drink, and a long, long sleep.' Taking him by the hand, she led him to their bedroom, turned on the taps in the bathroom, poured in a generous dose of eucalyptus oil and, with a reassuring kiss, went off to make some hot chocolate while he bathed. By the time she came back, Jake was sprawled face down, stark naked on their king-size bed, fast asleep, his briefcase on the floor beside him.

The round of golf seemed to go on for ever. Not only the golf itself, but the conversation over coffee afterwards, which encompassed the health, summer camp schedules, shopping aspirations and computer activities of several children. Now that her own children were beyond that stage, Ciara sometimes yawned surreptitiously, wondering whether she could ever have talked about kiddie activities as much as these younger mothers now seemed to. Could she? Surely not. At most, maybe she'd mentioned Tara's roller-blade craze, or Mike's fascination with Metallica or the occasional teacher not performing up to par, but she couldn't possibly have droned on non-stop about the price of designer trainers or homework or parent-teacher meetings *all afternoon*, could she?

No. Definitely not. That was all a blast from the past. She couldn't imagine ever having bored anyone as much as these mothers, she found with surprise, were suddenly starting to bore her. How much more fun to talk about fashion, or holidays! As soon as she decently could, she excused herself from the tip-swopping mums, explaining that she and Jake had a dinner date that night. Curiously, Sara Thompson raised a plucked eyebrow. Sara who owned the most exclusive boutique in town, and the priciest, and always dressed beautifully from it.

'Oh, really? How nice. Where, who with?'

'With the Hartes' she said, and was not entirely surprised when a small silence settled momentarily over the group of lady golfers. The Hartes didn't even live in 'an oasis of gracious living', they lived in an eighteenth-century converted church on nine acres, with stables for the older children's horses and a small lake on which the younger two sailed their little Mirrors in summer. Tom Harte was something in property development, currently snapping up whole streets in Prague or Budapest or somewhere.

'Well' Sara replied after a tiny pause, 'I hope you enjoy your evening. What are you planning to wear, Ciara?'

'My cream Louise linen' she replied, and blinked when Sara hesitated for the merest moment.

'Really? Oh, Ciara, don't you think it's a little cool for linen? I'd wear my black jersey, if I were you.'

Her black jersey? Certainly, it was a clingy, sexy little number, wrapped below the bust and tied tight around the waist, but what was wrong with. . . ? 'Thanks, Sara' she said airily, 'maybe I will. Let's see how Jake feels about it.' With a tinkly laugh, she waggled her fingers in a little wave as she departed, leaving the girls to return to their coffee-klatch and their talk of children, and vaccinations, and school fees, and who was having an affair with whom. Before going out to the Hartes' this evening, she remembered, she must read today's *Times* – the front page anyway – because she prided herself

12

on always having something interesting, up to date and amusing to discuss with any host or hostess. It was, as Jake said, one's dinner-table duty.

It was a lovely evening, and Ciara was glad she'd decided to wear her flattering black jersey after all, with a diamond pendant that gleamed in the candlelight, reflecting the burnished sheen of a refreshed, relaxed, much-revived Jake Lunny. He had given the pendant to her on the birth of the twins, and whenever she wore it she somehow felt enhanced, more beautiful, reassured of his enduring love for her. It was a reminder for him, too, of the importance of her place in his life. Not that he ever needed reminding. Sometimes she could almost palpably feel his devotion, see the silken ribbon that bound them together, even when they were seated apart as was the case tonight.

They had reached the cheese stage, and a decanter of port was making its way around the mahogany, late-Victorian table. Apart from the Lunnys and the senior Hartes, there was a visiting couple from Boston – a banker with his psychiatrist wife – and there were the two older Harte children. Fiach Harte was nineteen, a law student, with his sister Roisin who at twenty-one had just graduated in archaeology. Socially, both were almost as adept as their parents, keeping up an easy flow of conversation, and Ciara liked laconic, easy-going Fiach, who had long been a friend of Mike's. Roisin had never been quite as likeable, and tonight Ciara could clearly see why – she was so cool, so thoughtful, so much older than her years! Thinking of her absent daughter Tara, Ciara saw a bouncy, chatty, long-limbed, curly-haired extrovert, whereas Roisin Harte was . . . well, somehow almost Victorian, as if she matched the table. She wore a long flowery skirt and a white cotton top that drained her face of colour, with her rusty-coloured hair bundled up in a barette and a minimum of make-up.

No jewellery, no perfume; seated across the table from her, Ciara felt almost younger by comparison, as if their ages were reversed. As for the girl's conversation . . . Roisin was talking, for God's sake, about some long-dead old buffer who'd discovered Tutenkhamen's tomb. Poor thing, Ciara thought, she might have a brand-new degree under her belt but she's going to find it awfully hard to find a husband. Not with Tutenkhamen in tow. Not with those pale grey eyes begging for mascara, not with those five – six? – kilos she needs to lose. She looks as if she's never seen the inside of a nightclub, and wouldn't know the meaning of the word 'makeover'. Her poor parents are going to be hard put to get her off their hands.

Deftly, Georgina Harte manoeuvred the conversation out of her daughter's grip, out of Tutenkhamen's tomb into the twenty-first century, handing round a platter of brie and beaufort while her husband Tom looked after the port in its sleek Waterford decanter. With a smile, Ciara waved it away, passing it on around the table until it rested with Jake, who poured a little into his glass. How well he looked tonight, in that navy linen shirt, alert and fresh after only five'hours' sleep! And then, courteously, he turned to Roisin on his right.

'A little port?' he offered with a small, polite smile, and Roisin smiled back, no less politely.

'Thank you' she said, raising her glass for him to fill, and as he lifted the decanter he looked, very briefly, into her milky-grey eyes. With equal brevity, Roisin looked back before flushing, quickly dropping her gaze to the table, and Ciara froze as if the decanter had exploded in her husband's hand, as if shards of glass were showering down like scalpels.

Jake, she screamed silently. James Eugene Lunny, you are having an affair with Roisin Harte.

You are having an affair with the twenty-one-year-old daughter of our neighbours, our hosts, the parents of our son's friend Fiach.

You are having an affair with this fat, mousy *frump*!

You are in love with her. That was no flicker of passing interest; that was the look of *love*. My God. Oh my God my God my *God*!

Fighting for breath, she grasped the tablecloth where it skimmed her knees, unable to speak, to stand, to see the walls as they whirled around her. In spite of herself her eyes darted back to them, and there it was again – the briefest of glances, bright as a blade as it gleamed between her husband and Roisin Harte, seeming to spin on the air before plunging, like a dagger, into her very core.

Beaming, Georgina Harte handed her a cheese knife. 'Do try the brie, Ciara, darling? I know it looks a bit squishy, but it is delicious.'

2

At five in the morning, Jake Lunny was no longer the charming, attractive man who had set out to dinner with his charming, attractive wife nine hours earlier. His shirt rumpled, his eyes bleary and his face in need of shaving, he looked more like a man who had been held and interrogated by some secret police force whose methods depended on the resolute wearing down of its victim.

'Ciara' he groaned, 'for the last time, I have not slept with Roisin Harte. I swear it to you on a stack of bibles.'

'You're an atheist' she shrieked, 'you don't even have a bible! But I'll tell you what you do have, Jake Lunny. You have a fabulous family and a beautiful home and a great career and an absolutely *perfect* wife! How can you throw all that away on – on – on some dreary little *drip*!? How? How can you lie to me, treat me like an idiot, pretend there's nothing between you two when I saw it with my own eyes!? A blind man could have seen it! I'm not a fool, I want the truth and I want it now!'

She heard herself screeching – like a fishwife, as her mother would say – but she couldn't help it, couldn't calm down, couldn't believe his repeated denials. One picture truly was worth a thousand words. The image of him looking into Roisin Harte's adoring eyes, the complicity between them, sizzled on her soul as if stamped with a white-hot branding iron. It was what Hollywood called a smouldering look, as if he were Clarke Gable and that hideous girl, for God's sake, were Vivien Leigh. They *had* to have been to bed together. Why he kept denying it she couldn't grasp, because denial was both futile and frustrating. She couldn't handle the situation until she got the truth out of him.

'Look' he said at length, wearily, slumping onto the sofa, running his hands through his hair, 'I'm not saying I'm not attracted to Roisin, okay? Since you want the truth, I am attracted. In a certain way. But what I'm telling you – what matters – is that it's not physical, and I haven't done anything about it. I haven't seduced her, haven't been to bed with her. I'm not a total fool, for chrissake, nor a bastard either. I have no desire to hurt either one of you. If I wanted a fling – which I don't – I'd have it with some passing trolley dolly.'

What? Either one of you, he said? He was daring to put that little witch on a par with her, as if they were *equals*? Suddenly, gasping as if punched, Ciara was very, very frightened. This was worse than a confession of adultery. Much worse. Had he said 'yes, okay, I had a silly fling, so what, it didn't mean anything' she might – just might – have come to terms with that. Eventually. Instead, he was looking at her very directly, very levelly, clasping his hands on his knees in front of him as if about to explain a complex maths problem to a bewildered child.

'All right. Since you insist on the truth, let me tell it to you.' Pausing, he unclasped his hands, threw them upwards, and clasped them again. 'The truth – the truth is that I . . . Ciara, I don't know how to put this, but I think I . . . I'm changing. Changing fundamentally, in some way I don't understand myself.'

Changing? 'But – !'

'I know. It sounds ridiculous. Call it a mid-life crisis if you will, or whatever you like. Maybe it will pass. But right now I feel as if – as if I can't *breathe.*'

Silently, she stared at him, wondering if he might actually be losing his mind. Maybe all the travel, all the changing back and forth into different time zones, had finally unhinged him? The pressure, the stress? Had it all become too much?

'Jake' she stuttered after a long, taut pause, 'I think – do you think – maybe – you need a holiday?'

It was the best she could come up with. Even as she said it, she saw it falling short, like a badly aimed tennis ball. They had frequent holidays, had come back from Florida only six weeks ago.

'Yes' he sighed, with a kind of wince, 'I think maybe I do. A break. Time out. Space. Time and space, in which to grow into the new Jake Lunny, whoever he may turn out to be.'

The new Jake Lunny. But dear God, what on earth was wrong with the old Jake Lunny? The Jake she'd met at eighteen, married at nineteen, lived with for nineteen years? That was the Jake she had married, the Jake she loved, the Jake she wanted to spend the rest of her life with. And what about—?

'The children' he said slowly, 'are growing up, Ciara. I've put myself on hold while they were doing that, but now they're up and running and I – I think maybe it's my turn to do some growing.'

No. This just wasn't making any sense. 'What – what do you mean? You're a grown man, already! You are my husband and I love you and I don't *want* any other – other –'

'Incarnation?' he supplied, with the merest glimmer of a smile. 'Ciara, I'm sorry. But it has to happen. I'm weary and I'm restless and I feel the very urgent need to – to take a break.'

Frantically, she leaned forward, aware how awful she must look, how haggard and angry and weepy. 'A break from *what*? From work, maybe, but you surely can't mean from the children or from – from *me*?'

It was unthinkable, incomprehensible, that he should nod. Nod in a way that confirmed yes, that was exactly what he meant. From her. From his gorgeous, efficient, devoted wife, with whom he hadn't even had a row for years. Not one single, stand-up, rip-roaring row.

He seemed to mull on it. 'Yes. From you, Ciara. From routine and from our endless social life and the whole – Jesus, I am sorry. I love you and I am so, so sorry to have to say all this. But the truth is that I am bored. Stuck in a rut, frustrated, caged . . . I don't know why, it's not your fault, it must be just age, the male menopause or whatever you call it. I'm not talking other women, I'm not talking divorce, I'm just talking about a . . . a sabbatical. A sabbatical from my career as your husband. A few months – maybe six? – to draw breath and regroup and try to decide where I go from here, where we all go.'

Bored? Bored, he said? With her? It hit her as hard as if he'd slapped her. She couldn't keep her lip from trembling as fresh tears quivered in her eyes.

'I think you must be going mad, Jake. Sandwiches are falling out of your basket all over the floor. You cannot for one moment seriously be – be thinking of –?'

She couldn't say it, couldn't bring herself to articulate the word. So he said it for her.

'Leaving? Leaving home? Yes, Ciara. I am. Just for a while. The children are away already, soon they'll be off at college, it – it has to be now. Of course I'll keep in touch, of course I'll come back eventually, of course you won't be short of money or anything else. But I hope, I really hope, you'll let me do it. I need a break very, very badly.'

His look was earnest, and quizzical, but she thought she glimpsed something else in it, too. Something steely, something determined; he was not a successful, decisive pilot for nothing.

'And what if I won't? What if I say no, this is insane, you can't just walk out on your wife, leave me as if I were some floozy you'd picked up for the night?' She heard her voice, rasping like sandpaper.

'You're not some floozy. You are, as you say, my wife. I have responsibilities and duties to you, which I will fulfil – but, Ciara, with or without your consent, I am going to do it. I am taking time out from our relationship. Time which I hope will pay dividends, and refresh us both.'

She must be having a nightmare. This was like being sucked into a horror movie. Soon she would wake up and the sun would shine and –

'What will everyone say?' That was the wild, ludicrous protest that burst from her lungs. 'How on earth am I going to tell everyone that my husband has walked out on me?!?'

He didn't immediately answer. Instead, he stood up, walked slowly into the centre of the room, caught sight of himself in the mirror, and winced.

'Ciara, is that really what you most want to know? Why don't you ask me how this has all come about? What's it about, how has it evolved? What's going on in my mind and in my heart? What we can do to travel through this together? H'mm? Why aren't we talking about counselling or spiritual growth or emotional nutrition or—'

'Stop it!' she shrieked. 'Stop it, stop it, I can't bear it! Why are you doing this, Jake? Why are you doing this to me and to us, what have I done to deserve to be tortured? All I've ever done is love you and have your children and run your home and play my role and look the part and—'

'And now' he interjected, 'you can take a break too, if you want, from me. From all your duties. You can look deep into the mirror and decide whether you're happy with the person you see.'

What? What did he mean by that? That maybe he no longer liked what he saw, was that it, when he looked at her? But she was beautiful! Yes, all right, nearly forty – but fit and toned and scented and polished and the acknowledged beauty of their entire set! What more did he want, what more could she possibly do? Floundering, growing frantic, she felt panic set fast in her mind like ice in a freezer. Panic, and agonising pain, and blazingly wounded pride.

'Jake' she eventually managed to gasp, 'I don't know what you're talking about. Or what it is you want. But I think you'll find it isn't Roisin Harte. Or any other woman.'

'No' he agreed, very quietly. 'Roisin probably isn't the answer. But I think Roisin is definitely the question.'

'And then what?' Lee Warner asked, with as much sympathy as anyone could reasonably be expected to muster after three days of doling it out, along with spectacular quantities of tea, tissues and reassurance.

'And then' Ciara howled, 'he put on *Madame* bloody *Butterfly*! In the middle of the night, the middle of abandoning his wife and home, he put on some shagging Italian opera! He's insane, he needs a doctor!'

Yes. Lee had heard all this already, over and over, but still Ciara kept repeating it, gushing tears, unable to grasp the reality that her husband, Jake Lunny, had packed a bag at six o'clock that morning, attempted to kiss his wife, failed, and left. The Jaguar had purred quietly away down the drive at dawn and that had been quite simply that. He was gone, and Ciara was whirling in a void, like Alice falling down the tunnel into Wonderland.

'Well . . . honey, I think we're going to have to do something about getting you some sleep. This can't go on. Drink some camomile tea, please, hit the sack and I promise you you'll feel better when you wake up. Sleep here, in the guest room, you don't have to go home.'

Holding out little hope of compliance, Lee was agreeably surprised when – oh, thank God, at last! – Ciara nodded and said yes, maybe she should try to sleep a little. Exhaustion, Lee saw, was setting in, shock was taking its toll: Ciara's bone-white face looked like a porcelain doll's. A doll that had been dropped, chipped and damaged.

'Come on.' Gently, Lee slid an arm around her, helping her to her feet, steering her through the hall and up the stairs, finally depositing her shattered, babbling charge in the bedroom. Wide-eyed and wan, Ciara suddenly grabbed a sleeping pill from her pocket, gulped it without water, kicked off her shoes and flopped, fully dressed, onto the bed.

'Thank you, Lee' she managed to mumble, 'I know I'm being a pain . . . pathetic . . .'

'Don't be silly' Lee replied cheerfully, silently thinking that yes, she was, but feeling sorry for her all the same. Ciara was one of those women who – well. Life without Jake was not going to be any picnic for her. Where the hell had she got that sleeping pill?

Pulling up the duvet, she tucked her in and glided away, uneasy and yet relieved to think that Ciara must surely sleep, now, for hours. For the rest of the day, with any luck, which would leave her free to callously get on with her work in the garage that had been converted into a jewellery studio.

But, she reminded herself as she crept downstairs, I'm not her mother, am I? Nor her sister nor best friend – only her neighbour. It's just chance that I happened to buy the house next to hers, and we got chatty and . . . who is her best friend, anyway? She's never mentioned anyone in particular, for all her friends, all those women she plays golf with, goes shopping with, to parties and the races and what-not. We've never been anywhere together, unless you count the odd cup of coffee here in this kitchen, nor are we likely to go anywhere together. She's a socialite and I'm a – well, not a recluse exactly, but I like my peace, my solitude. Of which she has now stolen three days' worth. I'd better be getting a lot of brownie points for this. And I'd better get back to work. My wonderful work, that keeps me sane.

Making her way into her converted garage, Lee smiled as she sat down at her workbench, reminding herself that she might not be able to work at home if the Lunnys had not been so helpful. Setting up a place of business was officially forbidden in Huxley Wood, and they were the only ones who knew she'd done it. But Ciara and Jake had said they didn't mind provided there wasn't going to be any noise or traffic as a result. No, Lee promised; the garage would look exactly the same from the outside, with just an extra skylight in the roof – no noise, no vans or drills or anything. Fine, said the Lunnys, in that case they wouldn't tell anyone, and Lee shouldn't either. All the other houses were sufficiently distant that, probably, nobody would notice.

And then one day Ciara had come over carrying a cake, one from an expensive French patisserie, to ask how the new jewellery enterprise was coming along. Pleasantly surprised,

Lee said it was coming along fine, picking up more or less where it had left off in Vermont, and they'd got talking over the cake. Not garrulous by nature, she'd found herself answering Ciara's questions, which seemed prompted more by friendly interest than by nosiness.

Yes, she was American – you could tell, huh? American, and divorced, and childless. Thirty-four. A jeweller specialising in semi-precious stone pieces she designed herself. One-off originals, for sale in twenty expensive, exclusive American boutiques. Or maybe more, some day; she was planning a trip to California to negotiate with some outlets in San Francisco and Los Angeles. Oh, really? In that case, Ciara said picking up a garnet bracelet and holding it to the light, Lee should let her know whenever she might want any little packages flown over. Her pilot husband, Jake, would be happy to play courier. Such amazing jewellery, the kind of thing you'd see film stars wearing to the Oscars in *Hello!* magazine!

Even now, a year later, Lee still remembered Ciara's friendly, admiring smile. A guileless, happy housewife, she'd seemed genuinely impressed that 'such talent' had chosen to live in Huxley Wood. She'd never worked a day in her own life, she said with a giggle, wouldn't have a clue how to set up a business or even find the simplest job. The only thing she knew how to run was a home.

Nothing wrong with that, Lee replied; somebody had to run them. Running a business might sound more glamorous, but a lot of it was just graft. Paperwork and hassles and a lot of petty politics. Whereupon Ciara had nodded and clipped on the bracelet, stretching up her arm, waggling her fingers as she admired it in the sunlight. She had, Lee noted, the most beautifully manicured fingernails, the most fragile little wrists.

'Uh-huh. So what brought you to Ireland, anyway? D'you have roots or something?'

Yes. An Irish grandmother, Aine O'Donnell from Ardara in Donegal, who'd emigrated to America many moons ago. Now, her granddaughter had moved to Ireland in turn, not for any nostalgic reasons but because it spoke English and was reputed to be very Americanised. Reputed to be fun, too, a friendly place for a stranger to settle.

'God' Ciara responded wide-eyed, looking almost awestruck, 'I could never do anything like that. Move to a foreign country, I mean, all by myself – I'd be totally lost, I'd hate it!'

'Honey' Lee recalled saying, 'you'd be amazed what you can do, when you want to. I wanted a fresh start, as far away from Freddie Weinberg as possible. I gave Ireland some thought and decided hey, why not? So here I am, so far, so good!'

And then they'd talked about Freddie – 'a monster' – and Jake – 'a darling' – and Ciara's family, until abruptly Ciara leaped up. 'The children will be home soon, I have to cook dinner! Bye!'

Off she'd flown, perky as a little robin, leaving Lee smiling, pleased to have a neighbour who – if a little *Stepford-Wife* perhaps – at least seemed sociable, uncomplicated and un-demanding. Until now; until this summer's day when suddenly the light had snapped off in Ciara's sunny life, leaving her fraught, distraught, not waving but drowning. Happily married since her teens, she simply didn't know where to turn, what to do, couldn't grasp why Jake had moved out or what was happening. She looked, Lee thought, like a child lost by its mother in the Christmas crush, sobbing to be collected by some responsible adult, carried to the inform-ation desk and restored to its rightful owner.

Not that Lee could understand Jake's behaviour, either. She didn't know him very well, but he'd seemed like a nice man, a happy husband, certainly not the walking-out type. Which just went to show . . . men. Even if they weren't all nasty pieces of work like Freddie Weinberg, they were all untrustworthy, in the end. No woman in her right mind should ever depend on any one of them.

But Ciara wanted hers back. Wanted him urgently, desperately, she said; was going to drive into town and waylay him in the hotel he had moved into while he searched for an apartment. Lee thought this was a very bad idea.

'Give him time, honey. Let him be, for a little while. Let him cool off and start missing you.'

So far, this had worked for three days. Three demented days in which Ciara paced up and down Lee's kitchen rehearsing the speech she would make to Jake when she saw him, the speech abjectly apologising for not listening properly, not asking the right questions, not handling the whole hideous scenario properly at all. She'd been in shock, made a complete hash of the entire—

'Ciara' Lee pointed out, 'the man lobbed a live grenade at you. Very few people catch live grenades neatly in their baseball mitts and lob them back in a perfect curve.'

'Why?' Ciara wailed, unhearing. 'Why didn't I see this coming? Why didn't I realise he was unhappy? Why didn't he tell me? What could he possibly see in Roisin *Harte*? I just don't understand what's going on!' And then more tears, more gulping and gasping, in a way that somehow suggested she was to blame, mustn't have been nearly as good a wife as she'd thought.

Well, nobody was perfect. But Ciara Lunny, if you were to judge a book by its cover, came as close to perfection as any woman could. With her lovely husband, lovely home, lovely children, it was almost as if she'd learned the Wonderful-Wife textbook off by heart and could recite it verbatim. Almost as if she'd *written* it. Her only faults, that Lee could see, were a certain naiveté and a chirpy tendency to live life in Barbie mode, which you couldn't hold against her when she was so essentially likeable. A bit frivolous, maybe, a bit breathless, but those were hardly hanging offences.

Were they? Settling at her workbench, plugging in her soldering iron, Lee slipped on the glasses she wore for close work and peered into the glowing depths of an agate, holding it poised between the pincers of tiny pliers. This necklace, when it was finished, would never be worn by a delicate, feminine lady like Ciara Lunny; it would be worn by some urbane, original woman with the confidence to wear a striking, off-beat piece. Somebody who, while she might not have Ciara's laminated looks, would have attitude.

Was that, perhaps, what Roisin Harte had? Was that, perhaps, what Jake Lunny wanted?

Maybe. Or maybe not. Not knowing him very well and not knowing Roisin at all, Lee couldn't tell. All she knew was that, if she were a man, she'd go hatchet crazy married to a woman like Ciara. You might as well be married to a fluffy kitten or bunny-wunny or cheeping little chick, you'd have to sweep a dozen goddamn teddy bears off your pillow every night – and the worst part of all would be that you couldn't strangle their owner, because she would gaze soulfully up at you and bat her eyelashes and beg you, oh pleath, not to hurt them.

Not that Ciara actually lisped, wore anything fluffy or puffy – *au contraire*, she was trendily streamlined – but dear Lord, she was so *nice*! But then, Lee grimly reminded herself, nice cuts ice. I *wasn't* nice, I was candid and cynical and a hopeless housewife, and now I'm divorced. Ciara is the exact opposite so, logically, she should stay married. Yes? She hasn't committed any crime that Jake could possibly accuse her of. Not unless . . . except . . .?

Absorbed, lost in her work and her thoughts, she didn't hear the studio door open, didn't realise Ciara was standing behind her until a euphoric squeal suddenly shattered the silence.

'Lee!'

The pliers and necklace clattered to the floor, the agate rolled under the workbench and Lee flinched from the scorch of the soldering iron as she whirled round to confront a hugely smiling Ciara. A Ciara who, apparently, had not been able to sleep after all.

'Lee, I've got it! I know what to do, I know how to get Jake back!' Her grin was appalling, like something etched into a pumpkin at Halloween. Very cautiously, Lee stared up at her.

'Have you? Do you?'

'Yes! I've worked it all out! I'm going to rejuvenate myself! I'm going to have plastic surgery!'

3

No. There was absolutely nothing Lee could do to put her off, Ciara insisted, so would she please stop trying? She was going to find a surgeon who could take at least ten years off her, and that was that. A super-surgeon who could turn her into Elle Macpherson II, irresistible to every man and, specifically, to Jake Lunny.

'Have you considered' Lee mused a few days later, over drinks on Ciara's teak deck, 'how you'll look if your mouth ends up in your neck? If your ears swop places with your eyes?'

'Lee' Ciara sighed, 'don't be ridiculous. We're talking the finest surgery money can buy.'

'I saw a documentary once. This woman whose op went wrong. Her left eye was all droopy and sort of ran down into the corner of her mouth, like a river running into the sea.'

'Well, mine won't. Mine will make me look divine.'

'Or suppose you react to the anaesthetic? Suppose you spend the next forty years wired to a life-support system, looking like a turnip, being spoon-fed by your grand-children?'

'Lee, stop it! You're being deliberately negative.'

'I'm just trying to point out the pitfalls, is all. Surgery is a serious undertaking. I'd never have any I didn't urgently need. Besides, you're way too young, and far too pretty. You don't need it!'

'I do. I'm nearly forty. My eyelids . . . my chin . . .' Touching her hand to them, Ciara grimaced as if touching something at the bottom of the bin, something soggy, squelchy.

'Are perfectly fine. Anyway, whatever's going on with Jake hardly has to do with your chin or your eyelids, does it?'

'All I know is that it has to do with a woman – a fat frumpy girl – half my age.'

'But he said he wasn't sleeping with her! He said he was bored and frustrated, that he wanted time and space to think . . . it could be quite an innocent friendship. Platonic.'

'Platonic?' Intently, Ciara frowned. 'What do you mean?'

Whaat?! Was it possible she didn't understand the word? Lee stopped in her tracks. 'You know . . . just good friends?'

'Hah! Fat chance! I'm just thankful the children are away. Maybe he'll come home before they do. He—'

'He didn't marry you just for your looks, did he? There has to be more to a marriage than that, Ciara!'

'Yes. But my looks were what first attracted him. He told me so. A good-looking woman, he said, embellishes a home. Eye candy, as you Americans call it. And she gives a guy status.'

'So what's he doing with Roisin Harte?'

'I don't *know*! He won't tell me any more about her, says they've only ever had coffee and a few chats . . . I don't believe him.'

'Has he ever lied before?'

Ciara considered. No, not that she knew of. But there was a first time for everything. Thank God the senior Hartes hadn't seemed to suspect anything, hadn't noticed anything amiss at that fatal dinner party. Or Fiach, Mike's friend . . . ? She could only pray that he knew nothing either. Mike was only eighteen, only a child, must be protected from his father's new and awful perfidy. As must Tara – dear God, what was she going to say, when next she spoke to either child? Thus far she'd managed to keep Jake's departure secret from them both, chatting lightly on the phone, telling them he was just away on long-haul. They were not due home until September, by which time she would have – have figured all this out, and got Jake back. For now, nobody knew except Lee, who knew none of her friends and was not a gossip.

Suddenly, out of the blue, Ciara had an appalling flash. Sara Thompson, at the golf club, advising her to wear her sexy black outfit that evening. And that long silence, when she'd said she was dining at the Hartes'. Surely . . . ? Oh, God, no! Surely not! They couldn't know. Couldn't possibly. She was imagining that they even suspected.

'Lee' she said with new urgency, 'do you know anything about plastic surgery? Where to have it, I mean? Should I look in the Yellow Pages or what?'

Lee recoiled. 'Lord, no! If you're serious about it – and personally I think you're nuts – you must research it properly. Look it up on the internet, to start with.'

Bemused, Ciara gazed at her. 'I don't know how to use the internet.'

'What?'

'I mean . . . I've never needed to. Jake always did whatever needed doing on the computer. Did everything . . . a dozen bills have arrived since he left and I can't make head nor tail of this stuff about paying by direct debit or online or – he said not to worry. Said to give them to him and he'll take care of them. He called me last night, you know.'

'And – and what else did he say?'

Her eyes clouding with tears, Ciara scanned the garden, focusing on a bed of immaculate pink roses. 'He said he was fine and I mustn't worry. He's found an apartment on a short-term lease. He's going to live in it until he – gets – his head sorted, he says. He wants us to meet once a week and be civilised and I'm to go shopping to cheer myself up, spend as much money as I like.'

Shopping! Lee could only marvel at that. Even if it was Ciara's favourite hobby, even if she did buy every new fashion . . . was Jake pulling her leg, actually *laughing* at her? Shopping wasn't going to solve anything. It sounded to her as if Jake was trying to buy time. Or compensate his wife for her trouble. Guilty conscience, of course. Money was merely a bandage, wouldn't heal any wounds. As she well knew, having taken Freddie to the cleaners solely for the satisfaction of stripping his assets. Most of her divorce settlement had been lying in the bank ever since.

'Ciara, I'll show you how to use the computer.'

Ciara baulked. 'Oh, no! Thanks, but I'd never learn, I'm useless at anything technical.'

'And I'll show you how to change a fuse and a plug and a lightbulb. Show you how to decipher bills and bank statements and—'

As if she hadn't heard, Ciara smiled at Lee. 'Would you be able to get the plastic surgery stuff off the computer? I mean, put it on paper, so I could read it?'

Lee hardly knew whether to laugh or cry. 'No. I won't baby you the way Jake apparently did. But I will show you how to read it online or print it out yourself. Especially the e-mails posted by women whose surgery went wrong.'

Ciara snorted. 'Lee, stop trying to put me off! I tell you, I'm doing this, I'm having it! I am going to be *gorgeous!*'

'Ciara, you're gorgeous already! You look way younger than thirty-nine, you dress like a dream, it's brain surgery you need, not plastic! Talk to Jake, find out what's going on with *him*! Whatever it is, it's in his head, it has nothing to do with the way you look!'

But Ciara shook her head, adamantly. 'Lee, every woman's marriage has something to do with the way she looks. Right now, I look like a woman on the brink of middle age.'

'You are on the brink of it! And you can't change that. You should be glad you've got this far, be trying to go forward, not back! You'll never be a teenager again no matter what you do – nor should you want to be. You're the *mother* of two teenagers!'

Even as she said it, Lee saw it striking some nerve, something flinching in Ciara's face. When she answered, her voice was low.

'Yes. I am. I'm the wife of a man who's left me and the mother of two children who are also about to leave me. I am going to be all alone here in this house and I – I –' Terror scudded through her eyes, and Lee began to glimpse what she was feeling, the vast void that she was leaning into. Having only ever been a wife and mother, knowing how to do nothing else, Ciara had no fall-back position, nothing to cling to, nobody to reassure her of her personal value or anything to even divert her attention. She was like an employee suddenly sacked, made redundant, pensioned off with nowhere to go, no demand for her outdated old skills. She genuinely did believe her face was her fortune, her key to survival. Desperately, Lee made one last effort.

'Ciara, why don't you do some kind of course? H'mm? You have access to plenty of money, you say, so why not invest some of it in yourself? How about interior décor, or fashion – you could set up as one of those advisors who streamline people's wardrobes! Or you could do a massage course,

beauty therapy . . . cooking maybe? You must know something about that, having raised a family and thrown so many
dinner parties—'

'Lee' Ciara interrupted, 'you don't understand. You simply
don't see that I'd never be any good at any kind of job. I don't
want one. Don't want to go out to work at all. I belong here
at home, with Jake, this is the only place I want to be. I've been
happy with him for twenty years and I want twenty more.
Thirty, forty. That is *all* I want.'

Imploringly, yet with a kind of resolution, she looked at Lee,
and for some moments they sat in silence, pondering it over
their half-empty jug of mint juleps. Mint juleps were the only
recipe Lee knew off by heart, and Ciara had seized on it,
saying American drinks were all the thing this summer.
Contemplatively, Lee sipped from her glass, trying to get her
head around all this, to accept that there were still women in
the world whose lives revolved exclusively around their
husbands and their homes. Women whose marriages were
their careers.

And who was she, to decide whether that was good or bad,
right or wrong? Thus far, Ciara's chosen 'career' had been
rewarding, she had been happy. She had been loved. Love
was worth something, and it had shone on Ciara for many
years, could not just be switched off like a light. In her field,
if you wanted to call it that, Ciara had been successful. Not
everyone wanted independence or solitude or challenge or the
things that she, Lee, preferred for herself.

Even if Ciara was going about her scary new situation, now,
wrong way round, she was trying. Trying to save her marriage
and be happy again. She was also vulnerable, facing the
empty-nest syndrome, frightened and insecure. Plastic
surgery wasn't going to fix any of her problems, but. . .

36

'All right.' Standing up, putting down her glass, Lee held out her hand and smiled at Ciara. 'Come on. Let's go take a look at this computer and see what we can find.'

Eagerly, like a child grasping a lollipop, Ciara took the outstretched hand and let herself be pulled to her feet.

'Thanks, Lee. I know you think this is madness, but I – I want to feel good about myself. Better, anyway. My confidence has taken a hammering and I just don't know any other way to get it back.'

When websites were found and Ciara was shown how to make her way around them, she sat glowing under the light of an Anglepoise lamp, one that illuminated the few, tiny wrinkles she did have. Just little laughter lines, around her mouth . . . but puffy eyes, too, from all that weeping. Sitting beside her, leaving her to learn as much as she could for herself, Lee studied her, wondering.

Who was Ciara Lunny, exactly? Was there anyone inside that pretty package? Did the glitzy wrapper contain only some silly, easily broken toy, a child's disposable Christmas doll? Or was there a spirit to match the body, a spirit capable of soaring high, of flying far from its earth-bound box? Was there a soul, and if so, what did it seek? Glancing around the room, she scanned for books that might provide some clue to Ciara's psyche: but all she could see were Jake's aviation textbooks, a stack of gossip magazines and a thriller with a lurid jacket. Nothing to indicate anyone who ever delved deep into anything, thought or even wondered about anything very much. Not even one volume of Shakespeare, or poetry, or Jane Austen or Tolstoy, anything that could normally be found in any home in the civilised world. Nothing irreverent or funny, or moving or marvellous, at all?

Music, maybe? There was a system in the corner, a stack of CDs, and while Ciara surfed Lee got up, gliding discreetly over to it. This was only the third or fourth time she had been in the Lunny house, the first chance she'd had to look around . . . sliding some CDs from their rack, she riffled through them curiously. Abba, Stevie Wonder, Ronan Keating, Robbie Williams, a lot of unfamiliar rock stuff that must belong to the kids and, looking almost sheepish, a volume of Mozart.

'Ciara?' Holding it up, she turned around. 'Do you like Mozart?'

Ciara shook her head, her gaze not leaving the computer screen. 'Oh, no – that's Jake's. He's got into some really dull stuff lately.'

Yes. Like Roisin Harte? At random, Lee pulled out another fistful of discs: easy-listening compilations, teenage warblers, Christmas carols. Nothing, absolutely nothing, that could be described as basso profundo. Or any kind of profundo. Nothing that would stir a soul to delirious joy, or black despair, or inspire anything more than, maybe, a craving for an Aero bar.

Food. Could that be the key? Maybe Ciara liked to cook. Stealthily, Lee selected a strategy, and smiled brightly.

'Ciara?'

'Mmm?'

'If we're going to be hours on this computer, maybe I could . . . uh . . . stay for supper this evening?'

'Sure!' Ciara still didn't look up, but she did sound enthusiastic. 'What'll I make? What would you like?'

'Oh, I dunno . . . tell you what, why don't I have a leaf through your cookbooks? Where are they, in the kitchen?'

'Mmm.' Ciara's gaze was riveted to a petrifying post-operative close-up, depicting a face so bruised it appeared

38

fresh out of a butcher's window. Stifling a groan, Lee drifted out to the kitchen, her stomach heaving over the two solitary cookbooks when she found them. One was a dated Delia Smith, the other gruesomely entitled *Nibbles For Newlyweds*. Oh, God! Was that supposed to be soul food? Shuddering, Lee glanced through it, and shoved it back on its shelf. And then, surreptitiously, she opened a cupboard.

The cupboard was neatly stacked, full of convenience foods: bags of rice and pasta, tins of peas, beans, tomatoes, packets of savoury sauces, jars of sweet ones. Tea bags, instant coffee, flour, mustard, Saxa salt, Chocopops, Horlicks, Oxo, Nutella. And then the fridge, might as well be hanged for a sheep as a lamb, Lee muttered guiltily as she opened it to confront skimmed milk, low-cal tonic, processed low-fat cheddar . . . three eggs, mineral water, two low-fat yogurts and a tin of fruit.

But – ?! Ciara could afford the best of quality – so where was everything? Where was the *vitality*? Where were the great heaps of herbs, the rioting piles of fruit and vegetables, the pungent onions and garlic, the ocean-fresh fish? Virtually everything here was packaged, with a dead look about it, as if the fridge were a miniature morgue. Nothing sang out, nothing teased a taste bud, nothing indicated any connection whatsoever with earth, or sky, or sea. Glumly, Lee shut the fridge, and trudged thoughtfully back to Ciara at the computer, peering over her shoulder when she reached it.

'What's that? A dead camel?'

'Lee! It's a woman who's just had her nose done – wait till you see, she'll look smashing in a minute – look, here, isn't that amazing?'

Well. At least Ciara was able to move the pictures on, clicking with confidence – so she was able to learn something new, then, when she was motivated! Lee smiled. 'It's amazing how fast you seem to be mastering that computer.'

Almost guiltily, Ciara shrugged, shrinking back a little. 'Oh – well – I'm only doing what you showed me.'

'Mmm.' Reflectively, Lee looked at her, another question cropping up in her mind. 'Tell me, Ciara – you're so fashion conscious, what's your definition of a well-dressed woman?'

Ciara giggled, eyeing her archly. 'Why? Don't tell me you're thinking of ditching all those brisk black trousers and white tops of yours?'

'No! I'm just wondering, is all, how you define stylish?'

'Hah – easy! A Fendi bag, of course, Jimmy Choo shoes or Manolo Blahnik, Mac for make-up, anything by Prada, Versace, DKNY . . . why d'you ask? Do you want to try on some of my stuff?'

Eager as a little girl, she looked ready for a dressing-up session, but Lee shook her head. 'No! I'm just curious . . . do all those brands actually suit you? Do you like them? Or are they just labels? If you had to wear an outfit with no label on it, what would it be?'

'Huh?' Ciara looked blank.

'I mean, if you had to design your own! Something to suit your looks, your figure, your colouring, the season and occasion, without regard to fashion? A look defined by you, not by a magazine?'

'But that's why I buy magazines! To see what's in, what everyone else is wearing!'

'But how can any one look suit everyone? Mini skirts, crop tops, bell bottoms, whatever . . . Ciara, you're an adult! Only kids follow fashion, until they find their feet, find their style! You're a grown-up, you're meant to be the boss, to know who and what you are!'

Pouting, Ciara swivelled round from the computer. 'Lee, you're the one who wears black and white all the time, only ever varying the accessories or the hairstyle . . . I think that's really boring. I think a flick through a mag would brighten you up no end, since you ask.'

Lee laughed. 'I asked about you, not me! And you haven't answered my question.'

As if she hadn't heard, Ciara whirled back to the screen. 'Look! It says something here about cosmetic dentistry, too – I could get my teeth done, as well!'

'Indeed you could. If blue is in fashion this year, the dentist could probably dye them for you. Or why not get an emerald like Mick Jagger?'

'Oh, very funny! Did you find something you'd like me to make you for dinner?'

Yes, Lee thought. I'd love a big, fresh, steaming plateful of reality. It would do Ciara Lunny no end of good too, even if it did give her indigestion.

'Why don't we eat out? My treat, to cheer you up?'

To her surprise, Ciara looked touched. 'That's really nice of you, Lee. I'd love to eat out. I haven't been anywhere since Jake left.'

Quizzically, Lee raised an eyebrow. 'What – nowhere at all? But what about – your friends –?'

Ciara looked alarmed, her voice rose on a kind of imploring note. 'Oh, Lee, I can't tell them! Can't tell anyone! Nobody must know about Jake! It would only be so – so awkward, when he comes back. You're the only one who knows and you mustn't say a word to anyone. Promise?'

But – but what on earth were these friends *for*, if Ciara couldn't talk to them? If she couldn't be honest, couldn't seek comfort in their support and help and understanding? Lee was mystified. And suddenly sorry for her neighbour, who seemed so alone. More alone than she was herself, although Ciara was the one with the busy social life?

'I couldn't tell anyone even if I tried, since I don't know anyone! None of your circle, anyway. Don't worry, Ciara. If you want me to keep your secret, I will. Nobody will hear anything about Jake from me.'

A flood of relief washed through Ciara's features. 'Thanks, Lee. You're being so great . . . I don't know what I'd do without you, really I don't.'

And then she spun back to the computer. 'So what do you think? Come here and look – should I go for the classic straight nose, or this kinda cute one, it's called retroussé? There's a whole range, the Nicole Kidman and the Meryl Streep and the Amélie Poulain . . . plus a choice of chins, to complement them? What do you think is really *me*?'

Now, Lee thought, there's a good question. Does a real you actually exist? Is there a genuine original Ciara in there somewhere, or are you merely Mrs Lunny? A spouse selected off the shelf, and now plonked back on it, past her sell-by date?

She grinned. 'Oh, be brave! I'd go for the General de Gaulle if I were you.'

4

At least I can manage this computer, Ciara thought at two o'clock one bog-black, sleepless night. At least now I can do that much – see, I'm not just a pretty face! And soon, I'll be a much prettier one. I don't care what Lee says about cosmetic surgery, don't care how expensive it is or how much it might hurt. I'm having it. I'm doing it. In a few months I will look like Claudia Schiffer rolled into Cate Blanchett, and Jake will come scorching back to me. So why can't Lee be more encouraging about it?

Because she's weird, that's why. I never knew anyone so weird. She hardly seems to care how she looks, just goes on wearing those black or white outfits as if they were uniforms, as if she were serving coffee in Bewley's! She says those colours show off her jewellery, people notice it and ask who made it, but I'd go mad if I never went shopping or bought anything new or had any fun. She says her work is fun. As if! Work is something you do so you can afford to have fun. Being cooped up in that garage all day at that workbench has to be a total drag – she just won't admit it, is all. Won't admit she'd love to party and let her hair down, do something wild like this. Wait till she gets to be forty, and see what she does then.

As for her house . . . all those dreary books, all that awful music, that half-raw food . . . I never knew anything like it.

43

Never knew anyone who asks so many peculiar questions, either. What did she mean that night she started on about religion, for God's sake? When I said I couldn't get divorced because of being Catholic? She said something weird about religion not being the same as spirituality . . . is she a closet witch or something, will she soon be chanting spells? I wish she'd chant one over Jake, if she is . . . oh, Jake. When are you coming home? I miss you so much. I wish you'd just come back, no questions asked, wish the children would come back too, and we could all be a family again. That's all I want, just my home and husband and family. How can this be happening, how can I be sitting here at your computer in the middle of the night?

Because it distracts me, that's how. Keeps me from crying into your pillow until the sun comes up – which is another thing I don't get about Lee Warner. What does she mean about getting up at dawn some morning to walk down by the lake and have a champagne picnic? You only drink champagne at a *party,* with your *husband*! If you're celebrating something, not if he's left you. I can't see one reason in the wide world to get up at dawn or go walking or drink champagne with Lee Warner – Jesus, people would think we were lesbians or something, as well as bonkers, if they saw us.

Do that, and next thing she'd have me doing the rest of it, as well. Reading those barmy books, listening to that Mahler maniac, growing herbs as if Tesco didn't sell them by the jar. And then she might try to haul me off on one of those awful trips she calls holidays. I cannot believe all that stuff she told me about her 'travels' – hiking in India, sleeping outdoors, no hotel, no bathroom! Uhhh. And she hiked in the Amazon too, with leeches crawling into her boots and giant spiders into her bedroll – uh, my skin creeps just thinking about it! And she was a shepherd on a French mountain . . . how can that be? I thought shepherds were men. The sheep had ticks, she said, her whole life seems to have been full of insects. And then she married Freddie, 'the real insect'. She fell in love with him because he was the only man who ever took her to the theatre – what?! And then when they divorced she took him to the cleaners. Hah! At least she makes mistakes. Her marriage only lasted three years, she didn't have a *real* one like mine. Didn't have children, either – God, I miss Mike and Tara like hell, when are they ever coming home? When is this house ever going to *be* a home, again?

I wish Jake would talk to me. We used to talk, he never went all silent like this before. I can't believe he'd spring something so awful on me with no warning. Just don't know what's going on with him, can't stand meeting him this way, in cafés as if we were strangers on blind dates, can't bear the way he keeps saying everything is 'fine' and will be 'fine'. Why won't he tell me about Roisin, be honest, admit he's having an affair? And why is he having it with someone like her, of all people? The plainest, dullest little creature in creation! It's just not him, and I just don't understand it.

I don't understand anything, any more. I feel completely lost, stranded, so unsure of everything. Gutted. Betrayed, and horribly alone. I simply cannot bear being alone. Which I suppose is why I'm having supper so often lately with Lee, and she with me – even if we're chalk and cheese, it's still better than being on our own, whatever she might say about enjoying her own company. Admittedly, she hardly ever gives any dinner parties, or goes to many, only socialises with people she likes . . . but if we all did that, nobody would ever go anywhere! I reckon she's trying to avoid meeting men, because Freddie Weinberg was such a disaster. Her pride probably won't let her make another mistake. Why didn't she try harder to get him back, like I'm trying with Jake? I don't believe she really dumped him, the way she says she did, 'with a clang'. You don't leave your husband unless he's *really* awful, and she says he wasn't violent or anything, only a bit bossy.

Do you leave your wife, unless she's really awful? Does Jake think I am awful? Have I done something I don't even know about, injured him or disgraced him in some way? I wish he'd tell me, if I have. At least then I'd have a reason for all this, something to get a grip on. This feeling of being in limbo is sheer hell. I will lose my mind, if I – if I don't do something about it.

Twenty thousand. That's what it says here this surgery is going to cost, if I'm adding it up right. A lot of money. But Jake said to go shopping, didn't he? Said I could spend all I liked? There are more than twenty thousand shares in his portfolio, as he calls it, so . . . new nose. Chin. Eyelids. New Ciara! When I start looking really good, maybe I'll start feeling really good. Looks are so important, no matter what Lee says. If I take the plunge and get it all done right away, it could be finished and healed by the time the children come back from America. This is the ideal time, with nobody around to see the . . . the yukky bit.

I certainly wouldn't want Jake or Mike or Tara to see the way I look when the bandages come off. Those pictures on the internet were gruesome. I would want somebody, though . . . it says here you should bring somebody with you, in fact. Why? To sort of hold your hand I suppose, while you come round from the shock.

It will be a shock. Let's face it, it will be. It'll hurt, too. But it will be worth it. I will be the woman of Jake Lunny's dreams!

46

I'll be visible again, to him and the children and everyone else, photographed at all the social events and receptions, maybe even get into *VIP* magazine. I might even buy something from Versace, something really slinky. All the golf girls will be green with envy and Roisin Harte will simply fade away, Jake would look *stupid* with her compared to the new me.

Right. Let's go for it. Let's take the plunge and contact this clinic. How do you do an e-mail?

And who's going to come with me, through this awful ordeal?

Well, Lee conceded, you've got to come up for air sometime. Got to go to town now and again, if only to buy some new wire and pliers and stuff. I might as well hit a few book-shops while I'm here, see what's new, and then when the shopping's done I think I'll have a pint in that bar that does real, proper, creamy Guinness. The one beside the train station that hasn't been themed, practically the only one in Ireland that hasn't been tarted up to look like a Barcelona bodega or a Bordeaux brasserie. What is it with Ireland, that it keeps trying to look like somewhere else? I like living here, but sometimes I really think this country is having a major identity crisis.

Ciara Lunny is having a major identity crisis, too. She's Irish, but she looks like she was cloned in California. They all do. Where have the freckled redheads gone, those cute colleens we Americans always think of when we read Synge or Joyce? What's with all the blondes, and what's with this plastic surgery? Ireland's actually getting crazier than California. Next they'll be choosing the sex of their children and the chil-dren will be divorcing their parents, suing their dentists . . . anyway, let's get the shopping over and the pint pulling.

It was a small bar, when she finally made her way to it, with rickety wooden tables, brass pumps and a cheerful elderly barman who pretended to remember her from last time. 'Same again?' he winked, making her laugh, and then stare as he began pulling a pint. Good grief, he actually did remember! Amazed, she waited for the pint to settle, draping her raincoat on a coat stand and dipping into her bag of newly purchased books with that same delicious sense of anticipation she'd always felt as a child dipping into a sherbet fizz. With a full hour in hand before the train departed, she settled comfortably into a chair under a window offering enough light to read by. No neon here, no thudding music or fajita menu: just the quiet murmur of conversation from other tables, invisible voices floating up from banquetted little booths.

Her pint arrived with a smile and she sipped it slowly, sinking with a sensation of sheer luxury into her new Jennifer Johnston, a writer she'd only discovered since coming to Ireland. 'Oh, no' some people said, 'it's Edna O'Brien you should be reading.' And certainly Edna did look the part, a dazzlingly beautiful author with a properly Irish mane of red hair; but she lived in London, whereas Jennifer lived in Ireland and had – when Lee saw her on television – a delightfully breathless, scatty air about her. You could imagine her here in this tatty, genuine pub, while Edna would be sipping cocktails at the Shelbourne. Plucking distractedly at a packet of Tayto, Lee began to read.

How long had elapsed, she couldn't say, but it was quite a while, maybe thirty or forty minutes, before the voices started impinging on her mind, distracting her. Neither the man's nor the woman's was loud, but both were distinct, and quietly assertive. They were debating something, their words streaming from a table outside her line of vision, and as phrases gradually fell into context she realised they were talking, with low urgent passion, about Yeats. William Butler Yeats, arguably Ireland's greatest poet – or was Seamus Heaney better? That was the subject of their discussion, and Lee found herself eavesdropping shamelessly, fascinated to find that some Irish people did, after all, still read poetry.

And then, as if a spotlight had swivelled on her, she froze with shock. The woman's voice meant nothing to her, but the man's was Jake Lunny's. Jake Lunny who, until a few weeks ago, had been her next door neighbour. Had been Ciara's husband. Pilot Jake, who had flown six bracelets and six necklaces to New York for a boutique that needed them in a hurry.

Oh, God. What to do? Ignore the whole thing, pretend he wasn't there? Or say hello, get a look at the woman who was, presumably, now his mistress? Lee's own curiosity was surmountable, but Ciara would go mad if she heard this chance had been missed . . . with a kind of fascinated desperation, Lee put down her book and listened.

'Yes, but you have to remember – Willie was a mystic – disillusion set in – Maud soured him – personally and politically – that doesn't excuse – Seamus so pragmatic – great technician – less lyrical maybe, but –'

The words sputtered and fizzed in snatches, some inaudible, some ringingly vehement, while Lee's embarrassment billowed like a bubble; this seemed to be a very intense, very personal conversation. Undoubtedly, she should finish her drink and slide quietly away to her train. Closing her book, draining her glass, she stood up and made for where her coat was hanging. And that – oh, no – was the precise moment at which Jake also stood up, looking around him as if for the barman or the men's room. With glassy fixation, each gazed at the other, until there was nothing for it.

49

'Hello, Jake.' Inwardly cringing, Lee extended her hand, and after a moment's hesitation he took it.

'Hello, Lee! How are you?' His smile was warm, his tone genial, nothing in his demeanour suggested anything clandestine in the company he was keeping. He'd gained a little weight, she thought, since last she'd seen him, but he looked well, fresh and somehow rested, wearing his usual easy grace like a Ralph Lauren sweater. Beside him, still seated, a young, bespectacled woman with a mass of coppery hair smiled pleasantly up at her.

'I'm well, thanks – how are you?'

She was astonished when he laughed aloud. 'I'm great! Destressing, letting off a bit of steam – Lee, this is Roisin Harte. Roisin, my neighbour from Huxley Wood, Lee Warner.'

Left with no option, Lee shook the younger woman's hand, which was firm and friendly, and gazed into a pair of frank, pale grey eyes like opals. Intelligent eyes, with humour in them, and something beyond their owner's years. Something confident, serene.

'Nice to meet you, Roisin.' At speed, she mentally clocked all the details Ciara would want: Aran sweater, red muffler, long ginger-brown skirt. Boots, satchel, dangly amber earrings. Student look. And a wisp of Guinness froth on her lip. Nothing of the siren whatsoever. Nothing of the hideous hag, either. Just a pretty girl losing the last of her puppy fat. A girl with some interest in Nobel-prizewinning poets. In men way older than her, in earth years at least?

'Will you join us?' Jake asked with sudden unexpected enthusiasm, turning to Roisin with a grin. 'Lee makes jewellery. I flew a few pieces to the States for her. Sculptural stuff.'

50

Sculptural? Did men notice details like that? Hastily, Lee shook her head. 'No, thanks Jake, I have to make my train. Enjoy your pint in peace. Good to see you.'

And with that she fled, her head full of horror. Poor Ciara. A gorgeous rival was one thing, but a clever one was quite another. Roisin Harte looked as if she might well have grasped that she was not playing her rival on a level pitch. She also looked like a woman who might understand the word 'voluptuous' in all its shapes and forms.

To tell, or not to tell? All the way home the dilemma haunted Lee, pushing her one way and then the other. Of course Ciara would want to know all about the encounter, every drop of detail, any woman would expect a friend to supply whatever ammunition came to hand. Ciara would rightly feel that, the more she knew about Roisin Harte, the more she would learn about Jake Lunny's inexplicable infatuation. Had the pair been kissing? Cuddling? Intimate in any way?

No. Not physically. Sighing, Lee wondered how to explain to Ciara that the conversation she had overheard had been more intimate than any kiss; it had been heartfelt, passionate, the emotional engagement of two people tuned to the same music. It was *committed*. And it was – dear God – literary. When Ciara heard about Yeats and Heaney, she'd probably wonder whether they were a new brand of shoe, or had a hit in the charts. The names that had sounded so important to her husband would, Lee suspected, mean nothing at all to her. Jake wasn't just having an affair; the Lunny marriage was in way worse trouble than that. Jake had not looked at Roisin with any degree of desire, but – far more fatally – he had sounded intrigued by her.

The train rolled on, and Lee's mind with it, pondering the

problem. Looking at it from the outside, she would guess that Jake Lunny was one of those men who, having married too young, was now disenchanted by the ageing woman he had chosen primarily for her pretty face. Which was outrageously unfair, but Lee was realist enough to accept the way the male mind worked. In America, she'd seen enough men ditch babe after babe, no matter how cute, the minute they hit thirty; if anything Jake was lagging behind in the male chauvinist stakes. But, in America, new young babes invariably supplanted the ageing ones: what didn't add up here was that Jake had supplanted Ciara with a girl who, while certainly young, was neither blonde nor babe. A girl who looked nothing special, but could keep up a flow of conversation like the Orinoco river.

Which, Lee concluded with mixed emotions, seemed to indicate that Jake wasn't merely tiring of his wife's looks. He was tiring of her *presence*. He was growing up, moving on to something, someone more stimulating – and wouldn't be remotely attracted back by a cosmetically enhanced new version of the same old wife. Ciara was about to waste both her time and money. Thousands, on pointless, painful, surgery! A fraction of that money, invested in books or travel or adult education, would probably yield way higher dividends. Jake didn't seem to be seduced by sexy; he seemed seduced by stimulating.

But would Ciara see that, if it were pointed out to her? Somehow Lee didn't think she would. She would pout and say that was the silliest thing she'd ever heard, of course a pretty wife was a trophy wife, of course rejuvenation would pay off. Already she worked out every day, religiously attending her gym or dance classes – but when was the last time she'd taken her mind to a gym? Had it ever had a work-out?

Unlikely, Lee reckoned as she gathered up her things and the train slowed into the station. Ciara was a masterpiece of show over substance, probably didn't even know where the local library was. Probably had never been in it. For nearly twenty years she'd existed for, lived through, her husband and children – and now, when she looked into the mirror, suddenly there was nobody there any more. Which must, Lee thought with a shudder, be absolutely terrifying. Talk about an existential whammy.

Loudly, instinct muttered to her that she should stay well out of this. The Lunny marriage was none of her business, and besides she was no good at domestic stuff, never had been, nobody had been much surprised when her own marriage collapsed. And yet . . . when it had collapsed, she had unexpectedly experienced so many of the emotions that Ciara must be experiencing now.

Even though she was the one who'd walked away from Freddie, she'd still tasted the bitter tang of failure, still known moments of sheer panic and gaping loss, moments when flying solo had been as terrifying as leaping off Kilimanjaro. Airhead as Ciara might be, she was still a human being, a woman, and they had this in common, the bond of betrayal. And besides, maddening muppet and all as she was, Ciara was the first person who'd ever been neighbourly to her in Ireland. That heroically chocolate cake, that welcoming smile, that conspiratorial promise not to tell the neighbours about working in the garage . . . that had all mattered, a year ago when she, Lee, was finding her feet in this new country. Ciara's casually generous friendship had been a warm, comforting little flame. Should it be extinguished, now that it was less essential? Could Ciara simply be snuffed out, when she was the one who needed support?

Of course she could be. But only a monster would do it. Walking home from the train station, gritting her teeth and shutting her eyes against the strong breeze, Lee sighed as she recognised and accepted the inevitable: if Ciara was now the one in need of help, then it was Lee Warner's moral duty to furnish it. Clearly, for whatever reasons of her own, Ciara didn't want to turn to any of her other, closer friends. Maybe they didn't have any broken marriages, didn't know how it felt? Or maybe she didn't trust their loyalty? Or maybe . . . if word got out that Ciara was newly single, semi-detached at any rate, her girlfriends would start circling the wagons, fearful that she might set her sights on one of their husbands? At least she couldn't do that to Lee Warner, who didn't have a husband. Maybe Lee Warner was, now that she thought about it, not such a dumb choice of confidante?

All right. Okay. I'll do it. I'll stick with Ciara. She makes me nuts at times, she's as dippy as a lollipop, but she . . . she's vulnerable, and I know how that feels. And – for all her flibbertigibbet faults – she's what the Irish call a 'decent skin'. She means well. Probably her kids have scooted away for the summer because she's a bit of a smother-mother, they felt stifled, but still . . . she'd bring you chicken soup if you were ill, and a huge box of chocolates and a stack of absolutely idiot magazines. I won't let her get too close, because I don't want to end up watching soaps or celebrity trash with her, but I will . . . listen to her. Let her talk. And tell her I saw Jake.

'Everything' Ciara insisted, sitting lotus-like on Lee's futon, 'I want to know absolutely *everything* about this. How did he look? What was he wearing? What was she wearing? What were they doing?'

Reflectively, Lee paused, a chopping knife aloft in her hand

and a stack of chives awaiting execution below. It was important to go about this the right way. 'He looked . . . relaxed. He was wearing chinos and a turtleneck sweater, a sports jacket I'd seen before. Not exactly dolled up for a date.'

Ciara frowned. Was this good news, or bad? Had Jake got past the stage of 'dating' Roisin? Or what?

'She wasn't dressed to kill either. Kinda muffled up. No make-up.'

'No. I've never seen her wear any. Hideous little hag, isn't she?'

Lee hesitated, thinking that beauty truly was in the eye of the beholder. 'I wouldn't go that far. Let's just say low-key?'

'Huh. She could hardly look much worse if I were to slash her ears off with a hacksaw. Which I would if I got the chance.'

It was so unexpected, Lee burst out laughing, surprised to discover some small sense of black humour in sweet-as-pie Ciara Lunny. She'd never once said anything nasty before. The effect was as refreshing as peppermint tea. Unless – she couldn't actually mean that, could she!?

'As for what they were doing . . . no kissing that I could see, no canoodling as you Irish call it. Not even holding hands.'

'Well, that's something, I suppose.' Ciara's tone was begrudging. 'But then, what *were* they doing?'

'Drinking pints of stout. And talking about poetry.' Lee released the word in a kind of apprehensive whistle, and Ciara's eyes widened incredulously.

'*Poetry*!? But Jake knows damn all about poetry. He wouldn't know a poem from a packet of popcorn. No more would I.' On a vaguely triumphant note, she smiled and shook her hair, as if to confirm the impossibility of the topic. Silently, Lee groaned.

'Well, he seemed to know something about it today. They were arguing Yeats v. Heaney. He sounded . . . interested.'

Ciara blinked, and smiled again. 'Lee, Jake has never once in all our years of marriage read a poem, or owned a book of poems, or had the faintest interest in any of that stuff. Your pint must have gone to your head, you must have been hearing things.'

Carefully, Lee considered. 'Ciara, Jake never used to like opera, did he, or listen to it? You told me he'd only recently got into – what did you call it? – a lot of dull music?'

Oh. Oh . . . visibly making the connection, Ciara furrowed her brow, remembering, linking. 'Yeah. Uh. That's true. Lee . . . d'you reckon maybe that's where Roisin Harte fits in? With all this other dull stuff he seems to be getting into?'

'Yes. Yes, Ciara, I do. For what my opinion's worth, I think Roisin Harte is part of some bigger picture. My guess would be that Jake is looking for . . . um. Stimulus, of some kind? New horizons, new challenges? If you thought about it a bit, if you grasped it the right way, maybe you could –?'

'Well' Ciara's words burst across her bows like bubbles, 'am I ever glad you told me about this! Jake's new challenge is going to be *me*! I am going to be so gorgeous after my makeover he will *beg* to be let back into this house, and I am going to make him *grovel*!'

Oh, God, Lee thought despairingly. She's deaf as a post. And thick as one too. She's not getting the message here at all. Does she actually look a little bit manic? Her eyes are glittering – Jesus, I hope she's not doing anything stupid, is she? Not *on* anything?

Clasping her hands, Ciara smiled widely, raptly. 'Lee, would you . . . I was wondering . . . would you do me a favour?'

. 56

Lee thought of the welcoming cake. And the garage. And the jewellery urgently flown to New York. 'Sure. If I can, I will. What is it?'

'Would you come to London with me? I've booked into a clinic there. For the first facelift. Next week.'

5

I should be working, Lee muttered to herself as they waited for their flight to board. I should be finishing that consignment for that boutique in Boston, it'll be late and they'll blow a fuse. What on earth am I doing going to London with a woman who – sweet swizzlesticks, she's not actually buying a Danielle Steel, is she?

Beaming, Ciara brandished it. 'See, you think I don't read, but I do! This will keep me amused in the recovery room!'

Honey, Lee thought, you will more likely keep me amused in the recovery room. You are going to look like an Egyptian mummy. Then when the bandages come off you will look like Picasso's *Guernica*. I hope this doctor of yours has briefed you fully and you are braced for the reality of this. Somehow I can't see you being a stoic little soldier when the painkillers wear off.

The flight boarded and took off and Ciara smiled happily as she became airborne. 'Oh, this is so exciting! A new me – and I get to go shopping, too! I adore London, you know. Love to travel.'

Lee eyed her. 'Really? To where – Macchu Picchu? Myanmar? London hardly counts, it's so near. Where have your real travels taken you?'

'Oh – we had a fantastic time last year in Gran Canaria! Jetskied all day. It was brilliant. I was hoping Jake might buy a jet-ski for us to use back home. He said he'd rather get a wind-surfer. But the children would love it.'

Lee squirmed in her seat. 'Yes. And everyone else would hate it. Just one jet-ski ruins an entire coast, an entire lake, for everyone. Screaming motorbikes. Users should be executed.'

Dimpling with amusement, Ciara opened her book. 'Oh, Lee, you're such a killjoy. Not everyone's idea of fun is herbal tea with the monks, you know.'

Serenely, Lee said nothing. Soon Ciara would be un-conscious, with a tube up her nose and, with any luck, her mouth tightly swathed in bandages. The prospect was alluring enough to make her wonder whether there might actually be, after all, a God.

Yes, she was certain, Ciara nodded adamantly. Yes, she understood the risks. Yes, she was hearing everything the doctor was saying to her, accepting that the facelift was only a start, that the nose and chin would have to come later. Rome, as he pointed out, was not built in a day. Yes, she would be paying by credit card. Yes, she would report back to the clinic for surgery at nine tomorrow morning. And then, the counselling session over, she grasped Lee's arm.

'Let's go shopping!'

'For what? A supersize packet of Neurofen Plus?'

'Oh, you are so boring. Come on. Harrods. Bond Street, Regent Street. I want to get tons of stuff.'

'What do you need tons of?'

'Lee! You have no sense of adventure – what do you want to do, then? Go look at statues in some museum?'

'Actually, I have an appointment. With a shop in Hamp-stead that might be interested in taking some of my jewellery.

So why don't you go shopping and we'll meet up later? At Selfridges, say, at six?'

Ciara shrugged. 'Oh. Okay. Whatever.' And then, looking crestfallen, she melted away, leaving Lee feeling inexplicably guilty, like a mother parking a child in a crèche. But she couldn't babysit Ciara all afternoon, swan round London for stuff they didn't need! Resolutely she set off in the opposite direction; after all, time was money. Even if she didn't need money, and rarely had time to spend any. Even if, she belatedly wondered, Ciara maybe needed company today, and reassurance?

Damn, she thought. Dammit, I am going to have to do better than this.

Well, yes. It seemed to be a very good clinic, Lee conceded next morning, with nice efficient staff and every sign of being properly, reputably run. Ciara had chosen well, made a good job of it. Drowsy now with some preliminary drug, her blonde locks swept up into a plastic cap, Ciara was tucked up on a trolley waiting to be wheeled away, and Lee hardly knew whether to laugh or cry when she saw what she was clutching: a fluffy, minuscule teddy bear with a blue ribbon around its neck.

'Would you like me' she said straight-faced, 'to mind the little guy for you?'

But Ciara did not release her grip. Licking her lips, looking around her, she seemed befuddled. 'I wish . . .' she whispered, apparently to the ceiling.

Lee leaned closer. 'What do you wish? Can I get something for you?'

'I wish . . . Tara was here. I want Tara.' And suddenly she looked distressed, her expression pleading as if she were the child and Tara were her mother. Stricken – after all, surgery could go wrong – Lee gripped her hand.

'Don't worry, Ciara. I'm here. And you'll see Tara soon.'

Momentary silence. And then Ciara was gone, briskly wheeled away by a smocked attendant, leaving Lee with an awful thought: if anything did go wrong, how on earth would she explain it to the Lunny family? None of them knew Ciara was doing this, because 'they'd only try to talk me out of it'. For next-of-kin, Ciara had given not Jake's name but her mother's. Abruptly Lee was left with a vision of Ciara's fragile, frightened little face, and a powerful wish for everything to go right. And a dreadful feeling of responsibility, for not having succeeded in talking her out of it.

Ow. Ow ow owww. Swimming to the surface, which seemed to keep rising just out of reach, Ciara was conscious of one exclusive thing: pain. Pain that felt like an icepick chipping into her cheekbones. Pain that made her feel the same way she'd felt when having the twins, hugely resentful that nobody had warned her it would be this bad. 'Maybe a little discomfort' her doctors had said on both occasions. As if they'd know anything: when did men ever have twins, or plastic surgery? Ow. Ow ow ouchh! Sucking her teeth, she tried not to screech aloud.

'Ciara.' A voice was wafting through the fog. 'Ciara, can you open your eyes? I'm going to count to three and then you're going to look at me, okay?'

It took the full count to prise them open, and when she did some man's face nodded into hers, smiled with apparent satisfaction and then faded out of focus. No, she thought, don't go, give me drugs! I want a mug of morphine!

A hand touched hers. Some light cool hand that seemed

to belong to someone she couldn't quite identify.

'Tara' she mumbled hopefully. 'Tara . . . Jake . . .'

'Ciara. It's me. Lee. Here beside you. You're just waking up.'

Striving to concentrate, she frowned. 'Have you . . . have you . . . ?'

'Have I what?' The voice sounded sympathetic, as if it might be wheedled into supplying painkillers.

'Have you . . . done . . . your homework?'

A ricochet of laughter, as if she'd said something other than whatever she'd meant to say. What was it, that she'd meant to say?

'Yes. Only I had trouble with the math.' More muffled laughter.

'Then . . . go ask Daddy. He's good at . . . maths . . .' God, it hurt to speak! Wincing, she exhaled with the effort. When would the drugs be coming, spinning her back into blissful oblivion?

'Okay. I will. You just relax now, don't try to talk. You're pumped to the gills with painkillers, you know, bit fuzzy. But they'll wear off later.'

Wear *off*? But –?! But that must be wrong. She couldn't have had any painkillers. If she had, this chain-saw wouldn't be slicing into her skull and her teeth would not be throbbing like tom-toms. Somebody, she thought dimly, must be a bit mixed up. Totally mixed up.

No, Lee conceded grimly. Propped up on her pillows four days later, Ciara was not a pretty sight. Thank heaven they'd had the sense to rent an apartment for the week, because no hotel would have let Ciara in. She looked as if she'd been beaten up by her pimp. Black, violet, navy, emerald, fuchsia, primrose . . . every colour of the rainbow shone from Ciara's football-size face, in which her eyes resembled two fine-nib lines of calligraphy.

'Lee' she croaked, 'do I look any better today?' As yet, the doctor had vetoed a mirror. All, he said, in good time. End of the week.

'Honey' Lee spluttered, 'you look fabulous. Would you like another spoonful of jelly?'

No. Wincing, Ciara shook her head. Jelly and soup were the only things she could swallow, and Lee was heroically attempting to spoon them into her, but she couldn't taste or chew. The swinging icepick had been replaced by a boxer's glove, which kept punching her non-stop, dhunk-dhunk-dhunk. Flopping back on her pillows, she sighed.

'Remember this' Lee admonished. 'Remember this before you get the nose done, okay? Or the eyes or the chin.'

Yes. It might be irritating advice but it was undoubtedly well timed. Right now, Ciara thought, she would sooner jump off the Eiffel Tower than ever again let anyone near her with any sharp implement of any kind. How could that bloody doctor possibly think she was 'doing well' when her face felt like a beaten drum? If this was good, what on earth was bad?

Patting her hand, Lee nodded encouragingly. 'Don't worry. You're getting there. And I – uh, sorry – I'm starving. Would it be awful of me to order in a pizza? Or I can go out for one, if you'd rather?'

A pizza. Ciara's stomach flipped and churned. She would never eat again. Never, ever. If only God would make the pain stop for one minute, the swelling shrink for ten seconds, she would totter to the bathroom and – quietly, without any mess or fuss – slash her wrists.

★

'Well, Mrs Lunny, that's excellent. I think we can have a look at ourselves today. Nurse, bring a mirror, would you?'

Yes! At last! For the first time since the surgery of a week ago, anticipation outstripped dread. The pain was still thundering, but now there were brief respites before David Beckham's boot slammed back into her forehead. Attempting to smile, Ciara nodded.

'Well. So. What do we think?' The mirror gleamed, the doctor beamed, and Ciara . . . uhhh. Oh, no! No! Gasping, she recoiled appalled, as if from Frankenstein's monster.

'But I look – hideous! Horrible, horrific, awful! I – I'm *deformed*!' Hysterically, Ciara's voice rose on a note of operatic anguish as her mind grappled with the unspeakable: she was, after all, one of those rare cases of failure. Sheer disaster. Her surgery had left her looking worse – waaay worse – than Michael Jackson. Giddily, she clutched at the doctor as if drowning, feeling bubbles pop in her nose.

Chuckling, the doctor patted her shoulder, glancing at Lee for confirmation of his patient's folly. 'Not at all! You look lovely – or will do, in a few more days! Everything is healing perfectly. You have such good skin. And youth on your side, of course. Trust me, Mrs Lunny, you go back to Ireland now and let me know in a week's time if everyone's not saying you're gorgeous. There is . . . ah . . . um . . . someone there to look after you, is there, just in case –?'

Awkwardly, the question lay on the air, until Lee spoke up. 'I'll be looking after her. Staying with her for a little while until she's – er – out of the woods.'

Good. That seemed to settle that, then. Standing up, the doctor genially dismissed them with not impolite speed – there were five more women in the waiting room, although their exit route would not take them through it – and as Lee waited for Ciara to settle her bill with the receptionist, she wagged an impatient metaphorical finger at herself. 'Only at night, that's all! I'll sleep over with her, but during the day I'll be working in my workshop! She hasn't been mown down by a truck, she only has residual bruising and besides, it's self-inflicted! Tea, but no sympathy!'

For another week, back at home, Ciara lay low, not exactly licking her wounds because, as Lee grinned, her tongue wouldn't reach them, but preening, patting, studying herself in a hand mirror from every conceivable angle. Day by day the swelling receded, day by day her skin smoothed out, her new face emerging, taking shape like moulded clay and . . . and starting, suddenly, to look startling.

Startlingly, stunningly, lovely. There could be no denying it, until finally one morning Lee nodded, whistling in admiration.

'Wow! Ciara, you look beautiful! It's worked! You look truly, totally amazing!'

Eagerly, Ciara looked up at her, like a child congratulated by teacher.

'Do I? Do you really think so, Lee?'

'Yes!' She honestly did. 'That facelift is a miracle, the work of Michelangelo! You were always pretty, but now you – you – you've been ironed! It's taken at least ten years off you. More. Fifteen. You don't look a day over twenty-five.'

'Really?' Peering back into the mirror again, Ciara considered. And agreed. And exulted. Not only was her facelift a masterpiece, but she'd lost weight too, after all those tortuous mouthfuls of soup. She really did look wonderful, just as Lee said, not a day over twenty-five. She had been given back her fading youth. Gripped by some powerful emotion, she felt literal tears of joy rising to her wide, perfectly clear blue eyes.

'Oh, Lee! I can't believe this! It's even better than I'd dared to hope! You're right, I do look younger – much, much younger! I could almost be mistaken for my own daughter! Wait till Tara sees this – oh, I can't wait for her to come home, and see the new me! For everyone to see me!'

All but levitating with excitement, she jumped up, grabbed Lee and hugged her. Laughing, Lee hugged her back, relieved and delighted that the gruesome surgery had been such a success. A veritable triumph. Mike and Tara Lunny would, indeed, be astonished when they got home from America and saw their remoulded mother. As would Jake Lunny, when he saw the nymphette he was married to.

'But right now, let's go to the golf club for lunch! I want to show all the girls what I got in London! They won't believe their eyes, when they see this – come on, let's go!'

Grabbing Lee's hand, Ciara hauled her to her feet and spun her out in the direction of her big, metallic-blue, must-have Range Rover.

'I can't wait to see their faces! And then – and then, if they think I look terrific, I'll go show it to Jake! He is just going to pass out stone cold, when he sees the new me!'

6

Not all of 'the girls' were ever in the golf club at any one moment. But it was their headquarters, especially at lunchtime; Ciara knew she could count on finding at least five or six of her pals ensconced over salads and spritzers, chewing on the latest gossip. Today, she could hear Marie's loud laugh long before she saw her, and on walking into the lounge she saw Sara too, surrounded by Sue, Trish, Jean and Bernie. Not all of her buddies, but enough of them to make up a kind of mirror, that would reflect her fabulous new face back at her. This would be a dress rehearsal, before she showed it to Jake. Unable to contain her excitement, she all but ran up to them, hauling Lee in her wake.

'Hi, girls! How's everyone?' Eagerly, breathlessly, she sat down as nonchalantly as she could, rummaging in her bag for her mobile phone; somehow you felt naked until it was re-assuringly parked on the table. Besides, Jake might call.

There was a silence. A total, resounding silence, as her friends' conversation squealed to a stop in a way that was hugely satisfying. A way that said they were amazed, awestruck by her new appearance.

She couldn't suppress a huge smile. A smile that stretched, literally, all the way up to her ears. Visibly, they were too stunned to speak.

'Eh? Cat got our tongue? Nothing to say for ourselves,

today? Well . . . this is Lee Warner, my neighbour, let me introduce everyone.'

Somehow managing to keep her smile just the decent side of smug, she presented everyone, noting how their eyes barely swung to Lee for long enough to say hello before returning, fascinated, to her.

'Ciara . . .' It was Sara who spoke, finally. Sara Thompson, the leader of the pack. Sara in her Jimmy Choo shoes and Paul Smith shirt, sounding strangled for the first time in living memory. 'Ciara . . . what on earth has happened to you? To your face? What have you done?'

She simpered. Just couldn't help it. 'Oh, just a little bit of work! I mean – well, we're none of us getting any younger, are we? I thought it was time to give mother nature a helping hand. Nothing much, just a little tweak.' Airily, she waved a dismissive hand, as if she'd dropped a decade overnight by waving a wand, had felt no pain, spent no fortune. Just a click of the fingers and – hey presto! Youth on tap.

The silence settled. And deepened. For several seconds, nobody said another word, absorbing the shock, absorbing the smooth, creamy, incredibly rejuvenated Ciara Lunny. Even Lee, she noted, was silent beside her.

And then, at last, somebody spoke. Marie, who was over fifty and wrinkled as a walnut. 'But . . . Ciara . . . it's incredible! Where did you get it done? When? What did it cost? Did it hurt?'

Her eyes were round as marbles, and Ciara giggled in the schoolgirlish way she felt she could afford. 'Oh, it was nothing! Went to London. Marvellous man. Never felt a thing.'

Beside her, Lee stiffened. Blithely, she prattled on. 'Cost a few bob, I suppose, but hey – great value, don't you think? Worth every cent?'

There could be no arguing with that. Almost in unison, her friends sank back into their chairs, reaching for their spritzers without taking their incredulous eyes from her hypnotic new face.

'Well' Sue exhaled at length, 'yes. Worth whatever it cost. You look amazing, Ciara. This is way beyond Botox. You look like . . . like your own daughter!'

Laughter, and nods of confirmation, and then she saw what she most wanted to see, dawning in every eye – admiration. Envy, almost, naked lust. They'd all love to look like this. Ponderously, Sara stirred her spritzer.

'And you never said a word! We'd been wondering where you were, why we hadn't seen you lately . . . so tell us, Ciara, what does Jake think of this new you? He must be thrilled, huh?'

Conspiratorially, she smiled, and Ciara wondered. Wondered just for one split second, whether Sara knew about Jake and, if she did, whether she was deliberately being a prize bitch? It wouldn't be beyond Sara Thompson, who at forty-one was positively corrugated with lines. No doubt she'd be discreetly disappearing off to London herself, now – not that any amount of surgery could ever make anyone warm to her, really, or like her any better. It struck Ciara that Sara Thompson's social life was held together exclusively by money. Money, and that aura she somehow exuded, of being head girl, captain of the team. Even though she'd long socialised with Sara, she'd never actually liked her. Beside Lee, she looked somehow fake, her beady eyes sharp and malign as a raven's.

'Oh' she said casually, flicking back her freshly streaked hair, 'Jake hasn't seen it yet. I've only just got back, and he's away on long-haul.'

Sara skewered her with a sharp look. 'Again? Good grief, even for a pilot he seems to be away an awful lot lately. Sure he hasn't run off with a trolley dolly?'

Maliciously, she grinned, and everyone giggled dutifully. Except Lee, who had yet to say a word, was staring at them all as if they were a coven of witches. At speed, Ciara groped for some response. And then, smugly, she hit on the perfect one.

'Why would he want a dolly' she drawled archly, 'with a wife like me?'

Either nobody could answer that, or nobody dared. There was a further contemplative silence, in which Lee glanced at her watch and declined the offer of a drink. Defiantly, Ciara sat up and stared at them all, her shoulders squared and her stance challenging: go on, say it! Who's going to be the one to suggest that my husband has left me? Huh? Which one of you has the guts to come out and report the rumours?

No. I thought not. Well, don't bother. When Jake sees the new me, he'll be back at my side in a flash. So there. While you all go running off for facelifts of your own – not that I'd fancy any of your husbands in a fog. Huh! Even if Jake is going through a funny patch, it's only temporary, he's not a fraudster like some I could mention, nor a fat old toad . . . he's a prize hunk, and I will get him back, now, with a snap of my fingers. So don't anyone say anything she might regret, okay?

'Was it' Bernie Riley breathed reverently, 'very expensive?'

Again, Ciara flicked her hair, and shrugged. 'Oh . . . depends what you call expensive, I suppose. I just call it an investment. Money well spent, because I feel absolutely fantastic.'

And you look it. That's what you're supposed to say, girls! Go on, spit it out, compliments cost nothing you know. Okay, Sue and Marie have conceded that I look amazing, but what about the rest of you? What about you, Sara Thompson, is jealousy strangling you or what?

No response. Slowly, Ciara's elation began to deflate, as if they were letting the air out of her tyres. This was not quite the ecstatic reception she'd envisaged. Where were the congratulations, the clapping of hands, the awed gasps of admiration? Clearly, everyone was impressed, but why did nobody seem delighted, why was she getting no joy out of this? All anyone seemed interested in was the pain and the price, both of which were already forgotten in her own mind. Vaguely baffled, she turned to Lee.

'Lee, d'you play golf? We could sign you in as a guest if you do, maybe get up a fourball . . .'

Whereupon Sara Thompson tossed back the last of her drink and stood up, sadly shaking her head. 'Sorry. Count me out. I have a hairdressing appointment this afternoon.'

And then Trish Kavanagh got up too. 'Gotta fly too – manicure at three.'

As if some storm cloud had gathered overhead, they all scuttled away one after another, Jean and Bernie and every last one of them, until only Lee was left sitting beside her. Never, Ciara thought, had she felt so punctured, so disappointed in or so rebuffed by her friends. Barely ten minutes after her triumphant arrival, the table was deserted, surrounded by empty chairs. It was as if, instead of receiving a standing ovation for her starring role in a Broadway play, she'd been forced to watch the entire audience walk out.

Bewildered, trying to make sense of it, she turned to Lee, plucking at her sleeve.

'What happened? Where did they all go, what did I say, what did I do wrong?'

Thoughtfully, sadly, Lee sighed. 'I think' she said at length, 'what you did, honey, was show them up. Even I couldn't help noticing that, compared to you, they all looked like hags. Well – maybe not hags exactly, but not goddesses either. Middle-aged harridans way older than you. I get the awful feeling, Ciara, that you've maybe created a monster.'

'What?'

'A scary monster, that frightened the wits out of them. They all ran off because they feel they can't afford to be seen beside you now. Let's face it, the comparison is odious! They look menopausal while you look miraculous. Even if this facelift works like magic and gets your husband back for you, it might be going to cost you your friends.'

'My . . . friends?' Looking punched, Ciara clasped her hands together, held them to her mouth as if wielding off a blow. These women were, after all, allegedly her friends. They'd all been in this blasted golf club together for years! Even been away on weekends together, sometimes, to dinner parties in each other's homes . . . how could they all just fade away, like this, in five minutes flat?

Seeing the hurt in her face – her brand new, girlish little face – Lee squirmed, wondering how to soften the blow. 'I mean, you might not see them again until they all get facelifts of their own! You look so beautiful now, they might think you could be a threat to their marriages, run off with their husbands –'

Ooops. Too late. She hadn't thought that out properly, and watched it sink in with dawning horror. 'You mean' Ciara queried, 'they're afraid I might pinch one of their husbands now that – that I no longer have one of my own? Is that what you're trying to say?'

Glumly, Lee nodded. 'I guess it is. Let's be honest, Ciara, your new look is kind of intimidating. If beauty is in the eye

74

of the beholder, then they're probably all making up their minds that their husbands are not going to behold you.'

'But – but they're my friends! They've known me for years! They couldn't simply drop me, clang, just like that!'

Your friends. Who've known you for years. So how come it was me, Lee, you took to London? How come it's me, Lee, who's been looking after you ever since? Oh, Ciara. Next time you look in the mirror, I wish you'd see the full picture. Is there any mirror to reflect the full, three-dimensional picture?

'And the worst of it is' Ciara continued bitterly, 'they never even said hey, well done, you look wonderful. I so wanted at least one of them to say that. Any one of them.'

'Did you?' Even though she could understand that, Lee couldn't see that it mattered. Ciara knew she looked wonderful. If her so-called friends were jealous – well, what kind of friends were they? Their opinion was hardly worth the time of day. Somewhere, she must have other, closer, better friends, surely?

'Yes. I really did. It would have given me such a confidence boost, for when I meet Jake. Oh, God, Lee! What if he goes weird, too? What if he jumps up and says he has to run? What if he doesn't like the way I look, after all?'

Ciara's face filled with apprehension, the kind a child might feel on presenting itself for inspection with a view to adoption. Hands scrubbed, shoes polished, skirt straight? Cute enough to take home and keep? Sensing that her wretched 'friends' had not only hurt her but dented her confidence, Lee felt inexplicably sorry for her. Leaning over, patting her shoulder, she gave her a reassuring hug.

'He'll love the way you look, Ciara. No man could possibly resist the way you look.'

Looking abruptly unconvinced, or maybe vaguely grasping the implications of that, Ciara nodded, gazing into the depths of the vacant chairs around her.

Huxley Wood, that evening, felt very quiet. So quiet that Ciara found herself almost wishing she lived in a slum, in one of those teeming estates where there was always noise, always people coming and going. Anything would be better than this discreet upmarket silence, this big echoing house, this reverberating silence inside her own head. Never, in all her adult life, could she remember having had absolutely nothing to do before, nobody to talk to, no agenda or purpose whatsoever. Every minute felt like an hour, gaping dark and deep as a canyon, and nothing seemed to hold her attention. Leafing through a magazine, she put it down unfinished; switching on the television, she clicked through twenty channels without finding anything interesting. Even the shopping channels, tonight, only seemed to be offering kitchenware, and she really didn't need a nutmeg grater.

Slowly, gradually, the silence billowed out around her, feeling as if it were filling every available space from the inside of her skull to the core of the planet. Hugging her cardi around her, because it was unnaturally chilly for a summer evening, she thought of calling Tara in America, or her mother in Spain, or Lee next door, but somehow couldn't pick up the phone. Some voice in her head kept whispering that they had their own lives, that she was somehow going to have to get through this evening by herself. And maybe other evenings, as well? Dozens of them, hundreds, thousands, without any husband any more, any family?

All on my own! But I've never lived on my own, and I can't do it now, I don't want to do it! Why haven't the twins called, neither one of them, for ages? Why am I not out celebrating the success of my surgery with the girls, why did they all go off like that when we met today? Lee can't be right about them being jealous, or afraid of the way I look now. She can't. Not all of them . . . even Jean, even Sue? Why did they do it? Why is it so damn quiet?

Why did Jake leave me?

I can't bear it, without him. Even when he was away on flights he'd always call me, I can't remember the last time the phone didn't ring once all evening. He was so far away, sometimes, but he was always near, we were always connected in our heads, I never felt the way I feel now.

As if he weren't coming back.

But he will! He has to! He says himself it's only temporary, only a patch he's going through. Only a break, that's all he needs. From what? I wish I knew from what, wish I understood what this is all about.

Should I call him?

He says I shouldn't. Not unless it's an emergency. Does this count as an emergency?

Yes, it does. It does to me. I feel as if I might be going mad, losing my grip. I can't even go out anywhere without him, to a movie or a restaurant or anywhere, I never realised before how many places a woman can't go on her own. If I don't get out of this house, go somewhere or do something, I'll crack up. Just when I've got this lovely new look, I can't show it off anywhere to anyone. I'm a *prisoner*!

I'm going to count to ten. And then, if I can't stand it, I'm going to call him. Even if it means losing face. I'm going to ask him to meet me and tell me what the hell is going on, why he's holed up in some rented apartment 'thinking', when he should be here at home. With me. How am I supposed to know, to understand, when he never explained, never gave me any warning? Why didn't he?

He has to come home soon. He has to. This can't be anything more than some passing crisis, a storm in a teacup. He's just stressed, overworked. He couldn't possibly be thinking of . . . of divorce or anything. Even if he's not a Catholic, I am, he knows I'd never agree to a divorce. So far, he hasn't even mentioned it, and if he does I won't listen. Just will not listen.

You can block out anything you don't want to hear, and I won't hear of divorce. He hasn't even any grounds for one. I've been an exemplary wife and mother, done nothing wrong at all that I know of. And how could I know of anything, if he won't tell me?

How is this ever going to get sorted out, if all we do is go on having these 'civilised' meetings once a week, talking about the children and his work and the house and everything except – except us? Meetings at times and places chosen by him, too, as if my wishes or opinion didn't count. I wish I could tell him to go to hell. But I can't. Because if I did, maybe he would. Maybe he'd say 'all right, then, let's not meet any more' and go waltzing off with that awful girl.

Is he living with her? Is he? Can he really be having an affair? With the likes of Roisin Harte? What on earth could he see in her?

Whatever it is, it can hardly compare to what he's going to see in me! I look almost as young, now, as she does. He'll be knocked out. Maybe I should call him, right now, tell him it's important . . . after all, it is important. Not only is his wife a new woman, but if she doesn't see him soon, hear his voice and touch his skin, she's going to lose her mind.

Any minute now, I'll start bouncing off the walls, walking

round and round in circles, I'll lie down on the carpet and scream into it. I can't *stand* this silence, this awful hollow feeling! This suspense, wondering why he's done this and when it will all be over, when he's ever going to come back to his senses and back to his family. He has to come back, before the children do, they must never find out that their father had a – a little bit of a breakdown – while they were away. Tara would be distraught and heaven only knows what Mike would say or do. They're still only children, and it's my job to protect them.

I'm going to do it. Going to pick up that phone and ring him and tell him I must see him, it's important, it's about the children. He loves his children, he'd never refuse to talk about them.

Never. Not if there's one shred left of the Jake Lunny I've known and loved for twenty years. He will agree to meet me and we will talk about our children. After we've talked about my new face, after he gets over the lovely surprise of that.

An hour later, Ciara walked into the 'neutral venue' of Jake's choice. Given a choice, she'd have nominated Fitzers or Roly's or one of the other high-profile, gossipy places where word would stand some chance of going round: 'saw Jake and Ciara having dinner together last night, yeah, she was looking great!' Instead, Jake had met her request for an 'urgent' meeting by proposing a low-key pub in the suburbs. An obscure suburb at that, one where they would stand no chance of running into anyone they knew. It was like being asked to wear your new Donna Karan to a bingo night.

But, if nobody got to see them, at least she would get to see him. And he would get to see her. Which was why, sealing a smile onto her brand-new visage, she sailed into the pub on

79

three-inch stilettos, waved brightly when she spotted him and blew a kiss across the room.

Frowning, he blinked back. Screwed up his eyes, stared, and continued to stare fixedly as she approached him, beaming resolutely. He was not going to know that, barely an hour before, she had been almost exploding with loneliness, with the aching need of him. She was going to play this the way all the magazines said you should: no whining, no accusing, nothing alienating. Just a big smile and a big kiss.

Puckering her lips, she delivered one on his forehead, revelling in his evident fascination. Looking wrenchingly attractive in jeans and a light silk shirt, he was drinking in her new appearance as if it were fine wine, an incredible new one he'd never tasted before.

'Hi' she murmured into his ear, as sexily as she dared in these impossibly unromantic surroundings. The pub was big and boxy, filled with loud young drinkers shouting into mobile phones and at each other. Why on earth had he chosen such a horrible place?

'Ciara?'

He gazed at her as if he genuinely wasn't sure, and a flash of delight ignited the blood in her veins. There could be no mistaking his surprise, the double-take in his eyes.

'Yes, Mrs Ciara Lunny, your wife – the same, only different!'

She beamed, and he sat perfectly still, his gaze roving over her, searching before slowly, gradually, apprehending.

'Jesus Christ.'

Playfully, she pouted. That was hardly the romantic response a man made to his newly minted wife, was it? Of course, the shock. It would take him a few moments to adjust, to focus properly. Even her girlfriends, before evaporating from the golf club, had grudgingly conceded that she looked a knock-out. She'd seen that much in their envious eyes. The surgery was superb, she could smile without fear of anything slipping or snapping, and she did.

'What do you think?'

Her look was a kind of pleading pride. His was that of a man hit with a baseball bat.

'I – Ciara, what is this? What have you *done*?' He sounded genuinely, totally bewildered.

'I've had a facelift. Isn't it fab?'

No reply. Instead, he inspected her, taking her chin in his hand, turning her face this way and that, peering, squinting and, it seemed, playing for time.

And then, at last, some response. Not just any response, but admiration. Candid, ungrudging compliments.

'Yes. It is – quite – extraordinary. I scarcely recognise you. You look much younger. Nobody could possibly think you were anywhere near forty.'

'No! And the funny thing is, Jake, I don't feel anywhere near it. I feel as if my entire body clock has been turned back. Full of energy, absolutely fantastic.'

Quizzically, he continued to stare at her, still assessing, reflecting.

'Why didn't you tell me?'

'Oh, I wanted it to be a surprise!' She laughed, and he nodded, catching her agreeably unawares by taking her hand.

'Well, it certainly is one. You look very – pretty. Extremely attractive.'

There now. Why couldn't Sara and Marie and the rest of them simply say that? Conscious of some distant but deep relief ebbing through her, she smiled again, gratefully.

'Thanks, Jake. I'm glad you think so.'

Getting up abruptly, he went to the bar and ordered white

wine for her, Mexican beer for himself. On his return he stood gazing down at her for a minute, and there was a silence. And then, digesting his shock at last, he smiled back at her, in some new way she'd never seen before.

'You always were a good-looking girl, Ciara.'

'But now' she riposted, 'I'm even better!' And feeling better, too; he had taken her hand, he was being gallant and – and receptive to her.

'I only wish you'd told me.'

'Why? You wouldn't have tried to talk me out of it, would you?'

Lifting his beer, he sipped it, and put it down without answering. 'So. What's the problem? What's happened, that you want this urgent meeting? I spoke to the children last night, both of them, and they sounded fine.'

What? But he couldn't be calling her bluff already, surely, steering the conversation off her facelift round to the *point*? With an effort, she kept her tone carefully light.

'Yes, well, they are fine, so long as they're in America and know nothing about this – situation. I still haven't told them, since you say it's only temporary. But Jake, they'll be home in September, and meanwhile the strain of keeping this secret is half killing me! We are going to have to discuss it, and . . . and make sense of all this, somehow. You can't simply leave your wife for the whole summer and expect her not to worry, not to ask any questions.'

Nodding as if conceding the point, he grimaced. 'No. Of course not. Actually, Ciara, I'd be delighted if you *would* ask some questions.'

Well. That was a surprise, and encouraging. 'Then I will! Like, when are you coming home? What is going on with Roisin Harte? Do we need a marriage counsellor? Do you want me to have a tummy tuck, as well, or liposuction, change anything else about the way I look? Or our sex life? Or the way I run our home? Jake, I wish you'd tell me. I really do wish you would.'

He looked at her so oddly, she was almost unnerved; it was as if he were scrutinising her, raising an eyebrow the way he sometimes raised one over ludicrously inflated bills.

'No, Ciara. No. I don't want you to have liposuction or a tummy tuck or anything else.'

Oh. Good. Not that he wouldn't be pleased when she had her eyelids done, and her chin.

'Tell me, apart from this surgery, what else have you been doing lately?'

'Oh . . . nothing much.' Pride wouldn't let her add how little she could do, without him. Socially, she felt stripped.

'But you must have been doing something? Reading the papers, even?'

No. She'd only ever read a newspaper so she'd have dinner-party snippets at the ready. Since he moved out, she'd fended off three invitations, gone nowhere solo.

'No. Not really. It's only ever bad news, isn't it?'

He grimaced. 'Yes. I suppose it is. I only ask because . . .'

His voice tailed off, and he turned from his beer to look sidelong at her, scanning in some uncertain way.

'Because what?'

'Because . . . oh, God. Look, you're not to worry or anything, we'll be fine . . . but . . . it's just that – the stock market isn't great at the moment.'

Briefly, she was baffled. Until she remembered the shares portfolio, snoozing in the bank. Or wherever portfolios lived . . . suddenly, alarm flared in her as if he'd struck a match off her skin.

'What – you mean – you don't mean – there's any problem?' Stifling a gasp, she clutched at his arm for reassurance.

'No. Not as such. Not for the moment. We're just going to have to – to watch our spending a bit, is all. For the moment. Until things pick up.'

'But Jake – Jake, I've just spent a fortune! In London, on this facelift, I had to pay in sterling and – oh, my God!'

Her hand flew to her mouth, and she was only marginally reassured when he took it, gently, between his own hands, cupping them around it.

'It's okay, Ciara. That doesn't matter. I told you to spend what you liked and if this – surgery – makes you feel good, then it's worth it. Only – look, just don't have any more, okay? Not for the moment. If you want to treat yourself, buy something a bit cheaper!'

Cheaper? Fighting tears, she gazed at him. 'Like what? What do you mean? Shoes? Clothes? What can I afford now?'

Somehow, when he smiled, it was almost worse than if he hadn't. A weird, twisted kind of smile, that she didn't like and didn't trust.

'I was thinking of . . . maybe . . . something more like a book, a CD or a DVD? Sometimes, small things can be as rewarding as big things, you know?'

Whaaat? Things were as bad as that? He wanted her to buy a *book*? But he knew she didn't read, nor listen to any music beyond whatever might be on the radio. If he was trying to reduce her to that kind of petty spending, things must be far more serious than he was letting on. Really bad.

'Jake, are you – trying – to tell me – we have financial problems now, on top of everything else?'

She could hardly bear to ask. But his response was just a little bit soothing.

84

'No. We don't have problems, exactly, as such. We just need to be careful for a while, that's all, until things settle down. I still have a good salary, we won't starve.'

Careful? But she'd never had to be 'careful' in her life! Wouldn't know where to start. Abruptly, something clicked in her head.

'Jake, if we have to economise then I think we should start by saving the price of this apartment you're renting. And what about Roisin? Do you take her out to nice places, give her nice things? Is she the reason I have to be "careful" now, as you call it?'

She couldn't help it. And he didn't appear to like it.

'No, Ciara. She isn't. Roisin has nothing to do with this, I do not give her anything and wouldn't dream of seeing you short on her account. Roisin is, as I've told you before, merely a friend. A friend who, despite being only half my age, is somehow helping me to deal with whatever's going on in my head. We talk and walk and go for the odd pint and that's all.'

'Jake, what *is* going on in your head? Tell me, I want to know!'

Keenly, intently, he scanned her face, as if searching it, as if wanting to know something in turn. When he spoke, his voice was calm but clipped, as if he were telling his passengers to fasten their seatbelts.

'Ciara, if you want to know, then I'd really like you to try to think it out for yourself. Just think a bit, okay? Meanwhile, I'm going to continue to rent my apartment for the moment. For as long as I can afford it or – more importantly – need it. I'm sorry, but that's how things have to be. I am not coming home in the immediate future and I am not ready to discuss the reasons why. Not until you're ready to figure them out. As for the children – Ciara, you do realise, don't you, that they are not children any more?'

Yes. Yes, somewhere deep down inside, she had been wrestling with that realisation for months now, reluctantly recognising the slowly growing distance between herself and her twins. Her babies. But to say it aloud – had he slapped her, it could hardly have been more painful. Recoiling, she looked at him with eyes full of hurt and reproach.

'Jake, they are our children. They will always be our children.'

With a sigh, he released her hand.

7

'Lee, I'm worried. Really worried.'

Clasping her hands around one knee, chewing her lower lip, Ciara wasn't sure how far she dared go with Lee. Was 'worried' too strong a word to use with someone who – until now – had never been part of her inner circle? Somehow it didn't seem right to use the words she really wanted to use, words like 'desperate' and 'frantic' and 'wretched'. Every day, Jake's absence seemed to get darker, and deeper, and more distant, she simply could not believe that he had admired her new look and then gone on to talk about other things. About money, which was now gnawing at her on top of everything else. How could Lee just sit there sewing a button on a shirt, so – so *nonchalantly*?

Glancing up, Lee surveyed her. 'Are you? About Jake, you mean? Or about the twins? Or about the stock market? Or your girlfriends at the golf club?'

Ciara flinched. Lee made her sound almost neurotic, as if she were toting the worries of the world into her house! Yes, she was worried about all of those things . . . so why did articulating them make her sound, and feel, so petty, somehow? Almost petulant, as if her problems were neither real nor acute? How could Lee be so calm, as if there were no crisis at all, never mind several?

'Yes. I *am*! My family, my friends, my entire life seem to

87

be just slipping through my fingers . . . whenever I call Mike or Tara they're too busy to talk, if I call Sara or Jean or any of my friends they're busy too, they seem to be avoiding me like the plague . . . I hardly dare call Jake because I don't know what to say to him . . . and now money's a problem too!'

Her voice tailed off on a wail, and Lee looked briefly at her, stabbing a needle through the cotton in her hands.

'Yes. The stock market's in freefall. Some of my own investments have been hit a bit.'

'Have they? Well then, you know how I feel!'

Taking a pair of scissors, Lee snipped off the thread in a way that was, Ciara thought, not very sympathetic.

'Yes, honey, I can imagine. The one fashion accessory that would never suit you is a tight belt.'

What? Well, the nerve! Ciara bridled. 'It's not exactly tight. I mean, Jake still has a perfectly good salary and can well afford to support me. It's just that – well, how am I going to afford the next bit of surgery? I'd so love to get that Victoria Beckham nose!'

Stuffing her sewing materials into a painted wooden box, Lee snapped its lid shut. 'Well, if Jake's pockets don't seem to be quite as deep as hers, my suggestion would be that you go out and get a job.'

'A *job*?' Appalled, Ciara recoiled as if punched. She'd never had a job in her life. Not unless you counted six months working on a cosmetics counter in some department store years ago, in the brief interlude between school and marriage. That had been easy and relatively fun – whereas nowadays, from what she gathered, you practically had to have a doctorate to get even the simplest job. You had to be under twenty-five, and you had to have been to university for at least a decade. Even if she wanted to work, which she screamingly didn't, she wouldn't stand a chance. None. Who on earth would want an almost-forty-year-old mother-of-two with no experience of anything?

'Yes' Lee rejoined, glancing at her watch, 'a job. Work. You know, paid employment. You render somebody a service and they reward you with money.'

'But Lee, have you any idea what chins and noses cost? It would take years to save up! Besides, nobody would hire me, at my age—'

'Ciara' Lee interrupted, 'you may be nearly forty, but you sure as hell don't look it. The advantage of having had such a fabulous facelift is that now nobody could take you for more than twenty-five or twenty-six. All you have to do is tell a tiny white lie, nobody ever checks birth certificates, nobody cares so long as you look the part.'

'But—'

'I hear that the new restaurant at the far end of the village is looking for staff. Cooks. Waitresses. Table hostesses.'

'Lee, are you out of –?!'

'And I think somebody mentioned that boutique, too – what's its name, Zaza? The owner needs a sales assistant apparently.'

Ciara gasped aloud. 'You expect me to work in a *shop* –?'

'And then there's that nursery over near the tennis courts, it's expanding so maybe they might need minders? You're a mother, experienced with kids.'

Babies? Lee was suggesting she spend all day minding a horde of screaming *babies*?

'Unless of course they might only be taking qualified people. Nursery nurses, trained in pediatrics . . . anyway, try the boutique. And the restaurant. And there's a new gym near

Bray, they might want a fitness coach – you are really fit, aren't you?'

Yes – but – this was absurd!

'Why d'you want your chin done anyway, or your nose? They both look fine to me.'

'Then look closer! Look at the lines, the puckers . . . they really stand out against the rest of my face now, it's as firm as alabaster and they're so saggy by comparison.'

Drily, Lee laughed. 'So you've created a monster, huh? The more you get fixed, the more needs fixing? Can't have forty-year-old eyelids ruining twenty-five-year-old cheeks? And then when the face is perfect the neck will need firming . . . and then we can't have that silken pillar atop droopy shoulders or baggy boobs? Or orange-peel thighs? My Lord, Ciara, you'll be at this for ever, it's a vicious circle! It'll go on for years and you'll need ten jobs to pay for it all.'

Wham. A ray of startling light hit Ciara right between the eyes, a light illuminating a long, permanent path to the operating theatre, so bright it all but took her breath away. Lee was right. One thing was indeed going to lead to the next, was leading to it already.

But she couldn't stop now! Couldn't leave that upper lip to bleed lipstick, ruining the work that was already done above it . . . oh, what in hell could be happening to the wretched stock market, why couldn't Jake just give her the money for all the surgery she needed?

'Lee – do you know anything about this – this financial crisis? Is it serious?'

Her tone was pleading, and Lee skewered her with a wry look. 'Yes, it's quite serious. Global. Jake and I are just two amongst millions of people to be hit. Everyone's hoping for an upturn, but it won't be overnight. If you want any luxuries, Ciara, such as more surgery, then my advice to you would be to go out and earn them. If Jake's money is tied up, as you say it is, in bonds and other investments, he'll have precious little spare cash to jingle.'

Work. A job. Ciara still couldn't still get her head around it. Mrs Jake Lunny . . . working! Even if she could stomach such an idea, Mrs Jake Lunny was over the hill and under quali-fied. Nobody would want her for anything. Even if she wanted to do it, which she didn't. My abilities, she thought, are nil and my confidence is minus nil. I just don't belong in that world out – out there! I've never been in it and I know nothing about it! I'd only mess up and everyone would laugh at me!

So . . . what am I going to do, then? How am I going to afford my new nose? And what am I going to do, when the twins go off to college and I'm home alone all day? They'll only be back from America for a week or two before college starts. I might as well face it, nobody needs me at home any more now. Not even Jake.

Oh, Jake! I'm so mad at you, and I miss you so much, I could howl! I have howled, night after night, all on my own. And then I look awful next day, daren't even have lunch with the girls at the club in case they ask what's wrong . . . if they don't just all get up and scatter again, like they did last time. Is it true what Lee says, that I make them all look like grannies now, by comparison? Do they really not want to be seen with me any more?

That hurts. They might not be very close friends, but still, that hurts. I'd never have thought it would, but it does. Does nobody want me any more, am I being thrown on the scrap heap by *everyone*? My husband, my children and now even my so-called friends? What have I done to deserve all this, what am I going to do?

I don't know. All I know is, I can't sit at home going mad for very much longer. I can't even go shopping, now that money is tight, daren't risk making Jake angry. Or doing anything that might drive him even further away. I've got to get him back, and spending lots of money right now is not the way to endear myself to him.

'Lee. You don't really think anyone would hire me, do you, to do anything?'

The phone rang, and Lee called over her shoulder as she went to answer it. 'I don't know, Ciara! All I know is that you've nothing to lose by trying, if you want to earn money, if you want to get out of the house and meet some new people, maybe even have some fun.'

Fun? Glumly, Ciara thought about it. Nothing, surely, could be less fun than working. Getting up early, getting stuck in those awful traffic jams, having no time for oneself, taking orders from some stroppy boss . . . ? Nobody in their right mind could call that fun.

'All right' she sighed, to bat Lee off, 'I'll think about it. Who was that on the phone?'

'My date. Sorry, Ciara, don't mean to throw you out or anything, but I'm going to a concert in town tonight. Gotta get ready, gotta fly.'

Date? Her *date*, she said? 'With who? A man, d'you mean?' Surely not. Lee was divorced, well and truly divorced, had said herself she had no intention of ever marrying anyone ever again.

'Yes, of course, a man! Nice guy, I met him in a garage getting petrol last week – he pumped up my tyres for me!'

Gurgling with laughter, Lee suddenly grinned like a naughty little kid. 'Don't know if he's my type, but what the hell, we're going to hear some music together tonight, at any rate. I'll let you know on Monday how we get on.'

Monday? But today was only Friday. Surely Lee couldn't be planning to spend the entire weekend with this man, a virtual stranger? No. Hardly. She must have some other plan for the weekend. Which was suddenly looking exceedingly empty, if even Lee wasn't going to be around. Inexplicably deflated, Ciara barely managed to sound civil as she stood up.

'Do. I hope you have a lovely time.'

And then, politely but inexorably, she found herself escorted to the door, waved out into the gathering dusk. As she trudged bleakly down the drive, Lee called to her.

'And stop frowning, it'll furrow your new forehead!'

Mike. Suddenly Ciara couldn't wait to see her son, to hear his loud hearty voice, feel the house filling up with his vigorous masculine presence. Nor could she wait to see Tara . . . only how to tell both twins about Jake? How to explain this appallingly empty house?

Briefly, she thought of decorating their bedrooms, surprising them with lovely new colour schemes. But that would cost money. Not just the materials, but Mr Johnson who always did the painting and papering. And they might not even like the result; teenagers were notoriously touchy about their 'space', didn't like parents 'invading' it.

What, then? How to fill these resoundingly empty hours? Some women of her acquaintance did some charity work, got involved in community projects, meals-on-wheels . . . but how depressing! All those old people, poor people, miserable little houses, it would be the last straw. With nothing to show

93

for it either, not a cent. No. Definitely not anything volun-tary, with anyone doddery or decrepit. Old people were a vision of the future, and poverty was a vision of hell.

The computer. Apparently some people spent hours on computers. Doing what, exactly? At least, she thought, I know how to work it now. Up to a point. But I can't think of any way to make money out of it. Besides, if I messed it up, broke it, Jake would be furious. New ones are so expensive. I can't buy new anything, he might go ballistic. God, this stock market blip is such a bore, when will it be fixed?

Read a book? I'd rather put my head in the oven. Join a club? There's that women's walking group . . . Lee says walking is what people did before God invented gyms. But I'd much rather go to the gym! It's warm and bright and there's no howling gale to ruin your hair. No mud, no rain . . . I'll start going to the gym more often, then. I want my body to look as good as my face. Play more tennis, too. At least that doesn't cost much.

And then, some day, something will happen. Something will snap between Jake and Roisin, he'll come to his wits and come home. And then I'll have a purpose again, I'll have a husband to look after and a home to run. I'll be able to forget all this nonsense about getting a job.

Jake did not come to his wits. Nor come home. Instead he phoned Ciara punctiliously every other evening and met her once a week for dinner, sometimes at a restaurant, more frequently in the house that had been their home. Was, osten-sibly, still their home.

'I hope you don't mind cooking?' he asked one evening. 'I know you love restaurants, but prices seem to be going up on an almost daily basis.'

94

Shaking her head, lifting a roast duck from the oven, Ciara assured him that she didn't mind. On the contrary; she loved cooking for him, loved having him back home under any circumstances at all, even if it might be better not to tell him so. You had to act cool, the magazines advised, if you wanted to get your man back from whatever little harlot had temporarily ensnared him. You had to smile, and cook his favourite dishes, and offer to do his laundry, and pretend everything was absolutely fabulous. No tears, no tantrums, don't mention the war.

'Not at all' she smiled serenely, 'it's a pleasure.'

Pouring wine, he paused for a moment, looked at her across the dining table, and then struck a match to the candle she had set on it.

'So . . . what have you been up to?'

'Oh' she replied brightly, 'I've been busy.'

'At what?' Curiously, he raised an eyebrow.

'At the gym! I've lost three pounds and an inch off my hips.' Proudly, she wiggled them as she carried the duck to the table; whereupon he seized the carving knife and plunged it in just above the breastbone.

'Mike! Tara! Over here, here!' Waving like a windmill, standing on tiptoe, Ciara heard herself squeal, but couldn't help it. At last, both children, back from America, home where they belonged! Meeting up in Manhattan, they had flown home together, and as they emerged into the arrivals area Ciara felt an overwhelming urge to cry. She had missed them so much it had been like toothache, throbbing relentlessly, only unlike toothache it had had no remedy. Unable to contain herself, she plunged through the milling crowds and ran euphorically up to them: first Mike, then Tara.

'Oh, let me look at you! Tara, you're so tanned, Mike, you've put on weight, you look wonderful!' Seizing them, throwing an arm around each, she hugged them; in turn they took a joint step backward, gaping at her.

'Mum – my God – it can't be – ?' Looking thinner, and somehow taller, than she had been four months earlier, Tara Lunny stood rooted to the spot, mouth open, clutching at her brother as if for confirmation of the vision she was seeing. Saying nothing, he gripped her arm in a way that was somehow warning: don't move, don't say anything, let me handle this. And then he smiled, his beautiful, broad, brown-eyed smile.

'Mum! How are ya! Great to see ya!' Scooping her up, he lifted her off her feet with ease; at barely nineteen he was a full-grown man, muscular, masculine, deep-voiced and a good six inches taller than his mother. Kissing her on either cheek, he held her at arm's length, looked at her and laughed lightly.

'What's this? What's happened? You been drinking the elixir of eternal youth or something?'

Shyly, she touched her hand to her cheek, and smiled. 'Oh, I – I just got a tiny tuck, that's all.' His stare was surprisingly penetrating, as if searching for the mother he had been expecting to see.

'Well, we wouldn't have recognised you' – why was he blotting out Tara, behind him? – 'but you look terrific! Like our kid sister! You'll need ID in a pub to be served a pint!'

'Oh' she murmured, 'I don't look all that young. Mid twenties, Lee says.'

'Twenty-five. On the nose.' Abruptly, it was Tara who spoke, emerging from behind her brother like a genie from a bottle. Scorchingly beautiful Tara, with her waist-length skein of shimmering dark hair, her amber skin soft as suede and her mahogany brown eyes cooling, suddenly, like iced molasses. Shrinking back a fraction, Ciara recognised that look, the one that had been exclusive to Tara ever since baby-hood, when confronted with something she didn't want to see or hear. Sometimes, charmer and all as she could be, Tara had a way of making people feel . . . what? At this moment, Ciara felt very faintly rebuffed, almost rebuked. As if roles had been reversed and Tara were her mother.

'Don't you like it?' She'd thought Tara would love it, go into gales of giggles, say her mother was a hoot and bang up to the minute, too, on the fashion front. After all, half the women in the western world were having facelifts. Tara must have seen plenty of hot jobs in America. And she'd always liked her mother to be trendy, on the scene as she called it.

Grabbing at a suitcase sliding off the stack on their trolley, Tara focused on its label for a moment; and then she looked back up at Ciara.

'Why don't you' she said in a tone that was unexpectedly clipped, with a faintly American twang, 'give me a raincheck on that?'

'So' said Jake, passing round beers to his wife, son and daughter in the Lunny living room, 'no need for anyone to panic. I just felt the need of a little – breather, that's all. Your mother and I still see each other on a regular basis. No ques-tion of splitting up or anything, I'm just taking a bit of time out . . . taking stock, is all.'

Slowly, as if on automatic pilot, Mike raised his glass to his mouth, where it remained poised, untouched. Looking at him, Ciara saw something new in her son, something that had not been there before he went to New York. Some kind of – of maturity, as if a line had been drawn under his child-hood. Of course he was not mature, not yet, but he was as grown-up as it got. She was very glad Jake had had the courage to break this news to his children himself, at home, under their own roof.

'I see.' Exhaling, Mike looked at his father, looked down into his beer, and then looked at his mother, examining her in some way that made her flinch. What did he see, what was he thinking?

Aghast, outrage written all over her, Tara was much easier to read, a storm coiling in her eyes. 'So' she said in the newly tart tone she seemed to have cultivated, 'when can we expect you back, then?'

The question seemed, bizarrely, to be equally directed at either parent. But it was Jake who answered. Uneasily, he shrugged. 'Soon. I don't know – exactly when. As soon as I sort myself out. It's nothing, not worth making a fuss over. Anyway, why don't we forget about me for the moment, huh, why don't you two tell us all about your summer in America?'

He smiled encouragingly, and like a geyser, Tara began to seethe and sputter on the sofa, as if she might erupt at any moment. But it was Mike who spoke, glancing at his sister, cutting across whatever she was planning to say.

'I had a great summer' he said in a voice that seemed to have deepened. 'I made lots of money for college and hung out with the guys at the beach and did Manhattan and met . . . a girl.'

A girl. In one dazzling, horrific flash, Ciara got the picture: Mike was in love. Mike, her only son, had met an American girl and – and that was what was different about him. Her son had returned only in body: his mind and heart were where he had left them, on Long Island. That was why, whenever they spoke on the phone, he'd been so brief. Without knowing it, she had had competition for his attention. Deep inside her, something started to writhe and struggle.

'A girl?' she said, fighting to sound enthusiastic, to keep her voice light. 'Was she nice, did you have fun?'

Gravely, he nodded. Nodded in a way that said he'd had more than fun. 'Yes, Mother, we did and she is. Nice, I mean. Her name's Jessica.'

'Well' Jake interjected, raising his glass in a kind of salute, 'good for you! Nothing like a summer romance, eh?'

His tone was carefully casual, but it raised the question Ciara couldn't bear to ask. Studying his beer, Mike nodded into it, his face ruddy but not flushed. 'Yeah . . . well . . . actually we'll be seeing each other again. At Christmas. We're going skiing in Vermont.'

Christmas. In Vermont. With Jessica. Presumably details of Jessica would follow, any moment now, but Ciara found herself stepping back, tuning out. Unable to listen, unable to take it: Mike, home at last, and gone again, already! Gone for good . . . gone, like his father, to another woman. No matter how often he might return to this house, she saw with chilling clarity, he would never live in it any more, never be her boy again. He would drop in whenever he got time, hug her, smile at her, tease her and punch her shoulder in that affectionate way of his – and then he would be gone. To Jessica, the important woman in his life, the one who mattered more than Mum. Even if Jessica changed over the years, mutated into Sally or Laura or Maria, Mike would henceforth always be focused on another woman. Briefly, physically here, mentally, emotionally he was already moving on. Moving out. Even though she had known it

99

must happen some day, Ciara could barely keep from screaming aloud. Not now, she wanted to weep, not now, not already! He's only a boy, he's my son, why can't we have more time together, how can he be going to America, to this Jessica, for Christmas!

And how can Jake be sitting there looking so unfazed, so *approving*? Has he no idea what this is doing to me, is it not doing anything to *him*?

Apparently not; quite calmly, Jake was listening to Mike's glowing account of his new girlfriend, a student at Vassar, from Maryland. Brunette, witty, athletic, Cherokee blood, mother an oculist, father a lawyer . . . the conversation had a man-to-man note about it that confirmed what Ciara dreaded to hear, and never would in so many words: Mike had slept with this girl, not once but often, they were an 'item'. A couple. Some day, if they married, he might well move to America, go to live there permanently. Unable to speak, she gripped her glass in frozen fingers.

Father and son seemed to talk for ever before, finally, Tara spoke in a tone tipped with steel. 'Can't say I was so nuts on American guys. They were like, all image, no substance. So, hey, Ma, tell us what's with the facelift, huh?'

Her voice was challenging, making Ciara again feel as if roles were reversed, and she was being called upon to explain to the grown-ups why she had done something exceedingly silly. The kind of thing a little girl might do, running amok in her mother's make-up, tottering round in shoes that didn't fit.

But maybe Tara preferred to discuss her mother's facelift than her father's mid-life crisis? Turning to her, Ciara groped for words, and stalled: Tara looked as if she thought the two might somehow be connected. As if the surgery might be not the solution to her problem, as Ciara had hoped, but the *cause* of it?

Ciara wasn't sure how Mike had managed it, since Jake wasn't even living in the house, but within a week of his return he had contrived to have a row with his father. Over what, he wouldn't say, but she presumed it must be connected with what he called Jake's 'behaviour'. Was he angry on his own account, or hers, or the whole family's? Try as she might she couldn't get him to talk about it; deflecting every question with a joke, he busied himself with preparations for college instead. Top-notch exam results had earned him a place at UCC, doing something so scientific she couldn't quite grasp what it was.

'Explain it to me again' she pleaded, and he looked at her with a kind of pity.

'It has to do' he said patiently, 'with the way different materials react to different temperatures. How extreme heat or cold, for instance, might affect the skin of an aircraft.'

Nodding, seeing he was simplifying, she could only be thankful he had inherited his brains from his father, and wonder what this Jessica had done to capture his attention. A photograph had confirmed that the girl was pretty, but might she be something . . . more? It was so hard, these days, to know what went on in the heads of the young.

Tara, also, was packing for college in Galway, where she planned to study history and politics. Whirling round the house, there was a kind of demonic fervour about her, as if she couldn't wait to leave. But . . . ? Grasping at straws, Ciara suggested they take a day out to go shopping together. Or to lunch, the cinema, whatever she liked. A girlie day.

As if she hadn't heard, Tara gazed at her over an armful of

clothes. 'Tell me, Mum, what does everyone think of this new look of yours? Do your friends like it? Does Dad?'

Wincing involuntarily and, she hoped, invisibly, Ciara didn't know what to say. Nobody seemed to be reacting to her facelift the way they were supposed to.

'Well' she said warily, 'yes. Your father said I look great. So did some of the people at the gym.'

'Uh-huh.'

'And what about you? What do you think, Tara?'

'I think' Tara said, turning her back to stuff shoes into a duffel bag, 'I'd rather have a mother than a sister.'

'What?' Instinctively, Ciara clutched at her throat, as if Tara had whipped a knife from her pocket. 'But I thought – I mean – you and I –'

Nodding, Tara did not look up. 'Yeah. You and I have always been good pals. Almost like sisters. But you're not my sister! I don't want you to be! You're my *mother*! God almighty, how can I ever take you anywhere any more, go anywhere with you, if I try to tell anyone you're my mother they'll think you must have given birth to me when you were six years of age! You look – you look *ridiculous*! And now I look ridiculous too, beside you, it – it's *unnatural*!'

Her voice quivered with rage, leaving Ciara speechless, flinging her up against the bedroom wall for support.

'And as for Dad – you look like his *daughter*! It's *sick*!'

As a toddler Tara had had a fiery temper, often making both parents laugh at her antics, until one day she had gone too far, kicking her mother's shins until they were black and blue. Feeling as if she were reliving that day again now, tears swirling to her throat and sticking in it, Ciara backed out of the room, wrenched in a dozen different directions by a slew of conflicting emotions. Chief of which was a violent urge to kill her prickly, insensitive, sabre-tongued daughter.

Instead, bolting from the field of battle, she ran down the stairs in tears, flying for the sanctuary of Lee's house. Lee, who seemed to be the only person left on the entire planet who was ever glad to see her.

8

'Yes, well' Lee said, somewhat callously Ciara thought, 'that's teenagers for you I guess. I'm sure they'll get used to the new you in time. Even if getting their heads around Jake's absence might take a while.'

'But we haven't *got* time! They're leaving for college next week. I was looking forward so much to having them back from America, to being a family again just for a little while, and instead everyone's fighting with everyone! Our time together is ruined!'

Ciara plucked wretchedly at a tassel on her cowgirl waistcoat, and Lee looked hard at her, thinking that no amount of plastic surgery could ever make anyone look happy when they weren't. Not even this top-model wannabee with her great legs, great looks, poised picture-perfect as if a photographer might leap from behind the curtains. If fashion were ever to decree an ostrich plume in one's left ear as the order of the day, Ciara would surely be the first to wear it, blithely oblivious of some couturier's little joke. And yet, behind the mask, Lee sensed a very lost, unhappy little girl.

'Well, that's a pity, sure enough. But honey, life changes, you know? Kids sometimes cope with change better than adults, they adjust and they move on. Mike might be mad at his dad right now, and Tara mad at her mother, but in a week or so they're going to be way too busy settling into their new colleges to worry much about what's going on with their parents.'

Yes. That was exactly what Ciara suspected, and hearing it only made it worse. Letting go of her children was like having her front teeth wrenched out, and their mutinous mood was punching a horrible hole in what should have been one last, lovely family gathering. Jake said he was willing to come to Huxley Wood and sit down to several suppers, if everyone wanted him to, but the atmosphere was all wrong. Plus, both children seemed to be out all the time, catching up on the friends who'd also been away all summer. There hadn't been even one peaceful, pleasant meal *en famille*.

'Huh. You're a great help, I must say. You don't understand, Lee – everything's changing, everything's collapsing! My marriage, my family, my social life – I can't handle so much so fast!'

'Ciara, you'd better. If it's any consolation, you're not alone. Millions of lives change everywhere, every day. Assuming nobody actually died, they can be reconstructed. People adapt when they have to. I'm even doing a bit of adapting myself at the moment.'

Oh? Guiltily, Ciara squinted at her. She'd been so caught up in her own anxiety, she'd forgotten to ask Lee how her date went.

'Are you? How so?'

'Financially, for one thing. A lot of my money was tied up in one of the companies that's been hardest hit on the stock market. It's a good thing I have my jewellery business, because my future's not looking nearly so secure as it was.'

'Oh, my God.' Genuinely shocked, Ciara shivered: financial insecurity was something she could never cope with.

Couldn't even bear to think about. What if – what if this was *contagious*, what if Jake's money was to take more pounding too? Appalled, she stared at Lee, who shrugged and, incredibly, laughed.

'But hey, that's showbiz! You win some, you lose some.'

'How can you sound so chirpy about it? It's horrendous!'

'I can sound chirpy because I can earn more money. I'm telling you, a career's a great comfort in an uncertain world.'

She grinned like a magician whipping a rabbit out of a hat, and Ciara cringed. Next thing Lee would be starting on again about work, getting a job, that awful prospect she didn't even want to contemplate. Hastily, she changed the subject.

'And – how did your date go? Who was he, did you get on well with him?'

Blithely, Lee flung herself down in an armchair and crossed her legs, arching her eyebrows as if amused, as if she'd already forgotten her money woes.

'He was an architect called Tony. Quite attractive. Courteous. Well mannered, well dressed. We went to the Haydn concert at the NCH and the music was fabulous.'

'Oh. And?' Curiously, Ciara leaned forward. This sounded promising, and besides men were one of her favourite subjects.

'And then we went on to a restaurant. French. Swish. He insisted on treating me. The food was delicious.'

'Yes – and – Lee, get to the point!'

Lee's grin mutated into a giggle. 'And that is the point! That's all, end of story!'

'What? But – why? You've just said he was nice and you had a terrific time!'

'No, honey. I didn't say that. I said the food and music were great. Sadly, Tony was not great. He was a crashing bore who talked for two hours solid about his car – a Mercedes, apparently – and about his great passion for Victorian lithographs.'

Eh? Ciara had no idea what Victorian lithographs might be. All she knew was that Lee was making no sense. Who cared what the man talked about, if he was well dressed, drove a Mercedes and treated her to a swish restaurant?

'I can't see what you're laughing at. Nice men are hard to find and you must be mad to – to bin him like this!'

'Ciara' Lee drawled, 'the man was a collector. I got the impression he was looking to add to his collection of – of objects! Playthings! The entire conversation revolved around him and all I was required to do was look impressed. When I tried to ask him what he thought of Haydn's music, he brushed me off, and I realised he hadn't the faintest interest in it. He'd simply chosen a classical concert because it was socially appropriate for a first date – no imagination, no spontaneity was my verdict. Dull as dishwater.'

'Lee' Ciara implored, 'see him again. Give him another chance. You might get to like him, he might grow on you.'

'Yeah – like a zit! Sorry, Ciara, I'm not that desperate. Not desperate at all, actually! Fancy a drink?'

Airily, she got up to fetch some wine, leaving Ciara baffled on the sofa. Surely a thirty-four-year-old divorcée should be a bit more, well . . . grateful? Lee was the only woman she knew who could be so flippant about a man, so unconcerned about her single status. Whatever she said, she surely couldn't be serious about never marrying again. You'd have to be very eccentric to airbrush the whole subject of marriage out of your life. After only two months without Jake, she was hating the semi-single life herself, absolutely loathing every horrible, miserable second of it.

'I think' she said, accepting a glass of chardonnay, 'you're crazy. This man Tony sounds very – acceptable –'

'I'm sure he is. To anyone who just wants a man, without fussing over which particular one. But I'm afraid Tony did not pass my desert-island test.'

'Huh?'

'If I were stuck on a desert island, is he the person I'd want to be stuck with? Maybe for ever? That's what everyone should ask themselves before embarking on a relationship.'

A thought struck Ciara. 'Did he ask you out again?'

'Yes. As a matter of fact he did. And he's phoned twice since. I wish he'd take off and find someone else. Someone yearning for a Mercedes full of lithographs.'

A Mercedes. And the stock market in freefall. Nonplussed, Ciara stared at Lee. 'I don't know how you can be so—'

'Blasé? God, Ciara, he was only some guy, who cares? But, speaking of men, what's the latest on Jake? Any progress?'

Tightly, Ciara gripped the stem of her glass. 'Not unless you count his willingness to spend time with the children. If they wanted him to. He did take Tara out for a pizza, but Mike wouldn't go, and I . . . wasn't invited. He said he needed to talk to Tara alone.'

'And did he? Have you any idea what he said?'

'No. She clammed up when I asked her. She's been so difficult since she got home, won't do anything with me, go anywhere . . . seems to hugely resent my having had a facelift. As if she were the only one entitled to look good! I'm sure she'll be quick enough to have one herself at my age.'

Out of the blue, Lee felt a prick of pity for Ciara. She looked so forlorn, so disappointed that her expensive, painful surgery was bringing her so little joy. For a moment she sat studying her wine, thinking.

'Well, Tara will be out of your – er – face soon enough! Don't worry, Ciara, it's just a phase, she'll grow out of it. Meanwhile, have you thought any more about what we discussed? About maybe getting a job, looking for work, getting out of that house of yours?'

Like a horse that might bolt, Ciara shied off immediately. 'No. I—'

'Tell you what. I'll come with you. You do up a CV and we'll go visit that restaurant, the boutique—'

Hollowly, Ciara laughed. 'Lee, what would I put in a CV? Forty next month, wife and mother for nearly twenty years, full stop?'

'Fake it! If you worked in a department store for six months, say six years! What's the difference? You've cooked thousands of meals – so, say you've worked in catering! You're mad about fashion, so put something about stylist, image consultant! You're only looking for some little job after all, not to manage Microsoft! So long as you give them some bit of paper they'll be happy, all you have to do is slap on a smile and look confident.'

Confident? With her world dissolving around her, Ciara thought she'd never felt less confident in her life. Did Lee have to look, and sound, so adamant?

'Oh, Lee. I don't know. I don't *want* to work.'

'That's as may be, honey, but you need to. Not just to get the money for that nose, but for your own rapidly slipping self-esteem. And for fun – I mean, you can't hang around at home alone for ever, can you?'

For *ever*? But Jake would be coming home. He said he would. Soon. Eventually. He was just going through a little –

'If you like, I'll do up a CV with you. Print out a dozen copies and hey, we're in business! Okay?'

Brightly, Lee smiled, forcing Ciara to smile wanly back, in the way one might politely smile at the gaoler leading one to the scaffold.

And then, overnight it seemed, Mike and Tara were gone. Off to college, off to their busy new adult lives, Tara still sulking, Mike vaguely protective of his mother, as if she were the child. Hugging her goodbye, he promised to call her regularly, and she got the sinking feeling that he would tick off the task twice a week on his palmtop. He was, she sensed, powerfully angry with his father, and sorry for her, in a way that felt somehow demeaning.

What was it with both twins, that they were making her feel so – so – juvenile? Just because she looked young didn't mean she was young, did it? She was their mother, not some ditsy little doll! A person, and a parent, to be respected! America must have done something to them. Just as Roisin Harte had done something to Jake, brainwashed him in some weird way. After three months he showed no sign of coming to his senses, and hadn't mentioned anything about their nest egg being safely back in its basket, either.

'All right' she said glumly to Lee at the end of September, 'do your worst. Do me up a CV and let's see if there's anyone out there wants me for anything.'

H'mm. So Jake was still resisting his surgically enhanced wife, was he? The golf club girls were still shying away? Tara had not melted, was not missing Mum the way Mum was missing her? Sitting down at her computer, Lee got cracking.

'Here you are' she said next morning, producing a fabulous work of fiction. 'Now get in your car and we'll go visit the boutique first, then the new restaurant, plus Snippets hair salon is looking for a receptionist, they have an ad up in their window.'

'What'll I wear?' Ciara fretted.

'A smile, honey, a wide white smile! And make it quick, because I'm only giving you this one day, I have my own work to get on with you know.'

Witch, Ciara muttered under her breath. Lee was doing her a favour, forcing her to look grateful when she wasn't grateful at all.

'Only lunchtime? Oh, what a pity. We'd want you to do the dinner shift as well. Are you a night student, is that it, not free in the evenings? Or do you have young children?'

The man peered at her, and despite herself Ciara preened a little.

'No – yes – I – mean – I' Oh God, why had Lee told all these lies, it was so confusing, what was she meant to say—

'Actually' Lee interjected with a note of perfect calm, 'she could get free in the evenings, if you were paying enough to make it worth her while – couldn't you, Ciara?'

Her tone drilled into Ciara like a Black & Decker, and Ciara stiffened. Yes, she was free in the evenings, but she didn't want to work them! Not as well as lunchtimes! After all she was forty next month, not getting any younger . . . Eagerly, the man, whose name was Robin, beamed at her.

'Well, that would be ideal, if you could do both shifts I'd offer you the job on the spot! You project exactly the right image of our restaurant – young, trendy, hip and attractive. Of course, our rate is slightly higher at night. And it would only be four nights a week – we're closed Mondays, and Dana does weekends. I'm sure someone like you would enjoy the buzz at nights, we have a young dynamic team here full of adrenalin.'

Was he actually clasping his hands? Saying that yes, he would give her the job, put her in charge of meeting and greeting his guests, if she would agree to do both shifts? It was a big restaurant, very popular and trendy – but what if Sara came in, or Jean or any of the golf girls caught her *working*? It would be too humiliating for words.

'Yes' Lee said in a tone of steel, 'she would. She'd love it. She can start next Tuesday, if that suits you?'

'Perfect' beamed Robin, 'I'm delighted to have got someone who so fits what this restaurant is trying to *say*! Now, let's all sit down and run through the details, hours, rates, house rules . . . you'll get friendly with our regulars, naturally, but the important thing is never to get *familiar* . . . make up and jewellery are permitted, but not perfume . . .'

On he rattled, Lee nodding cheerfully as he rummaged for pen and paper, and yet again Ciara had the feeling of being a child amidst adults, railroaded into behaviour that was not her choice. Railroaded by Lee into smiling frenetically, nodding enthusiastically, as if she actually wanted this damn job. Apart from a pretty good rate of pay, and an upscale restaurant that might have certain perks, she could see nothing to recommend putting in thirty hours' hard graft a week. She'd be on her feet non-stop, taking people's coats, leading them to their tables, making sure they enjoyed the meals she had once enjoyed herself, with Jake, in nice restaurants just like this one. Oh, the horror of it! If it weren't for Lee's determination, and needing something to fill the undeniable void of her life, and make enough money to get that new nose . . . she'd have to get it, and the little chin lift, to match the rest of her face.

'So, noon until three, and then seven until midnight, Tuesday to Friday inclusive. Welcome to our staff, Ciara, good to have you aboard!'

Genially, Robin was shaking her hand, and she was praying that none of the golf club girls should ever be overcome with longing for fusion food.

Flicking on the news that night, Lee sat down to watch it with a feeling of settling in, in more ways than one. With Ciara fixed up as a hostess in East Meets West, she felt she had done a good day's work, a favour for a neighbour. Whether Ciara liked it or not, the job would be good for her, if she stuck with it and could take the pace.

Trendy as the restaurant was, it would probably be frenetic to work in, and all the staff would undoubtedly be much younger than her. But she would look the same age as them ... Lord, how awful to have to pretend you were a decade or more younger than you were! That would be the really exhausting bit, and Lee marvelled at the optimism of anyone who tried to stop the clock. Granted, Ciara was fit – almost bionic, after all that work in the gym – but could anyone of forty really have as much energy as they'd had fifteen years earlier? Her own version of 'looking good' simply involved sleep, exercise and water; all she wanted was to feel good. Healthy. Happy. Who cared about age? It was getting to be as big a deal in Ireland as in America, an obsession she just couldn't get her head around.

And Ireland was getting more like America in other things, too. The top news story this evening was about the smoking ban, something she'd once thought of as neurotically Californian. And then there was an item about tranquillisers; the government was trying to dissuade doctors from dishing them out like Smarties. Prozac, apparently, was the new Marlboro, eagerly guzzled by a spectacularly stressed society. Fast food was flourishing, too, nobody had time to cook; like tranquillisers burgers were another quick fix, even if they might ultimately do as much damage as cigarettes – really the whole thing was insane, Lee reflected, thinking of Ciara and all the pressure people were putting themselves under. But hey, it was voluntary. Anyone who wanted to look dazzling, and earn the fortune they needed to finance all the clothes, the gyms, the surgeons, was bound to end up stressed.

It was a wonder they didn't all implode. What ever happened to the sleepy little Ireland of the postcards, the ruminating sheep, the cows ambling through misty fields? A truly representational picture of Ireland would depict a whizzing treadmill, or a bank statement featuring a massive overdraft or . . . at that moment the financial news came on, and she sat up with a jolt, staring at the screen. The Dow Jones . . . Jesus.

Whoo. Wow. Just like Freddie her former husband, her divorce settlement was whirling down the drain, so fast it took her breath away. Gasping, blinking in shock, she reached for the phone to call Jay, her accountant in Vermont, not caring what hour of the day or night it might be there. And then, fingers poised over keypad, she amazed herself by not calling him.

Why? What was the point? He'd be hysterical, yelping about all kinds of stuff she wouldn't understand, berating her for not listening to him and getting out while the going was good. She hadn't paid enough attention to her money, and now it had shrunk like a sweater in the wash, would no longer keep her warm if things got chilly.

Oh well. Easy come, easy go. At least one thing remained intact: a choice of whether to panic, or not. Clicking off the news, she returned to the newspaper crossword she'd been doing, and found her attention instantly absorbed by it. After all, as her mother was fond of saying, 'your health is your wealth', and she still had that. Which meant she could work, and earn her living.

There was even an odd, but distinct, sense of liberation in being rid of the last traces of Freddie. A feeling of emerging from a scalding shower washed clean, stripped bare, purged and purified.

Jake was astounded. And delighted. 'A job?' he repeated incredulously, as if Ciara had signed on for a NASA space probe. 'What a great idea!'

She decided against telling him it had been Lee's. 'Yes, well, as long as I don't have you to look after . . . I have some time on my hands.' Just a little bit of guilt, she thought, but not too much, don't pile it on.

'In that new fusion restaurant? You'll have great fun! Get out of the house, meet lots of people – brilliant!'

What? He wasn't going to try to stop her? Wasn't going to say anything about being well able to support her? About how infra dig it would look for a pilot's wife to be hostessing, *working,* instead of playing golf? A little frisson of alarm tickled her tummy.

'Yes, well, if I want to have any more nips or tucks –'

There was a silence. And then a kind of sigh. 'Ciara. You don't need plastic surgery.'

I do, she thought. I do, I do, I do! I'm going to be forty, middle-aged, everything will sag and look awful and nobody will want me. You wouldn't want me yourself, would you, if I looked like your granny?

'That's a matter of opinion, Jake. Let's not argue over it. Look, have you spoken to Mike lately? Or Tara?'

'Yes. Both. They seem to be settling well into college.'

Yes, she thought dismally, they do. Their phone calls are full of new activities, new people . . . Lee was right. I do need this job. New activities and people of my own – damn, I hate it, but I need it! And I need you too, Jake Lunny, I don't know how much more of this 'break' I can take.

Will you even remember my birthday, when it happens? Or would you rather forget that your wife's going to be forty? Rather forget your wife, full stop?

9

Thunk! Thumpa-thunka-*thunk*! The music was thundering, and Ciara was getting a headache to match. Over the pulsating racket, a hundred guests were shouting, striving to converse, and from her desk in reception Ciara gazed at them, wondering how they could possibly be enjoying the battle. Had she and Jake, when young, once gone to places as noisy as this, actually enjoyed yelling at each other over some infernal din masquerading as music? They must have, she supposed; but it was a long time ago and time had mercifully obliterated the memory. In latter years, they'd liked restaurants with live music, maybe a piano or guitar, pleasantly playing in the background . . . which was, of course, one of the hallmarks of getting old.

Old-er. Not old, not yet, not by a long shot! Bracing herself, she picked up the ringing phone at her elbow and shrieked into it.

'East Meets West, good *evening!!*'

Some man shouted back, attempting to book a lunch table for tomorrow: was he saying for two people, or that they'd be there at two? Unable to hear clearly, she wrote down both possibilities, looked up and smiled forcefully at the arriving party of six streaming in the door. Smile, Robin had instructed her, smile at everyone as if they were your long-lost millionaire uncle.

'Cleary' barked one of the men, looking and sounding as if he'd had a rough day. Her smile widened as she ran her finger down the bookings.

'Oh yes, table thirty-two, party of four.'

'Six' he snapped, 'as you can see, we've picked up company on the way.'

Which meant they'd have to be given a different, bigger table. If one was free. 'Let me take your coats' she beamed, 'why don't you sit down and have a drink at the bar while I check—'

'No thanks' retorted the ringleader, 'we don't want a drink, just had one, why don't you take us straight to our table?'

Her smile widened. 'Of course I will, as soon as we have one for six—'

Belligerently, the man turned to his party. 'Looks like we got a problem, folks.'

A problem. The one word Robin had warned her he never wanted to hear. There was no such thing as a problem, only a solution. Which it was her job to find. The customer was always right.

'Oh, no, not at all! I'm sure we can accommodate two extra – let me have a word with Neil our head waiter, the party at table nine should be leaving shortly –'

Desperately, she raced into the dining area and collared Neil, who shook his head. 'No, sorry, they've just ordered liqueurs, could be another half hour.'

Oh, no. What was she going to do with this lot for half an hour? Flying back to the lobby, she was aghast to see them hanging up their own coats, something else Robin had warned her must never happen.

'No problem, we're going to set up a table for six, if you don't mind waiting just a few—'

120

'Jesus' growled the impatient man, glancing at his watch, 'how long is it gonna be? We're hungry here, lady, what's the big deal about two extra people? Huh?'

He glared at her, and she felt her jaws ache with the strain of smiling. 'Only a few moments. Let me bring you the menu to read while you're waiting.'

Beaming, she furnished six copies, and Mr Charm-School snatched his from her grudgingly, glowering at the woman opposite him. 'What did I tell ya. We shoulda gone to Le Cirque.'

Oh, shut up, she thought, don't take it out on me that you've had a lousy day. And now I suppose I have to offer you a bottle of champagne, on the house, because that's Robin's policy if there's any delay or hassle with anyone.

She was reaching to get it when another party came in, 'Gregan, four for eight.' Yes, as booked, on the dot. Beckoning the way, she led them into the dining area, seated them, and returned to find the Cleary party standing up, closing their menus, reaching for their coats.

'We're leaving' announced the spokesman, 'if other people are going to be seated before us – what kinda place is this, anyway? You won't see us back here again.'

'Oh' she gasped, 'oh, but –'

Robin came flying up, a smile all but tied in a bow on his lips. 'Good evening, can I help, does something seem to be the matter?'

A thumb was jerked in Ciara's direction. 'Yeah. This lady here's the matter. Says she can't give us our table and then takes other people to theirs. What kinda service is that? You'd get a warmer welcome in Iceland.'

Quizzically, Robin raised an eyebrow.

'But –' she babbled, 'this gentleman only booked for four.

Now he needs a table for six. I was just about to offer him some champagne until table nine comes free –'

Not answering, Robin grasped the bookings ledger, studied it and nodded at the group as if Ciara were invisible. 'Well, isn't that a lucky thing! We can fit you in at table twenty-seven, I'll just get Neil to set it, follow me please!'

Without so much as a backward glance, he led the grizzling party into the dining area, leaving Ciara frazzled in the lobby. How could table twenty-seven be free? Squinting into the bookings, she ran her eye down them until – oh, no – she saw that a party of six, collectively called Becker, had cancelled. Somehow, it had escaped her notice that their table was free.

God, she groaned, this is a nightmare. Robin is going to kill me. My head is splitting. I need an aspirin.

'Hi, honey' boomed a voice, 'Becker. Chris Becker! We had to cancel earlier, but now three of us are able to make it after all, any chance of a table?'

Genially, the man grinned at her as he helped his two female friends out of their rain-pearled coats, and Ciara gulped, fighting a rising urge to scream.

'Of course' she smiled winningly, 'let me just take your coats and check the book.'

'So long as we're not by the door. Or the kitchen. Or under that goddamn ventilator we were under last time.'

I'm going to quit, she thought. I'm going to walk out, go home, swallow ten dozen aspirin and that'll be that. This is mayhem, this is Grand Central, nobody could cope with the likes of this. Jake Lunny's job is a breeze by comparison.

'Ciara. A word, please.'

Beckoning with raised eyebrow and crooked finger, Robin

summoned Ciara to his office and she trotted apprehensively after him, half-dreading, half-hoping that he was about to fire her. It was an awful job, she felt as if she were being whirled through a spindrier, her head was hammering, her throat was parched and her feet were like two croissants hot out of the oven.

I don't need this! I'm a married woman with a husband who can well support me . . . legally *has* to support me, no matter where he is or who he's with. Okay, maybe he doesn't have to pay to get my nose done. But I'm doing it for him, aren't I? Doing it so I'll look good for him and reflect well on him, nobody will be able to say he's married to an old bag, he'll be proud to take me anywhere or be seen anywhere with me. That's my real job – to look good for my husband! The only one I can do or want to do!

'Sit down.'

Politely, Robin indicated a chair and obediently she sat, feeling like a schoolgirl in the principal's office even though Robin was barely thirty. How ridiculous, she thought, to be working for a boss way younger than I am myself.

She was surprised when he smiled. 'Hard work, huh?'

'Yes. Very. Way harder than I—'

'Don't worry. You'll get used to it. Everyone finds it tough the first few days, but they adjust. That's why we only employ young, energetic people like yourself, people who can stay the course. Plus, the customers like a pretty face, they don't want to see any old wrinklies. How old are you? Twenty-seven, twenty-eight?'

Oh, God. 'Er, yes, uh – yes. That's right.' Is this legal, she wondered frantically, is there not some law against asking employees their age?

'I just wonder because we need to fill in a few forms for

payroll details. Here we are.' Extracting them from a file, he handed them across his desk. 'It's a bit late tonight of course, no need to do them on the spot, but could you get them back to me tomorrow?'

Her head whirled. What was she going to put for date of birth? If she told the truth, would he sack her for having lied? If she lied, on paper, would she go to prison?

'Uh – yes. Sure. Of course.'

'Great. Just a formality, but it's got to be done! Now, why don't you go home and get some sleep. I know tonight was tough, but you'll get the hang of the bookings . . . it's simple once you get used to it.'

Simple? The bookings ledger reminded her of her maths copybook at school, where she'd wrestled in vain to divide ninety-one by fourteen, or work out how many litres of paint would cover eleven metres of wall; there were always bits that wouldn't go, bits that fell off or didn't match or ended up dangling in space.

She flicked her hair. 'Oh, no problem. I can handle it.'

He beamed. 'Of course you can! Think of it as a big party. A sit-down dinner like maybe a wedding, where you just have to make sure there's room for everyone and they're all comfortable.'

Her mind flew to her long-ago wedding. A huge event with a hundred and sixty-nine guests, it had been a nightmare of what Jake called 'logistics', the seat plan had taken days and even then Julie Keegan had ended up beside Declan O'Neill . . .

'Right' she smiled weakly. On honeymoon, she'd been comatose with exhaustion, had taken days to recover. And Julie had never forgiven her.

'The other staff will help you! We're a team here, one for

all and all for one, the rule is that work should be fun! I'm planning a big staff party for Christmas, we're all going to go out and paint the town red, disco till dawn!'

Disco till dawn. Faintly, she remembered those days. Years ago. And years.

'That sounds great, Robin!'

'You better believe it. Now, off you go, get your beauty sleep and bring me in those papers tomorrow, okay?'

'Yes. Sure.'

As she tottered to her taxi, she scarcely knew what was worse: working past midnight, or faking forms that could land you in jail, or painting the town red with twenty colleagues half your age with twice your stamina.

'So I just sort of made a three look like an eight, and a four look like a seven . . .'

Lee grinned. 'Oh what a tangled web we weave, when first we practise to deceive!'

Ciara winced. That was what Jake used to say to the children when they were small, caught out in little white lies. Was shaving fifteen years off your age just a little white lie?

'I mean, nobody will check, will they? I'm not going to land up in *court* or anything over this, am I?'

She looked so anxious, Lee laughed again. 'No. Hardly. It's just red tape. All Robin cares is that you look the part. Which you do.'

'But I'm going to have to dodge the Christmas party! I can't go out on the town all night with a crowd of youngsters – I mean – it's bad enough working so late, I'm shattered by midnight – and then I have to get up next day for the lunch shift –'

'Well, honey, I guess that's reality for you! Think of the

nose. And the chin. Hold it high enough and it might not even need surgery.'

'Huh. Very funny. Plus, what about my birthday?'

'What about it?'

'It falls on a Thursday!'

'So?'

'So how will I get the night off? Jake will want to take me out somewhere nice – I'm sure he will! Will you call in sick for me?'

Lee considered. 'I guess I will, if need be. Why don't we cross that bridge when we get to it. Hey, guess what happened today?'

Ciara frowned. She hadn't finished talking about her job yet, or her birthday. 'What?'

'That boutique in London ordered forty more pieces! Great news, with things the way they are financially. I'd hate to have to give up this house or anything . . . but the jewellery is selling really well.'

'Give up this house? Why would you do that?'

'Because that's the kind of thing that happens when people's money takes a hammering! Mine's been hit really hard. But at least I can keep the roof over my head. And the workshop roof too.'

'Oh, Lee – is the stock market all that bad?'

'Yes. It is. Maybe you'd better be glad of this job, if Jake has as much money tied up in shares as you say he has.'

Ciara froze. There couldn't be any question, surely, of losing the *house*? 'But – but –?'

'I tell you, I'm glad I don't have any kids to put through college. No doubt Jake's salary will see Mike and Tara through, but still, he must be glad you're working, huh?'

Yes. Jake had been glad to hear it. But surely not because–?

126

Abruptly, out of nowhere, Ciara had a petrifying vision of Jake without assets, Jake losing every cent of that lovely nest egg in the bank, Jake coming back to Huxley Wood not because he wanted to but because he had to. Not a poor Jake, exactly – heaven forbid – but not a rich Jake either.

'Yes' she muttered, 'he says he's glad I'm working.'

'And then the twins can always work again during their next vacation.'

Suddenly, Ciara was tired of the word 'work'. Tired, full stop.

'If they have to. Maybe this will all have blown over by then.'

'Maybe. Unfortunately, in my case the damage is done! Most of my divorce settlement from Freddie is down the drain. Good riddance. From now on I'll be living on my wits, hustling hard.'

Ciara stared. How could Lee be so airy about all this, as if losing a fortune scarcely mattered? It dawned on her that there were aspects of Lee she had never explored, didn't know very well. Things it might pay to know?

'What happened, Lee? With Freddie? Why did you split up?'

Lee grimaced, and shrugged. 'We split up because he was a control freak. He thought being his wife should be my *career*. He wanted me to give up making jewellery to play hostess to all his business contacts, society friends . . . thank God I didn't listen. He was a wealthy man, and money was his weapon. It's a very potent weapon, and it damn near killed me.'

'But didn't you *want* to? Entertain his friends, I mean? Be a good wife?' Puzzled, Ciara peered at Lee. Why get married, if you weren't going to do what you were supposed to do? That was the deal, when you married a man with money.

'I tried. For nearly a year . . . until I was bored stiff, of both it and him, realised I'd made a terrible mistake. That was when he kinda turned nasty.'

'Huh? How, nasty?' For the life of her, Ciara couldn't make out how Lee could sound so casual, as if she were talking about a handbag that didn't suit.

'Oh . . . he started beating me up a bit. Not physically, but mentally. Trying to psyche me out, make me feel inadequate when I wouldn't play by his rules. Mental cruelty, the judge called it, when we finally ended up in divorce court. Lots of my friends gave depositions, and I fixed Freddie but *good*.'

Lee grinned, and Ciara gaped at her. Was playing by the rules not what marriage was all about? And was it not worth humouring a husband who had lots of money? Surely Lee couldn't have thrown away this Freddie just because he expected her to toe the line? After all, there must have been lots of rewards, treats, luxury goodies galore?

And then, out of nowhere, a tiny torch of anger ignited somewhere inside her. Flared up like a firework, fizzled out and was gone. Anger about who or what exactly, she couldn't say, anger she could neither explain nor retain. Anger was virtually a foreign emotion to her, she couldn't remember when she'd last felt real, scalding rage. Even when recently provoked by Tara, she'd immediately clamped down, fled the battlefield. As for Jake – she simply would not allow herself to include anger anywhere in her thoughts of him. Anger was not part of the life she had lived with him; at most she'd only ever got annoyed, and learned to handle that. Civilised adults discussed their problems, worked them out – whereas rage was a huge, dangerous, destructive force, way too risky to release.

For a while, she said nothing, mulling over what Lee had

told her. Mental cruelty, she said? Well, maybe that would turn you against marriage, if it went far enough for long enough. Maybe it would drive someone like Lee to divorce, even to revenge. Only, when you got divorce and revenge, what did you do then? Her own brief experience of life without a husband was appalling, she couldn't wait for it to end. Couldn't wait for Jake to . . . to stop this slow torture, this uncertainty, this soul-searching spiel! It might not compare with whatever Freddie had said or done to Lee, but it was a form of cruelty, just the same.

Calmly, Lee glanced out the window. 'It's brightening up, Ciara. Why don't we go for a walk?'

Yes. Without the faintest idea why, for the first time that she could remember, Ciara suddenly wanted to go for a very long, very fast walk. Grabbing her jacket, she threw it on, looking at Lee in a new light as she all but hustled her out the door.

'Okay. Let's do that. I want to hear more about this marriage of yours. About your husband, and your divorce, and how the hell you've been surviving since. I know lots of women who've gone off their husbands, but I don't know any who've actually left them. Even if Jake is playing around, I can't imagine divorcing him in a million years.'

IO

Forty. The dreaded birthday, as inescapable as it was somehow affronting. Both Mike and Tara were very sorry they couldn't make it home to celebrate with their mother – yes, it was half term, but they were so *busy*. Apologetically, Mike sent extravagant flowers and an enormous card, blowing kisses down the phone as he promised to see her soon. Tara also called, wanting to know whether Ciara had received the gift she'd sent.

'Yes' said Ciara, clutching the computerised skipping rope the postman had just delivered, 'it's terrific, darling, thank you!'

'You said you wanted one that would count how many calories you were burning off' Tara said, managing to sound both aggressive and defensive. Ciara nodded. She had mentioned that, a month or two ago before she started working at East Meets West. Now, she thought that what she'd really love was a week in bed. A whole week, unconscious.

'I did, and I'll count every last one! It's such a shame you can't be here, Daddy has booked a table at Brown's for tonight—'

'I know' Tara said shortly, 'I was talking to him last night. Mum, when is he – when are you –?'

'Soon' Ciara promised, wondering why she sounded so

swift, so certain. Jake's return to his home, to his senses, looked neither swift nor certain. A slightly cool note seemed to have crept into their recent conversations, she was finding it increasingly difficult to be 'understanding'. To keep smiling and pretending she believed his reassurances.

Was that why the twins were not coming home for her birthday? Because they couldn't stand the suspense, the strain? Mike, she sensed, had taken her side, while Tara seemed to be more on Jake's. It was only a guess, but that was somehow how it felt. Their absence could hardly be due to mere laziness, could it, or indifference? They were good kids, neither had ever missed a birthday before.

'Well' Tara sighed, 'I hope somebody's going to do a bit of growing up sometime soon. You're supposed to be the adults – forty is as grown-up as it gets, I hear.'

Did she sound angry, or merely exasperated? All Ciara knew for sure was that she didn't want to alienate her any further.

'Don't worry. Everything will work out. You'll see.'

'It'd better' retorted Tara, and was gone, leaving Ciara feeling totally unfestive. How could anyone celebrate, in these circumstances? As if forty were cause for celebration, anyway! Now that she worked in a restaurant, the attraction of eating in one tonight, even with Jake, was diminished. Of course Brown's was lovely, but . . . dammit, Jake, why can't we just stay home, here in our own house? Have champagne and a Chinese takeaway and cuddle up – I hate you for doing this to me, you bastard. I hate you for making me dress up and traipse into town and greet you with a kiss and smile all night and not mention Roisin Harte and act as if everything was *wonderful*!

And I hate you for what you're doing to our children, too.

132

To all of us, as a family. When you walked out, I thought you were confused or ill or something; now I'm beginning to wonder if maybe you're not just plain selfish?

I love you. I do still love you, and miss you, and want you back. Only it's been four months now. That's a helluva long time to indulge yourself. Especially without even properly explaining what's the matter. How do you expect me to cope, when I don't know what I'm supposed to be coping with?

I don't want to have dinner with you tonight. For the first time in my life, I'm not in the mood. So why am I doing it?

'Happy birthday, darling.' Stooping to kiss his wife on the plush sofa where she sat waiting for him, Jake smiled his widest Captain Lunny smile. Welcome aboard, we'll be cruising at thirty thousand feet tonight . . . unexpectedly he was not carrying the anticipated bouquet, but a giftwrapped parcel instead. A chunky, promising-looking parcel.

Jimmy Choo shoes? Manolo Blahnik? As she gazed up Ciara was glad there were no flowers: had he had the nerve to produce a romantic bouquet, she might have hit him over the head with it. Astonished by the very thought, she permitted him to kiss her cheek, sinking into her chair dazed by the mere idea.

Settling at their table, sipping an aperitif, he parked the parcel on a ledge behind him and appeared to forget about it, distracted by the menu as it arrived. Curiosity gripped her: but she would have to wait until he handed it over, she supposed, which he seemed in no hurry to do. Gifts on previous birthdays had included jewellery, holidays, clothes, lingerie, but forty surely merited something special? No matter how she dreaded getting older, presents were gratifying, some small compensation for the trauma.

Eventually they ordered pâté, shellfish, chicken, and heroically he rose to the bottle of champagne they always shared
on birthdays. 'So' he grinned as they chinked glasses, 'forty,
huh? Do you feel any different?'

Yes. To her surprise, she found that she did. She felt tired,
after a busy lunch shift at East Meets West. She felt sad, that
neither of her children was here tonight. She felt shocked, by
Lee's tale of marital and financial collapse. And suddenly
she felt annoyed with Jake, fed up with his mid-life crisis.
This farce had gone on long enough, she was entitled to an
explanation. To his exclusive attention, with no Roisin
Harte hovering between them. For the first time in her
married life, she felt truly impatient with her husband.

But impatience was not something you showed the handsome man who was wining and dining you. 'Yes' she replied
at length, with studied calm, 'I do. I actually feel forty.'

'Well, you don't look it!'

She struggled to share his smile. Of course I don't look it,
she thought. I've had an expensive facelift and worked my
butt off – literally – at the gym for *years*. I spent a full hour
on my hair, make-up and clothes before coming here
tonight. I don't look it because I make such a bloody huge
effort. Are you worth it, Jake Lunny, are you really worth it?
You always were before, but tonight . . . tonight, I just don't
know.

'Flattery' she said coolly, 'will get you nowhere.' Always,
that had been a jokey phrase between them. Tonight, it
seemed to ring hollow as a saucepan.

He looked surprised. 'Hey, Ciara, it was meant to be a
compliment! Are you tired, is this new job hard going? Or is
it fun, are you meeting people, enjoying the novelty?'

Was she? His smile was expectant, somehow hopeful. 'Yes.

The staff are fun, and most of the customers. But it's very hard work, I'm run off my feet.' Literally run off them, she thought; there are times when I'd give anything to swop my high heels for a comfy pair of flatties. If hostesses were allowed to wear flatties. If I owned a pair, which I never have yet.

'Well, you don't have to do it, you know. Even if our savings have taken a wallop, I can still support you. Maybe in slightly less style! But in comfort, nonetheless.'

Pointedly, she looked at him. Money was one of the subjects she wanted to discuss tonight. 'Enough for me to get my nose done? Five grand?'

Fork aloft, he paused over his prawns with some faint air of exasperation. 'Jesus, Ciara, how often do I have to say it – you don't need your goddamn nose done!'

'I do if I don't want to look my age. Do *you* want me to look it?'

He sighed. Which was rich, she thought, when her appearance had always mattered so much to him. Mattered from the moment they first met, mattered in the whole circle in which they moved. Wives were thin, and blonde, and youthful, and that was that. Those who failed the annual exam – the Christmas charity ball – had only themselves to blame if they were subsequently traded in.

'I just want you to look well. What is this obsession with your looks and your age? And what's that saying – "life begins at forty"?'

She sighed in turn. 'You're about the sixth person to say that today. Mum and Dad called from Marbella, the children called, my brother from Seattle –' And nobody else, she thought with a pang, because nobody outside the family knows I'm forty today. I'd sooner swallow crushed glass than

135

let anyone know . . . only it does fall a bit flat, then, when you don't get any cards. When nobody makes any fuss.

He frowned. 'What about Sara? Your pals from the golf club? Are you playing much lately?'

For one flying moment she yearned to confide in him. Yearned to be honest and admit what had happened, tell him of the callous retreat her friends had beaten from her sparkling new look. But pride wouldn't let her. 'No. I'm not playing at all. I haven't time any more, and anyway I – I've gone off golf.'

'Really?'

'Yes, really. In fact I never much enjoyed it. Besides, now I have the problem of what to say when people ask how you are. How long am I supposed to go on saying you're fine? Pretending to my friends and your friends and my parents and your parents and our children and everyone else that you still live at home and we are still a happily married couple? Huh? How long, Jake?'

Astonished, he stared at her, and she was astonished herself, had had absolutely no idea that all this was going to come pouring out. On the contrary, she had psyched herself up to arrive here this evening prepared to do what she'd done all her life, which was smile and be nice. Cause no waves, throw down no gauntlets. As the magazines warned, men hated to be cornered. Hated to even be asked any awkward questions.

'And, while we're at it, do the Hartes know you're having an affair with their daughter? Because let me tell you, I did not enjoy talking to them on the phone today. It was a nightmare. Of your making. In fact I spent the whole day telling lies, covering for you – how long do you expect me to continue doing that, Jake? How long do you expect me to believe that you're not having any affair? How long, *exactly*?'

Incredulous, she heard her voice rising, noted a woman glancing round from the next table, saw his face paling very slightly, the amiability freezing in his eyes.

'Ciara, for chrissakes lower your voice.'

'All right. I'll lower my voice. But I still want an answer, Jake. Now. Tonight.'

An ultimatum? But – horrified, she tried to haul herself back, tried to muzzle whoever was speaking. It couldn't possibly be her; Ciara Lunny had never, ever put Jake Lunny under any kind of pressure. Ever.

For a moment, he didn't answer, his gaze fixed on his plate so she was unable to see whatever was happening in his face. And then, in a gesture so apparently irrelevant she was flummoxed, he put down his cutlery, turned around and reached for the parcel behind him.

'Your birthday present. Why don't you open it now?'

Huh? Was he trying to divert her? Placate her? Or simply not listening to stuff he didn't want to hear? Did he think she was a child to be bribed?

'Jake, thank you, but I really don't think this is the moment—'

'Yes. It is the moment. Open it.'

One glance at his face sent her fingers plucking at the parcel; without warning he had gone into Captain Lunny mode, was taking charge in his authoritative way. Silently, she slid her long scarlet nails under the sellotape.

'Oh . . . ohh . . . but . . . what's . . . this?' Never, since infancy, had she failed to smile rapturously when unwrapping a parcel, whatever its contents, because that was what charming, well-behaved girls did when given gifts. They beamed and thanked prettily and kissed the donor, even if they hated whatever turned out to be inside the wrapping. Now, she felt her face deflating, heard her words hissing slowly out of her puckered mouth like air from a tyre.

His voice, along with the food on their plates, was growing cold. 'What does it look like?'

It looked very like – undeniably *was* – a stack of books. Half a dozen hefty great books, weighty as concrete bricks as she lifted out one after another, blinking blankly at their titles.

Sophie's World, by Jostein Gaarder. *Age And Guile*, by PJ O'Rourke. *The Prime Of Life*, by Simone de Beauvoir. *Excursions In The Real World*, by William Trevor. *The Bonfire Of The Vanities*, by Tom Wolfe. And finally a romance: *Wuthering Heights*, by Emily Brontë.

'But – Jake –' In her chest, something clenched, some confused knot was strangling her. The habit of a lifetime – 'Oh, thank you, you shouldn't have, this is so beautiful!' – wrestling with frozen incomprehension: 'But you know I never read anything like this, you idiot, is this some kind of stupid joke!' Both phrases raced through her mind, but neither would pass her lips.

After a long, baffled pause, she put the books down, sat back, stared at him and managed to whisper. To croak. '*Why?*'

Candidly, in a way that was both appraising and challenging, he met her eye. 'Because you asked me a question. Because you wanted an answer. Ciara, this is the answer.'

'What?' She felt her hand fluttering at her throat. 'Jake, I don't understand – I just don't –'

Without warning he turned around, summoned a waiter and requested the bill for their half-finished meal, congealing before them. Extracting a credit card from the inside pocket of his jacket, he studied it with a kind of grimace, as if what he had eaten had been distasteful.

'Ciara, these books are the answer to your question. Let me know when you've read them, and then we'll talk about when I'm coming home.'

All but grabbing the bill as it arrived, he waited with visible impatience for the card to slide through the machine, signed the resulting chit, stood up and pushed back his chair.

'I'm sorry, Ciara. I hadn't intended to give you those until we'd finished our meal. But now that I have, I can't stay any longer. I – goodnight. Goodbye.'

Before she could summon breath, he was gone.

Lights were still on in Lee's house when she reached it, sobbing and distraught, twenty minutes later. It was late, way after ten, but Lee led such a quiet life, she'd probably be glad of a visitor. Any visitor, Ciara thought, even if I do need sympathy and – and – I could murder a stiff Scotch, if alcohol wasn't so fattening.

Picking up the wretched parcel, she paid off the taxi and tottered to the door, ringing the bell so urgently that Lee appeared within seconds. A flushed, laughing Lee, accompanied by merry voices floating out from her dining room.

'Ciara!' Looking less thrilled and more surprised than Ciara had expected, she threw wide the door nonetheless, ushering her inside. 'What's the matter? You look awful!'

'I feel awful' Ciara admitted, 'but – you have visitors –?'

'Just a few friends for supper. They'll be leaving soon. Come on in and have a glass of wine.'

Before she knew it she was seated with a glass of chardonnay, surrounded by half a dozen cheery, chatty people at a table strewn with the remnants of supper, plates half obliterated under a large map spread between them.

'We're going to Vietnam' Lee explained, 'for Christmas. Hiring a camper van, heading off like those hippies in *The Drifters* . . . have you read any James Michener, Ciara, do you like him?'

Jesus, more books! Why was everyone so into them tonight? And what am I supposed to say, she wondered, 'No, the only things I ever read are *Hello!* magazine and dry-clean-only'?

'Uh, no. Uh, Vietnam?'

Lee laughed. 'Yeah. Can't stand consumer Christmas. Gonna get well away from it this year, huh guys?'

Cheerfully, her friends – since when did she know all these people? – agreed that they were. And then, sussing the situation, they stood up, tossing back their wine, reaching for jackets as they insisted they'd been just about to leave anyway. Five minutes later they were all gone, three men, two women, vanishing in a flurry of maps and books. Astonished and not a little embarrassed, Ciara watched them disappear down the drive; what on earth had made her think she was virtually Lee's only friend?

Returning to the warm, messy room, ignoring the rubble of supper, Lee sloshed red wine into a glass and flopped into an armchair. She looks lovely tonight, Ciara noted, her style's weird but those chunky red earrings do suit that white top, her hair's nice loose –

'Let me guess. Jake Lunny is leaving his wife for good, running off to Uzbekistan with Roisin Harte?'

Wretchedly – Uzbekwhere? – Ciara could barely manage a small, strangled laugh. 'No. It's worse than that, Lee. Even worse than that.'

'Oh wow. The bank has pulled the plug and the Lunnys will

be moving to a small cabin on Tory Island, of clay and wattles made?'

'Look.' Bending down, Ciara rummaged in the parcel at her feet. 'Look what he's given me, Lee. For my *birth*day.' Her face crumpling, she waved aloft *The Prime Of Life*. 'I mean, what the hell kind of thing is this to do to your wife on her fortieth fucking birthday?'

Lee sat up. Ciara, swearing? And – 'Today's your birthday? Your fortieth?'

'Yes. But please don't tell anyone.' Looking imploring, as if she were a spy clutching a state secret, Ciara muttered so guiltily that Lee spluttered.

'But you should have said, I'd have baked a cake!'

'Lee, I said forty, not four.'

'Yeah – and think of all the people who never make it to forty! Or even to four, sometimes . . . Ciara, birthdays celebrate survival. You should be real chuffed. Anyway, let's see the books.'

Without warning Lee was down on her knees on the floor, whisking through them, reading jacket blurbs out loud, nodding with . . . *approval*? 'Cool. I love all Simone's memoirs. PJ O'Rourke is a cranky bastard but he's so provocative – *Bonfire* blew New York away, when it was written – *Wuthering Heights*? Well, he sure can't be accused of giving you anything new, can he?'

Aghast, Ciara recoiled as if Lee had declared the books radioactive. 'You – surely – don't mean they're *second hand?!?*'

Lee's explosive laughter was as annoying as it was baffling. 'No – oh, Ciara! I only mean, all these books were written years ago, we're not exactly talking radical.'

Oh, no. Could she really know them all, have read them? All of them? Flushing, Ciara strove for dignity. 'Well, obviously, *Wuthering Heights* has been out for ages, it was a film you know.'

There now. See. I'm not that bad, I went to the Sacred Heart convent for—

'So' Lee was looking at her in that off-kilter, off-hand way she had, 'what's your problem?'

'My *problem*?' Was she shrieking? Okay, she was shrieking. 'My problem is that this is *it*! This is what he's given me for my fortieth goddamn bloody birthday!' Was she swearing? Okay, she was swearing. 'Lee, he's my husband! Where's my diamond bracelet? My mink coat? My week at Champney's? He didn't even give me any f-f-*flowers* . . .'

Was she sobbing? Okay, she was sobbing. Sobbing torrents, suddenly, gushing all over Lee's map of Vietnam, flooding the rice paddies. 'I mean, what have I done to deserve this? Why is he *torturing* me? And then – and then he stood up and walked out! Left me there, all on my own! On my birthdaaay . . .'

Silence. Complete silence, as Lee callously left her to wail and rail, flicking through the books as she waited for the storm to subside, raising an eyebrow at the William Trevor. 'Well, honey, y'know, it's not a mink-'n'-diamonds economy just now, Jake's having to breathe in like the rest of us . . . I only get to go to Vietnam because I sold those pieces of jewellery to London, and because Vietnam, God help it, is dirt cheap.'

Huh? Was that supposed to be some kind of consolation?

'And besides, these are great books.'

Well. I might as well, Ciara thought furiously, have gone home and straight to bed, for all the sympathy I'm getting here. She doesn't understand one single word I'm saying.

'Lee, he wants me to *read* them! The whole six . . . I asked him when he was coming back to me and he said he'd discuss that when I've read them! He's raving mad. He said they were the answer to my question. He's gone totally doolally.'

'In that case' Lee drawled, 'why would you want him back?'

Ciara's gaze shot up from Saigon like a Mirage jet pulling out of a loop. 'What?'

'I said, why . . . tell me, Ciara, what exactly is it you love about Jake Lunny?'

'Love?'

'Yes. It's a noun or a transitive verb. In this case, your husband Jake is the object of the verb . . . let's start at the beginning. Where did you meet him?'

With the distinct, infuriating albeit helpless feeling of not being taken nearly as seriously as the occasion demanded, Ciara wiped her eyes with her sleeve and what small dignity could be mustered when you were sniffling like a child.

'We met on the cosmetics counter of the store where I worked after leaving school. He was looking for perfume for his girlfriend's birthday. I suggested Youth Dew.'

'You witch. Knowing it's the perfume of choice of old ladies?'

Ciara's eyes widened innocently, but a blush betrayed her. 'Uh . . . well, he was gorgeous! And then I discovered he was a pilot. Only a cadet, at the time, but still.'

As if that explained everything, she paused, and Lee glanced at *Wuthering Heights* on the floor. 'So. Goodbye girlfriend?'

'Yes. Well, not immediately. But a few weeks later, he came back and asked me out. We went to see some barmy Woody

Allen film and then he took me to dinner. At Le Caprice. He told me I was even better looking than Jane Fonda.'

'Okay. So we've got ourselves a handsome pilot who does a fancy line in flattery. And ritzy restaurants. At what stage did you fall in love with him?'

Ciara stared. Surely even Lee couldn't be that thick? 'That night! Right then and there!'

'I see. And since? Has this epic passion plumbed even greater depths, soared to ever higher galaxies over the past twenty years?'

Frowning, Ciara eyed her. 'Lee, Jake is still a pilot. Still handsome. Still a good catch – or was until recently. He's a good father to our children – or was until recently. And he's always flattered me, fancied me –'

'Until recently?'

'Yes! Lee, what can he possibly see in Roisin Harte? It'd actually be easier to cope if she were stunning! Exquisite, sensational – but she isn't a looker at all, she's plain as a plate of porridge. It simply doesn't add *up*.'

'H'mm. Ciara, tell me, were you ever any good at math?'

'No, but—'

'Then might I suggest doing what Jake apparently wants, and reading these books? Unless maybe the gloss has worn off this communion of Lunny souls? I hate to say it, but if it has – well, why not cheer yourself up, take a toyboy off the shelf?'

A toyboy? Now there was an idea. An *inspired* idea. A younger man, to make Jake jealous?

'Lee, you're a genius! Oh, why didn't I think of this sooner – I could find one with a snap of my fingers, someone who'll appreciate my new facelift! Some guy who won't even know I've had one, who'll simply think I'm gorgeous, parade me all over town on his arm! Jake and the girls and everyone will be pea green – oh, you are brilliant!'

Leaping up, she flew to Lee, seized her and hugged her, trampling all over the books in her flurry of joy.

But, Lee silently gasped, I was only joking, you nitwit! It was meant to be a *joke*!

11

The Christmas party. The first staff party Ciara had ever attended, the first since her marriage she'd ever gone to without Jake on her arm. It was to be on the restaurant's own premises, but a firm of Mexican caterers was coming in to do 'something completely different'. Unable to decide whether she was dreading it or what, she hit the hairdressers that morning, the beauty salon for a manicure, and then a boutique where she treated herself to a sexy, silvery top in shiny lurex. With her drainpipe black velvet trousers and highest black heels, she would look easily as young and cool as the rest of them.

Easily, she thought with satisfaction as her nails were grown and glossed, the manicurist remarking on the success of her new blonde streaks. I am going to look wonderful and have a wonderful time. Okay, maybe it's not the hunt ball, but I don't want to go to that this year anyway. Can't go, without Jake, even if those old bats from the golf club weren't going to be there. So I'm going to this instead, and going to enjoy it with Robin and Neil and all the others. Even if I do have to walk in alone . . . Tara says lots of women go to parties alone these days. But how do they face it? I've never gone alone to anything before, have no idea how anyone can just walk in and brazen it out.

But at least it'll be a chance to meet the 'crew', as Robin

147

calls them, properly. Things are always so busy, I've hardly had a chance to talk to anyone I work with . . . and it'll get me out of the damn house, too. Why did Lee have to go off to Vietnam for bloody Christmas? Now she's not around I'm starting to miss her, hadn't realised how much I like her, really, even if she doesn't understand anything and makes fun of everything. She's the only person who's stuck around this year, who listens, doesn't seem to care what I wear or what mood I'm in. The only one who knows about Jake, too, the only one I can trust. So let's do as she says, go to this party and have a good time tonight. Try to find . . . well, if not a toyboy, someone who might cheer me up a bit? Someone who can take away this awful loneliness, even for a few hours, because I just don't know how much more of it I can stand.

'Wow! Don't you look sensational!' Handing Ciara a glass, Robin grinned rather luridly, and Ciara grinned back. Really, there was nothing like a compliment to lift a girl's spirits. This wasn't nearly as difficult as she'd dreaded. Taking the glass, she peered into it. 'Thank you! What's this?'

'A margarita. C'mon, let me take you round, introduce you . . . you've hardly met half the staff yet, have you?'

No. She hadn't. But tonight there would be time for everyone – even if she'd have to shout over that salsa music – and no, she wasn't overdressed. Lots of the girls were wearing even shinier outfits than hers, wild make-up, dayglo hairdos, jewellery that caught the revolving strobe lights that were turning the restaurant pink, green, blue . . . the whole place was pulsating, with a faintly frantic note to it, as if a moment's lull might ruin the whole thing.

'This is Zara – Sam – Kim – Mel – guys, say hello to Ciara, she's off the desk tonight!' With a friendly nudge, Robin thrust her into the midst of her colleagues, decamping to welcome other arrivals while she took a long pull on her margarita and plunged in. Somewhere, way out on the fringes of her mind, lurked the awful thought: these kids are the same age as my own. I'm old enough to be their mother.

Will anyone suspect? What's the shorthand, these days, in which teenagers and twenty-somethings talk? Of course I know most of it from Mike and Tara, but still . . . I'd better watch every word.

'Hey Ciara' offered Kim, a Malaysian youth with a mauve pigtail and matching stud in his nose, 'you look real bling tonight!'

'Thanks' she gurgled, twirling her drink, taking another slug, 'so do you!'

'Sorry we haven't had much chance to chat before' shouted Sam, from the shimmering depths of a gold waistcoat under which he was naked to the waist, 'but we're always in the vaults of hell while you're out front. Nothing personal. How're you enjoying the job, anyway?'

'Ooohh – great!' Airily, she waved a hand to indicate utter bliss, reaching for a canapé with the other; the margarita was surprisingly strong on an empty stomach. Was there going to be sit-down food, or what?

'Have you met Morgan Richards' vet?' shrieked Zara, a tall girl with orange hair who was, if Ciara remembered right, a dessert chef. Shaking her head, she strained her ears.

'Whose vet?'

'I said, have you met Morgan Richards yet?' Zara yelled, pushing forward an equally tall man who looked slightly older than the others. Ciara had only glimpsed him once, pan-frying something as she scurried past the kitchens, frowning intently into a cloud of steam.

'No – hi, Morgan.' Don't shake hands, she reminded herself, nobody shakes hands these days. Look as if you've just woken up trying to remember your own name.

Morgan, who looked as if he'd just done precisely that, raised a palm from the back of the group, which was beginning to fizz in some way, as if ready to disperse. 'Hey, Clara.'

'Ciara' she bawled back, '*Ciara!*' Dear God, the noise was even worse than on working nights. Closing his eyes, Morgan nodded so soulfully that it crossed her mind to wonder whether he was on something even stronger than the cocktails. Something about his unshaven, fuddled look suggested that he didn't much care whether her name was Klondike or Cleopatra, and would probably be calling her Kleenex by the end of the night, if he stayed upright that long.

Well, she thought, it's a change from the hunt ball, right enough.

Squid. That must have been what did it. Spicy black squid that had got churned up with one of those margaritas as she gyrated on the dance floor, her stomach spinning like a washing machine. Which margarita? The fifth, maybe? Or sixth? Or that beer Mel had insisted she slug by the neck with a wedge of lime?

Or it might have been the tortillas, squelching with spicy goo. Or that tequila. 'Tequila slammers' someone had called the little shots, thumping one down on a table before handing it to her, insisting she lick salt off the back of his hand first . . . who? Somebody big, kinda bossy, smelling of something vaguely sweet, a hulking presence she couldn't now put name or face to.

Oh well. That, apparently, was parties for you these days. Music that glued your ears to your skull, food that ripped the lining off your eyelids, drinks that put your tonsils through your toes. Moaning faintly, wincing as an earring dug into her neck – where was the other? – Ciara lay utterly still on her back, reaching for the clock without moving, wondering what time of day it was. What day it was. Not that it mattered: even if Tara had been drowning, Mike had been having a heart transplant or Jake had been forced by terrorists to divert at gunpoint to Taiwan, she could not have got up today. Could not even sit up, the mere thought sending her stomach scuttling to . . . ooohhh.

Still. It had been a fun party. An absolutely exhausting party, what with those spike heels and that conga line and that terrible dread of doing or saying anything that would date her, but not without amusing interludes, particularly that bit when someone threw her up to the ceiling and someone else caught her coming down. She hadn't felt such liberation, such exhilaration since she'd been a kid on the roller-coaster at Butlins . . . uhhh. Was there any way to reach the Alka Seltzer in the bathroom without leaving the bed? Lying carefully still, contemplating the ceiling as it slowed down, she tried to figure out if there might be.

Damn, she thought, if only Jake were here, he'd get it for me. Not that I'd need it if he were here, because I'd never have eaten or drunk the things I ate and drank last night. He'd never have let me behave like that. Thank God he can't see the state of me today. What on earth must I look like? It's a good thing there's nobody here to—

Dhuzz. Dhuzz, dhuzz, *dhuzz*. Puzzled, she screwed up her eyes, wondering. What was that noise? It sounded as if it might be the dishwasher downstairs, slurping and whizzing, but why would she have put it on? Without Jake and the children around, it took a week to fill . . . dhuzz, dhuzz, oh God,

151

it was doing her head in! Sitting up with a nauseating lurch, she groped to steady herself, and her hand clutched a fistful of some dry springy substance, as if she'd plunged it inside the mattress. Looking down, she stared, and gaped, and opened her mouth to scream, but nothing came. Frozen as stalagmites in Antarctica, her vocal chords emitted not the slightest squeak.

Dhuzz. Comfortably, the body attached to the fistful of hair shifted under the duvet, snored again, and snuggled itself down into ever deeper sleep.

With massive disapproval, a look of joint horror she had never noticed before, Ciara's children gaped down from their photograph on the dresser, silently watching their mother wallop the lump in the bed – the *marital* bed – beside her, squeaking incoherently at a man – a total *stranger* – who was evidently having enormous difficulty in waking up.

But, finally, he did. For a moment he said nothing, merely registering without comment that he was being assaulted; and then, yawning, he ran a beefy hand through tangled curls, turned to his assailant and smiled nonchalantly out of a black field of stubble.

'Hey.'

Hey? What did that mean? Hey as in 'good morning, madam'? Or hey as in 'hey, stop that before I hit you back'? Uncertainly, Ciara paused in her pummelling, staring appalled as the top half of a very large, stocky, naked man gradually emerged from the billowing depths of duvet, grinning at her with casual familiarity.

Oh my God, she thought. Morgan Richards. The chef. I work with. At East Meets West. Oh no oh God oh no God no no *no*.

'Well' Morgan drawled thoughtfully, hauling himself up on one elbow, 'just because I cook for a living, I hope you're not expecting me to fry any eggs this morning.'

No. She was not expecting any frying of any eggs. She was expecting to die, to move on any minute now to some other, mercifully distant new world, one in which nobody would know her . . . was that it? Had she actually died, of alcoholic poisoning? Was Morgan Richards St Peter in disguise? He certainly seemed to be inspecting her with some curiosity.

'Wouldn't mind a juice, though. You got any juice?'

Sadly, silently, she shook her head. Nobody could possibly expect her to know what was in the fridge here in . . .

'Nice house' Morgan commented, winching himself upright, swivelling his gaze around the bedroom, vaguely noting his surroundings. 'Whose is it?'

Whose *was* it? The nerve! What, did he think it was too good for her, was that it? Or that she couldn't possibly afford it, on her paltry pay? Or . . . suddenly, she winced as if he'd flung a brick at her head. Of course he thought it was someone else's. It was a family house. A middle-class, middle-aged house, completely unconnected with the single twentysomething she had been last night.

'It . . .' Her breath seemed to be rationed, speech proving remarkably difficult. 'It belongs . . . to . . . my . . . parents.'

Inside her head, some incredulous demon started dancing up and down, raving in disbelief. You've just woken up in bed with a man you spent the night with, a one-night stand you appear to have had *sex* with? And the first thing you say to him is that you live with your *parents*? Are you out of your *mind*?

Scratching his stubbly chin, Morgan nodded gravely, considering. 'I see. And are they – uh – at home, this morning?'

'No' croaked a voice Ciara had never heard before, 'they – er – live – in – uh – Spain.'

Well. That was true. Was it not?

'Right. And who's that?' His head nodded in the direction of the dresser.

Aghast, clutching the duvet to her, Ciara sat bolt upright, stomach lurching with terror. Jake. Jake had come home and . . . and somehow framed himself, alongside the twins, on the dresser.

'Oh, that.' Dizzily, she giggled, choking on a churning mixture of tequila, thundering horror and galloping guilt. 'That's myhhh – uncle.'

If he thought it odd to have a framed photo of one's uncle in one's bedroom, Morgan was too polite to say so. Instead he jerked a thumb in the direction of the twins. 'And the matching set?'

'My – urmm – kid brother. And – hahhh – sister.'

Take me, she thought. Take me now, God, to your bosom and peace everlasting, amen.

'Really? They around today? Any chance they'd get us some juice?' Hopefully, Morgan looked speculatively at them, and Ciara wondered how many years – decades? – it would be before she could ever face her son or daughter again.

'No, they . . . 're . . . away. At . . . college.'

'H'mm. Bonus babies, huh? They look a good few years younger than you – seven, maybe, eight?'

'Yesss . . . er, Morgan . . .' Her tongue felt stapled to her tonsils. 'I – ah – did – uh – do – you – remember – anything?'

Frowning, he looked at her. 'About what?'

Somehow she plucked the words from the depths of her diaphragm. 'About . . . last . . . night?'

Pursing his lips, he thought about it. 'Sure. Great party. You're a fun girl, Clara. And then you haul me home here and we start having sex that coulda been even more fun if you hadn't crashed out in the middle of it.'

Crashed? Out? In the middle . . . middle before, or middle after? *Which* middle?

'Morgan' she said, sitting up, forcing down the nausea that rose with her, getting a grip on the one thing of which she was sure, 'my name is not Clara. It's Ciara.'

'Right. Whatever. Anyway, gotta go.'

What? He was planning to *leave*? Just get up and go, without further ado, as if their sexual encounter – whatever it was, or wasn't – meant no more than an episode of *EastEnders*? Mouth open, duvet bunched in her fist, she watched agog as he threw back his half of the bedding, swung long chunky legs to the floor and stood up, stark naked, entirely careless.

'D'ya mind if I take a shower?'

Speechless, she eyed the bathroom, and he padded away to it, brazenly, bizarrely, snapping a hand to his forehead in salute as he marched past the photo of Jake. 'Good morning, sir!'

During the ten minutes of his absence Ciara managed to sit fully upright, lean back, stuff a wodge of sheet into her mouth and think. Not coherently, not painlessly, because her brain was still roaring with tequila, but to line up two or possibly three thoughts in random order.

By the time Morgan came back, she knew who she was. Ciara Lunny, restaurant receptionist, twenty-six-year-old spinster of this parish, raving alcoholic turned man-eating slut. Rejected wife of Jake Lunny, redundant mother of Lunny twins, bewildered rival of Roisin Harte. Rendered temporarily insane by alcohol. May eventually recover some motor functions or small vocabulary, but long-term prognosis poor.

'Morgan' she said when he eventually came back, towelled, dripping and smelling horrifically of Jake's cedarwood aftershave, 'where are you going?'

It wasn't what she meant to say. What she meant to say was 'Morgan, did you and I have sex last night? If so, what health precautions were taken? Did you happen to notice my biceps and extremely flat stomach, I work out at the gym, you'd never think I was the forty-year-old mother of those twins in that picture, would you? Oh and by the way, how old are you? Around twenty-six I'd guess, not *quite* young enough to be my firstborn? Now, before you leave, would you mind just putting this pillow over my face and holding it there until I stop breathing? Yes, that's right, thank you very much. Goodbye, Morgan.'

He grimaced. 'I'm going abseiling. If today's still Sunday . . . I abseil up some cliffs most Sundays, I'm in a club . . . hey, wanna come?'

Abseiling? Was that the thing where a bunch of lunatics clambered up and down sheer cliffs, dangling on ropes, swinging out over five-hundred-foot drops into craters, canyons or crashing oceans, their lives dependent on a couple of little metal clips? Briefly, she thought about it.

'Yes. That'd be fun, Morgan. Let's do that. Let's go.'

Ciara, hi! Happy new year! I hope you managed to have some fun, with or without Jake? Have you read his books yet? How are the kids, how was Christmas? Let me know what's happening?

156

Vietnam is wonderful. Mind-blowing. I have never encountered anything like it, such beauty of body or spirit, such serenity, it's like visiting some other planet. So tranquil . . . in fact we've fallen so much in love with it that myself and one of the other guys have decided to stay on for a while . . . not sure how long, maybe a few months, will update you later. D'you think you could possibly keep an eye on my house until things are more definite? Let yourself in with that key I gave you, just check everything's okay? Thank you! Will tell you more as we go along, meanwhile keep in touch, I visit this cybercafe every few days – you do remember how to e-mail, don't you?!

Love and hugs, Lee

Love? And hugs? Well, Ciara reflected, that was more than she'd had from her own family lately. What a shame they should come from a nutter. She'd never remotely suspected that Lee might be nuts, but you had to be fairly far gone to jump ship like this, stay on in a country like Vietnam . . . what did she mean, a few *months*? Where exactly, for how long, who with? 'One of the guys' she said, but Americans called everyone 'guys', male and female alike, that shed no light on anything. Amazed and intrigued, Ciara sat staring at the screen, wondering how on earth anyone could so blithely do something like this.

Could just *go*, and not come back? Put her current life on hold, to dip into another? So lightly, so casually, as if Vietnam were not thousands of miles away, a totally foreign country, culture, language? As Ciara recalled, when her former neighbour Deirdre Molloy had moved to Cork, the manoeuvre had involved an articulated lorry, three solicitors, four estate agents, five schools, six months of paperwork and eighty-nine packing crates.

Whereas Lee, on a whim, on a whisper, had just glided away to Vietnam. Vanished on a puff of wind?

Feeling bereft, somehow mugged, Ciara sat staring at the screen, trying to make sense of it and failing. Never in her life had she encountered something so airy, so unplanned . . . of course, Lee was single. No heavy baggage to carry. But still . . . could people really do this kind of thing? Without a blink?

Apparently they could. Jake could leave home and now so, too, could Lee.

Mulling on it, sipping a cup of jasmine tea, Ciara battled the sense of abandonment she knew was absurd. Lee hadn't abandoned *her*, there was nothing personal in it, she'd merely extended her holiday, was all. Extended it because, presumably, she was enjoying it. Eventually, she would be back. Meanwhile, she, Ciara, was to keep in touch. Simple as that.

So, she would keep in touch. After all, Lee was the one who'd taught her to use this computer. Lee was . . . a good friend. A much better friend than any of those damn women who claimed to be 'friends' but turned out to be no such thing. Writing an e-mail wasn't going to come easy – previous compositions had only ever included shopping lists and one letter each to the twins – but Ciara resolved to reply to Lee. Right now, when she had so much to tell her. It might take all day – in fact it might take a few days, on and off – but she'd do it.

Clicking gingerly on 'reply', she gazed astonished at the blank page that came up, already addressed, waiting for her to fill it in. No explosion, no curling smoke or bits of computer strewn on the carpet: she hadn't broken anything.

She was, apparently, able not only to get a job but now tackle technology as well, all by herself.

And seduce her colleagues within minutes of being introduced to them. Tapping on the keyboard with two fingers, gazing deep into it, she wondered what kind of monster she was in the process of creating.

12

Dear Lee,

What do you mean, you're staying on? Why? Who with?
Till when? What's happening? Tell me!

Yes of course I'll mind your house. I went over today and
watered the plants. Everything's fine. Except that you're
not here! I miss you. I can't believe anyone can just sort of
vanish like this. No warning or fuss or anything. Vietnam
must be fantastic. Tell me more? I've never been
anywhere like that. Can't imagine such a place. Majorca's
more me!

Christmas was awful. Mike went to America to visit his
girlfriend, which only left the three of us, me and Jake and
Tara. At least they did show up. But only to sit around the
table looking miserable. I couldn't invite my parents or
anyone else to join us because of the 'situation'. We still
haven't told anyone, it's all too messy and . . . I just don't
know what to do or say about it. Even though he's breaking
my heart, there are times when I could kill him. Times
when I wonder whether I really know who he is, at all. After
twenty years together, and two children! Can husbands
turn into strangers? Even nice, good ones like Jake?

No, I haven't read those books of his yet. I *can't*. They're too big and serious and he must know I never will . . . besides, why does he want me to? He didn't marry a college professor, he married Ciara O'Kane off the cosmetics counter!

But I have done something else. Something you won't believe, I don't even believe it myself. I've taken . . . are you ready for this? . . . a lover. Done exactly what you said, and got myself a toyboy. A guy I met at the restaurant. No, not even a rich customer! He's the chef. One of five chefs to be exact. When I wake up and look in the mirror in the mornings, all I see is this woman looking so *surprised*! And shocked. If Tara did something like this I'd murder her, tell her she was a little trollop. If she knew, I don't dare think what she'd say. Or Mike, or *Jake*, they'd faint if they found out. But then I think of Roisin Harte and I find myself wondering, why not? Why sit here waiting for my husband to come home, to start appreciating everything he's risking?

He's been gone nearly six months now and Morgan Richards is better than sitting around moping, going mad.

Much better, actually. He's not my type at all, in fact he's a bit scruffy (you know how young guys only half-shave these days, and wear horrible tattoos?) and love doesn't come into the picture at all naturally, but . . . he's twenty-six, and he fancies me! Thinks I'm about the same age, thinks I'm fun, he says.

The weird thing is, we're having fun. You can't imagine how exhausting fun is, when you're years older than people think you are! We've been abseiling and discoing and roaring round on his motorbike and last weekend we went on one of those things where everyone runs screaming up hills and through forests shooting ink pellets at each other . . . every bone in my body was aching like it'd been beaten with a cricket bat. I'd have slaughtered my granny for a hot bubble bath. But there never seemed to be time for one – I'd forgotten how men of Morgan's age are so obsessed with sex. Non-stop sex, round the clock . . . Jake was like that once, but he was away so much, and the twins got in the way so often. I can't believe I'm sleeping with someone else now, someone I don't even love – and worse, I'm enjoying it. Well – most of me is horrified, of course, but some wicked little bit of me is actually enjoying this adventure. He's very different to Jake – I never knew guys could be so different in bed – but he's great. Way younger than me, but knows so much more! He must have had dozens of girlfriends, whereas I only ever had Jake. The first time we slept together (deliberately that is, not counting the night we met) I felt like an idiot, he actually laughed, couldn't believe I was 'so innocent' at my age – Christ, imagine if he knew I was forty and married for years! Anyway, I've learned a few new tricks since. He makes me feel adventurous, and his energy is amazing. Plus, we're not married or even in love, so it all feels kinda – light, or free or something, like a really good work-out at the gym!

The only problem is, I'm shattered. Practically unconscious all day, can barely stay upright at work. Nobody knows anything at the restaurant, we hardly ever see each other there since he's in the kitchen while I'm out

163

front. But I tell you, I'd murder my mother for a massage, I'm black and blue from all this activity! For a week in bed – asleep – I'd murder my father as well. How am I going to go on like this, like a youngster with endless energy? And now he says he wants us to go abseiling again next Sunday – Jesus, the heights, the ropes, the terror, the knots in every muscle, you'd need a wheelchair at the end of it.

But I can't tell Morgan that! I have to grin and punch the air and say 'wey *hey*' as if I *was* loving every moment, before we go off to some thundering disco to drink and dance – *why* does the music have to be so loud? They'll all go deaf, that whole generation – mine, I mean. Us twenty-somethings.

Is it worth it? Can I keep doing it?

Yeah. It is. I can. I hope. Morgan is no Jake Lunny, but it feels great when he introduces me to his friends as his 'lady'. Feels much better than sitting home watching *Coronation Street* all on my own. I just wish he wasn't quite such a 'new man' about money – do you know that young women (like me!) pay their own way everywhere now, split all the bills?

Well, maybe that's only fair. Morgan doesn't earn nearly as much as Jake, plus I have a salary now . . . still, it's a shock! As you know, I'm a material girl, but maybe I'll get used to it? I suppose I'll have to, it doesn't look as if there are going to be many treats or goodies in this brave new world, as Jake would call it. Morgan calls it 'democracy', says he 'wouldn't insult' me by paying for anything.

So that's the news from Huxley Wood. It's taken me four days to write this lot! But at least nothing has vanished or exploded, you did a good job teaching me the computer. Are you okay? You seem so far away. Let me know if you need anything, I can post or Fedex stuff. Tell me more about Vietnam and whatever is keeping you there. You will be back by Easter, won't you? At the latest?

You're weird, Lee Warner! The weirdest woman I ever met, apart from this blonde who lives in my mirror when she's not off abseiling with her sex-mad toyboy or pulling ligaments in dens full of dope (yeah, they all do cannabis and some do a lot more). Will I wind up in therapy? Will you wind up in – where are you, exactly? In a hotel or what? Who with?

Love and hugs
Ciara

Morgan's breath was warm in her ear, a tendril of his caramel-streaked hair caressing her cheek. 'Hey . . . wanna go to a party tomorrow night?'

Suppressing a shudder – more screeching noise, teetering stilettos, drunken karaoke!? – Ciara turned to smile eagerly. 'Sure! Where, whose, what kind?'

'Friends of mine. Jim and Sandra. Just married. House-warming.'

Oh. Well. That didn't sound quite so bad. Brightly, Ciara nodded. Yes, she'd be ready at eight tomorrow night. Yes she'd love him to pick her up on his motorbike – motorbikes, she had discovered, were hell on wheels in winter, the icy wind whipped the very marrow from your bones – but babes didn't care about that, did they? Babes loved motor-bikes.

'Great. Oh, and bring a bottle, okay?' On that romantic note, Morgan returned to his kitchen, leaving Ciara to mull on the joys of democratic youth. In her previous, married life, Jake had always chosen clarets to bring to parties, while she selected exotic flowers and paid for them on their joint credit card. The card he bankrolled.

Or did he?

Well, yes. Admittedly he was the one earning the substantial salary. But, she suddenly thought, in my way I paid too. Being his wife was my *job*. And I was damn good at it. I was entitled to spend whatever I spent, it wasn't as if he was doling out pocket money to a child. Any treats I got, I earned. I ran his house and raised his children and entertained his friends and pushed his career and . . .

And now I have to buy a bottle of wine out of my own money. That's going to feel very odd. But at least I have my own money. I work eight killer shifts a week, and Robin pays me an honest wage. It's hard work – oh, why did I have to pick something where I'm on my feet all day? – but at least I can do it. I'm not too old, too useless, too redundant. In one way, working here makes me feel young again. It's almost like being back on the cosmetics counter. Meeting, greeting, making people feel good, feel welcome . . . I enjoy that.

And I'll enjoy this party tomorrow night, if it slays me dead. Of course I can jump up on the table in my red spikes and belt out 'Simply The Best', I'm only a young one! Ten tequilas? Size ten? Two hours' sleep? No problem!

★

166

Oh, bliss. Oh, relief. The party was only a dinner party: eight guests, no sweaty pumping throng, no acid or house or whatever that 'music' was called.

Jesus, Ciara thought, I don't know what it's called. Don't know what's top of the pops this week. I'm going to have to do a bit of swotting up on that, er, scene.

Steered by Morgan, clutching a bottle of chablis – the only one, she noticed, everyone else appeared to have brought plonk – she nodded laconic greeting to the other guests, camouflaging any spontaneous enthusiasm that might erupt. Cool, that was the keynote: and cool was easy when your teeth were chattering after an arctic ride on a motorbike.

'Sandra, Jim – this is Ciara -' Introductions were made, and Ciara cringed as Sandra smiled, as warmly as was permissible at twenty-two or-three years of age. A child! But she can't have just got married, Ciara thought horrified, she's only a baby. This should be illegal.

I can't have been only twenty myself, can I?

'Take your jacket?' Sandra offered, and Ciara cringed.

'Oh no – thanks – maybe later –'

'Whatever. Love your hair.'

She'd done it up high, spewing like a geyser from the top of her head with blue tips at the end of each gelled spike, but as she looked around her she realised she'd miscalculated. Compared to the other four girls – women – in the room, she was way over the top. Their hair looked as if they'd forgotten to do anything to it for at least six months. Christ, she thought, staring at Sandra's murky nest, if you were my daughter I'd ram your head under the shower and lather up a gallon of shampoo –

Handing her a bowl of crisps – crisps?! – Sandra drifted

away, leaving Ciara on the fringe of some conversation between the other guests, involving something or somewhere called Beyoncé. What was Beyoncé? It sounded like maybe some new African country.

'Give me J.Lo any day' Morgan grinned, and she nodded, making a mental note: find out what is J.Lo. A yogurt, a cereal?

'Naw. Brit's the biz' said a youth with a snake tattooed on his forearm, whereupon Morgan guffawed for reasons unclear.

'Matt' he said as an afterthought, 'this is Cla – er, Ciara.'

She raised a vague hand, and Matt surveyed her before winking at Morgan. 'Hey! Given up the babysnatching, have we? Mothers complaining, were they?'

Morgan's eyes seemed to inflate a fraction. 'Lay off, pal.'

That was all he said, but it was enough to send Matt, grinning, back to his own girlfriend, who looked about twenty and was wearing a dress identical to one Ciara remembered having worn herself circa 1985, minus the mountaineering boots. If only I'd kept it, she thought ruefully, Tara could have it now. It'd look good on Tara. How is Tara? I wish she'd ring me . . .

Eventually, after a bewildering discussion of someone or something called Macy – was that not a shop in New York? – dinner was flagged, and everyone drifted into the dining room where, open-mouthed, Ciara saw that someone had chopped the legs off the table. Barely a foot high, it was surrounded by cushions, bedecked with plates of pretty but chilly-looking food and – oh, no – chopsticks.

Sushi. Ciara had tried it once, under pressure from Tara, and hated every cold, raw, sticky mouthful. But everyone now purred approval; apparently sushi was in vogue amongst the trendy-somethings. As was sitting crosslegged on the floor, dutifully ingesting mouthfuls of that foul wasabi sauce, washed down with . . . good grief. Sake? Tiny thimbles of Japanese rice wine? But what about the Chablis –?

From nowhere, something came to her. Something she'd seen on TV or heard . . . had Lee said it? 'Fashion is for kids, it's what they do until they find a style.' Evidently Jim and Sandra had yet to find theirs; at their age, being fashionable was vital. The Japanese furniture looked absurd in their tiny semi-dee, and hellishly uncomfortable, the food would be horrible, the whole scene was almost screaming its need to be trendy. When you were young you did what the fashionistas told you. Next year, Japanese would probably give way to Mexican, Indian, Thai . . . it might be decades before Jim and Sandra grew up, gave in and bought a table adults could eat off. There was something almost touching about their desperation to be cool, Ciara thought – something that was making someone, somewhere, very rich, if all newly-wed youngsters were obediently investing in Japanese furniture this year.

Sinking down on a cushion, crossing her legs – ow! – lotus-like under her, Ciara took up some chopsticks and strove valiantly to look nonchalant, to pin down a seaweed roll as everyone admired the banquet before embarking on a heated conversation about global warming.

God, she thought longingly, what I'd give for some global warming right now. Some hot food to thaw me out, and would someone ever turn up the central heating? But they're so young, economising I suppose on fuel bills. Jake and I had to do that for the first year, I remember wearing two sweaters in winter. I wish I'd worn two today. Are they seriously calling this a house-*warming*?

Global warming led to sustainable agri-economy, which led to recycling . . . her mind drifting, Ciara remembered the Lunny household's recycling phase. Mike and Tara had insisted on it a few years ago, leaving their mountains of cans and bottles for her to take to the bank, a chore which had begun to pall after the first few hundred trips. One day, looking out at a wild gale and lashing rain, she had stuffed the whole lot into the ordinary bin, weekly collection of which was after all costing six hundred euros a year. Guiltily, saying nothing, she had continued to do this, rehearsing her argument for when the twins found out: what difference is it making whether we recycle or not? I can't see any difference! Our lives have not changed, has anyone's!? In what way, precisely? The only difference was that I was getting bloody pneumonia, not to mention bored stiff, spending an hour every Monday shoving your Coke bottles into eco-sacks, lugging them to the depot, shoving them into the green container! So now, if the planet explodes with Kro bottles, tough!

The subject had bored her ever since, but apparently she was the only one bored now: Jim, Morgan, Sandra, Matt and the others were getting agitated, their voices rising, faces flushing with what she recognised as the long-forgotten passion of youth. Sometimes she still glimpsed such fervour in Tara, but not in Mike . . . Mike, it hit her with a jolt, was a chip off her own block. Sleek, affable, fond of his creature comforts, privately indifferent to any social issue that might inconvenience him. She couldn't imagine him trudging to a bottle bank in a million years. Lip service: leave the actual job to someone else.

Whereas for this dirty-haired, fresh-faced group today, the question of plastic pollution was a blazing issue, setting fire

170

to their previously bored, seen-it-all young eyes. Listening as their debate reached fever pitch – some girl called Evie, more cynical than the others, was stirring it up – Ciara felt again somehow touched, almost moved by emotion more intense than any she'd ever felt. Even at their age, she'd never cared about anything the way this lot evidently cared. Nothing, except Jake, and getting married, and setting up a cosy home, and establishing a nice easy suburban circle. Which Jim and Sandra would probably do in turn, when their Japanese phase wore off. When sushi gave way to mashed bananas and the newly burning question of putting Baby's name down for school.

'So' shouted a voice in her ear, 'do you, Ciara? Huh? D'you think we should join NATO, or not?'

What? With horror she realised she'd got left behind, the conversation had moved on to . . . oh, God, to one she remembered from a dinner party of her own, at least ten or fifteen years ago. Jake had got revved up, said things she frantically tried to retrieve now. But in vain. She couldn't even remember what exactly NATO was, even if she cared, which she didn't. But Morgan was looking expectantly at her, and this whole evening, she thought, was becoming terribly trying. Jesus, if I didn't care first time round, why the hell would I care second time round?! At the Hartes' dinner parties, we discuss property prices! Cars and clothes and the best restaurant to be found in Marbella!

Do the Hartes know about Roisin and Jake? Do they? They must. Oh, Christ, they surely must. That's why they never sent a Christmas card this year. Next thing we'll be off everyone's list.

'I don't know!' she shouted, into an abruptly echoing, startled silence. Looking mystified and offended in equal

171

parts, everyone was shrinking back as if she'd ripped a sword from a hidden scabbard.

'But Ciara' said a slow, patient voice at length, 'you must have some opinion, surely?'

Wide-eyed, Matt looked at her, and it dawned on her: no. No I haven't. None. At all. So there. I'm a material girl and I don't give a damn about any of this pseudo-eco-political bullshit, nor will you when you're my age. When you're my age, all but the most naive amongst you will realise that the best anyone can hope for in this life is a good time, a bit of fun, your 2.2 children safely reared, a big comfy gas-guzzler in the drive – yes, a gas-guzzler, let's keep the Arab economy healthy, since you're all so concerned about sustainable economies!

Jake never hassled me like this. Never asked me any awkward questions or gave a fiddler's what I might think about the state of the nation . . . not until recently anyway, not until he went off his rocker and dumped me with all those blasted books. While he swanned off with Roisin Harte.

Suddenly, she stood up, feeling drained and lost, a fish out of water. Around her, seven intensely expectant pairs of eyes stared at her. 'Morgan, I – I'm not feeling very well. D'you think you could take me home?'

Looking not at all amused, much less concerned, he stood up reluctantly, apparently much more interested in NATO than in her, and muttered something grudging.

Oh, Christ, she thought, I've annoyed him. I've failed a test, let him down in front of his friends, behaved like a forty-something instead of a twenty-something. But I can't go on! This whole evening is like some sort of exam, one I already sat and failed two decades ago. I'm exhausted. Frozen rigid and bored rigid. I want to go home.

As she mumbled her goodbyes and overly effusive thanks, he steered her to the door and the last thing she heard was a muted but merry cackle from Matt: 'Hah! That's what he gets for dating women his own age! Shoulda stuck to the kiddi-winks!'

'Maybe' floated Sandra's voice, mildly reproving, 'but he is nearly thirty now, you know. His parents are desperate for him to settle down.'

No. Such a small word, but so hard to say when you were young! When you were still a child, so anxious to please . . . it took years of practice before you could say it easily, firmly, without guilt. 'No' it struck Ciara, was a very adult word.

'No. Sorry, Morgan, not tonight. Got a headache. See you tomorrow.'

With an aura of immense grievance, Morgan revved his motorbike and shot off, leaving Ciara toting a mixture of relief and unease into her house. She really, truly was not in the mood to humour or indulge him tonight – he was not a child after all, it wasn't her job to keep him amused round the clock!

Only then, might he lose interest in her, find someone more accommodating?

Jesus, she thought, I'm too old for this. This is the kind of thing I used to worry about when I was sixteen. When you had to have a boyfriend. Had to prove how gorgeous and popular you were . . . do I really still have to prove it? At forty? Why? To make Jake Lunny jealous?

Not if it means swallowing sushi amongst a bunch of doe-eyed children, I don't. Jake would have laughed if he'd seen the lot of us, squatting round that table waving chopsticks . . . I can't have spent more than two hours at that party, but it felt like two weeks. God, the way they all *looked*, so eager and

173

fervent and righteous! Matt and Evie seemed almost adult, but the others were so . . . sweet. So young.

Young the way you can only be when you actually are young. No matter how young I might look, I'll never feel like that again. Never be that fresh, that passionate, that *new*. They're all seeing the world for the first time, they *care* so much. Whereas I've discovered that nothing changes, all my sharp edges have been worn away by repetition and routine and . . . is that why I hardly ever read newspapers or listen to the news? Because I've read it before, heard it before, over and over and over? Nothing will ever shock me much again, or amaze me the way things did when I was twenty. If gorillas become extinct or Iceland vanishes under a rising tide, so be it. *C'est la vie.* It's selfish and callous and it's how most people feel after forty years on this eternally argumentative, self-destructive planet. Realistic, even weary. You finally realise you can only protect your own tiny patch, and maybe not even make a very good job of that. I wish I could get deeply worried about a Coke bottle floating in the North Sea and all the eco-mayhem it might cause, but I can't. I just can't.

I can get my eyelids lifted or my tummy tucked every year for the rest of my life and I'll still never look like Sandra or those other girls, with that fresh spring bloom on them, that eager spark in their eyes. No matter how I try, I'll never get that back. I can look fit but I will never again look breathless. Or blithe. I'm a mother and my whole being is stamped with the responsibility of that, I can never shake it off or duck out from under it. Never again hear or see or do things for the first time, never be starstruck or crusading or . . . my world has its limits and maybe, just maybe, it's time I started to see them.

Oh, Jesus. I really have created a monster. Have I? Now that I look young and have a young boyfriend, am I going to have to pretend to *be* young, all day every day for the rest of my life? In body *and* in spirit? Act like the whole world is new to me and hey, watch me sort it out?! Party every Saturday and climb cliffs every Sunday, work all week *and* work out with Morgan? Shriek and shout and dance and ride motorbikes, discuss the environment and smoke dope and stay a size ten? Dig gangsta rap, humour guys, pay for wine, eat sushi and never, ever mention the words 'early night'?

If that's the case, I'll be dead long before my time, of either exhaustion or slashed wrists. I'm on a spinning carousel and how in hell am I ever going to get off? What on earth was I thinking of, when I climbed aboard in my mini-skirt and stilettos and twenty tons of Lancôme Miracle?

And the worst of it is, I can't even tell anyone. The golf club girls have ditched me because I look younger than them, Tara hates me for looking as young as her, Mike is mortified by his mother and Jake thinks I don't need to do any of this. Jake would say it was all self-inflicted.

Yeah. Right. While he runs round with Roisin Harte, who's young enough to be his goddamn daughter. This whole thing is his fault and – and he doesn't even know, much less care!

It's late. I am worn out in body and soul. But I think maybe before I hit the hay I'd better write a quick e-mail to Lee and see what she has to say. Why did that bloody surgeon never warn me that acting young would make me feel so old? Or that nothing's as ageing as chronic exhaustion? There should be a huge health warning in his surgery:

'The New You Is Going To Need Endless, Serious Stamina'.

13

Dear Lee,

Help! What am I going to do? My life is out of control, I'm whizzing round in a blender! Work is so busy and life with Morgan is even busier, I had no idea that a toyboy could be so exhausting.

When we're not swinging from chandeliers we're climbing cliffs or screaming round on his freezing motorbike or going to his friends' awful parties. As you know, I love parties – but not these ones with his pals, they're half my age and we have nothing in common, it's like they're speaking a foreign language. It actually is foreign, sometimes, I hardly know what they're talking about. I am absolutely frazzled here. No matter how many vitamins I swallow or how much I exercise, I just haven't enough energy, can't keep up with this – even pretending to keep up is a nightmare. It's like running on an endless treadmill, up the down escalator, getting nowhere. It's awful and meanwhile I don't know where to turn next, what to do.

I suppose the next step is letting Jake know about Morgan. Arranging for him to 'accidentally' see us together. I just hope that works the way it's meant to, and will jolt him to his senses? Or maybe it'll have some other completely unexpected effect . . . I'm so afraid of making him angry, but I have to do something, try everything to get him back. What do you think? Please tell me, because I'm really kinda confused, nothing seems to be turning out the way it's supposed to.

And then, belatedly, a thought hit her.

How are things turning out for you? Is Vietnam very different? Do the women there do Botox or have facelifts? Do the kids go clubbing and drinking all night every night? Do you need Japanese furniture to keep up with the Joneses? Where exactly are you, doing what? Any financial news, are things okay? You're not very chatty, you know, a guidebook would give me more information!

Anyway, I hope you're happy and I hope you answer this soon, because I need advice and you're the only person I know who seems to see things differently.

Maybe different is good? It can't be any worse, anyway. Tara's all tied up with her new college and new friends, we just don't seem to be communicating, and Mike . . . well, he calls quite often but he's mainly interested in his new girlfriend, I think he's quite serious about her. Too young! But of course I can't say that, he'd only remind me how young I got married myself.

That can't be why things are going wrong now, can it? I can't see how. But maybe you can?

Lots of love,
Ciara

★

'Right this way, your table's ready . . .' Ciara said it so often at East Meets West it was like a mantra, she was all but reciting it in her sleep, sometimes watching arriving guests with envy when they were married couples, calm, smiling, come to enjoy a nice evening in each other's company. Once she had been one of them; now she was ticking off their names in a book, steering them to their tables, aware both of being invisible and of their happy complicity, the way in which they seemed to blank her. Did married couples really do that to single people, even if only unconsciously? Despite her fabulous new face, nobody seemed to see her in sharp focus.

If I ever get hold of Roisin Harte, she thought furiously on St Valentine's night when the restaurant was awash on romance, I'll break her shagging neck for her. I'd tell her parents what she's done if it wasn't so . . . embarrassing. So absolutely humiliating. As for Jake – I want him to know about Morgan. Want him to see how I can snap up someone else, how someone else has snapped *me* up.

Want him to be positively sick with jealousy. Challenge Morgan to a duel, reclaim me and boot Roisin out of his life for evermore. Shoot her, actually.

Whether Lee thinks it's a good idea or not, I'm going to do it. After all, what other point is there to Morgan? If there is any other, I wish she'd tell me what it is. Besides, he was her idea. He might be high-octane in bed, but that's all he is. And now that novelty's wearing off, there's something kind of soulless about sleeping with a semi-stranger. Even if Jake and I did take each other a bit for granted, at least there wasn't such awful pressure to perform. There were cuddles, there was love. I certainly don't want Morgan getting any ideas about anything long-term . . . what did that guy Matt mean

179

about his parents being desperate for him to settle down?

Not with me! Been there, done that, got the T-shirt!

'Ciara?' The voice on the phone sounded uncertain, and a little apologetic. 'It's Jean.'

Jean? Conroy? From the golf club? Ciara stiffened. 'Well – a blast from the past, huh? Haven't heard from you for a long time!'

Letting the guilt register, she waited, not asking how Jean was in turn. Some 'friends' that bunch had turned out to be.

'Yes, well, sorry, I've been so busy – besides, you haven't been to the club for ages!'

'I' Ciara replied shortly, 'have got a job.' Astonishing herself even as she said it, she suddenly found she didn't care who knew. What was wrong with working? Some people – Lee Warner for instance – worked even when they didn't need to, just because they enjoyed what they did. So feck that band of harpies and their idle lives, she thought, see if I care about them any more. Even if Jake and I get back together, I might well continue to work a bit. It gets me out and about, it's my own money, it's a new egg in my basket. One I made all by myself. It feels good.

'A job?' echoed Jean, sounding incredulous. 'What as?'

'As a restaurant hostess. Receptionist. Meeter-greeter.'

'Really! Well, I never . . .' Had Ciara announced a new career as a stripper, a lap-dancer, she could hardly have sounded more shocked. 'And what does Jake make of that?'

For one fleeting moment, Ciara was tempted to come clean, to tell Jean what Jake had done. But no. She would only regret that.

'He thinks it's great. He's away so much you know, and the

children are off at college, so I needed a new activity. I'm meeting all sorts of people and having a great time!'

There was a pause. 'I see. Well, if you feel you must . . . I suppose . . . you wouldn't be free for a fourball, then, on Thursday?'

Ah. Suddenly Ciara got the picture. Jean had been delegated by the rest of 'the girls' to make this call, to summon her back into the fold. They must have been having facelifts of their own, now to be shown off in turn. Either that or were planning to, and wanted information.

'No. Sorry, Jean. I wouldn't be.' Deliberately she did not add 'but thanks for asking' because, she realised with surprise, she was not at all grateful. Suddenly, she neither needed nor wanted these former so-called friends any more. They'd hurt her, insulted her, and she'd moved on without them. They'd shown themselves up for the mean little witches they were, and she wanted nothing more to do with any of them. Lee might be virtually her only friend now – and very far away – but she was a better friend. One who cared and understood and was *genuine*. Going back to this lot, now, would be like going back to Liebfraumilch after tasting Laurent Perrier.

My God, she thought in amazement as she put down the phone, what's happening to me? Did I actually stand up for myself, there? Did I confess to working? Voluntarily turn down a social invitation?

Scary. Morgan Richards must be wearing me out way worse than I thought. Either that or I'm going through some kind of mid-life crisis.

Mid-life. At twenty-eight. Physically, that's all I'm supposed to be. That's how I snared Morgan and that's why Robin feels free to work me to the bone. Sweet Jesus. I'm meant to be a sweet young thing and mid-life crises aren't meant to happen until you're forty. Is it my imagination, or are things starting to get horribly muddled here?

Things, Ciara had to admit, had cooled with Jake, and were not going well at all. In failing to read the birthday books he had given her, she sensed she had let him down, disappointed him in some way that was out of all proportion to the crime. Since Christmas she had seen him barely once a week, for stiffly polite encounters that made her feel they were looking at each other through a sheet of glass. They could see and hear each other, but were not making any contact.

She was surprised to find annoyance seeping into her increasingly mixed feelings for him, mounting irritation chipping away at the two decades of love that had once felt so solid, so unassailable. And yet love remained; only it was buried now, under the rubble of his betrayal, deep down in the gaping, smoking crater of his departure.

And still, she thought, I can't push him too far. He's still my husband, the father of my children, the breadwinner who pays all the big bills. My little job is great, but I only took it so I could afford more surgery . . . do I still want more?

I'm not sure any more what I want. Are a perfect nose or chin the way forward, after all? Is beauty really the key to happiness?

If not, then what is? Could I take Jake back now, if he showed up tomorrow morning? Clamp down on all this rising rage and go on as if nothing had happened, simply take up where we left off?

There's only one way to find out. I'm going to have to persuade Morgan to take me to that pub where Lee saw him with Roisin Harte, and hope he's there again, and see whether he goes into orbit at the sight of me with another man.

182

★

'But that's a very old pub' Morgan complained.

Yes, Ciara conceded, it must be a hundred years old or more—

'No, I mean old people hang out in it! Nobody under forty would be caught dead in it. Why d'you want to go there?'

'Oh, just for a change . . . I hear the Guinness is great.'

Eventually, reluctantly, Morgan agreed to go. But the pub was nearly empty when they arrived, and even three pints later there was still no sign of Jake. With great difficulty she persuaded Morgan to take her back five or six times more, until after some weeks his patience snapped.

'This is the last time, Ciara. I hate this place, don't know what you see in it.'

At that precise moment, she saw Jake. At last, he was here! Her heart flipped as she glimpsed him, partly because he looked so familiar, the man with whom she had shared her entire life, was connected with in some fundamental way. Partly because he was so attractive, and partly because he was deep in animated conversation with Roisin Harte. That girl looks like a bag lady, Ciara thought, what on earth *is* it he sees in her? If he didn't get his sight tested regularly at work, I'd say he needs to visit an optician.

But then, I'm not looking my best this evening myself. Damn! A sling is not the most attractive of accessories, but as Morgan says, a fractured wrist 'goes with the territory' when you go abseiling. As for that hat Morgan's wearing – well, I know it's trendy, but it's a pity it makes him look so like Benny out of *Crossroads*.

Not that he knows that. He's too young to remember *Crossroads*, wouldn't have a clue who Benny was. Still, I just wish it didn't make him look so . . . dim?

At that moment, following Roisin's suddenly distracted gaze, Jake turned, and saw her. Immediately, raising her good arm, she waved, smiled hugely and then snuggled up to Morgan in a way he could not possibly mistake. See, her body language shouted, two can play at this game! This guy's *my* new lover, what do you think? Cute, huh? Well – okay, so he could lose the hat. But then Roisin could lose that sweater, it makes her look like a ewe.

Frowning, Jake peered at her, taking in Morgan, baffled impact registering in his face. Still smiling resolutely, Ciara raised her glass in a way that said 'Cheers, here's looking at you', and sipped from it slowly, wondering whether his heart was turning cartwheels the way hers was. Jake Lunny, it had to be admitted, was a very seductive man, that navy polo neck could hardly look better on Pierce Brosnan, bringing out the jade hue of his eyes.

Was he swamped with jealousy? Speechless with it, over-whelmed? Was he going to get up, come over and swing a punch at Morgan?

Yes! He was standing up, in slow motion it seemed, he was making his way to their table, a smile very gradually rising on his face – a pinched smile, Ciara thought, positively pinched, as if the effort of it was excruciating. It must be stabbing him sheer through the heart to see his wife here like this, so visibly half of a new couple. As he approached, she sensed Morgan stiffening beside her.

'Who's this bloke?' he muttered, whereupon Jake, reaching them, eyed him narrowly. And then, without a word, he bent down and kissed Ciara on the cheek.

'Ciara! How nice to see you. And this is –?'

'Morgan Richards' she purred, 'Morgan, this is Jake – er –'

Suddenly, panic set in. She hadn't foreseen this, hadn't

planned any neutral way of introducing Jake. What was he? She could hardly say husband, not when he was so clearly over forty. But 'ex' wasn't right either, and 'friend' sounded even worse.

Extending his hand, ignoring her confusion, Jake reached forward and obliged Morgan to shake hands with him, his grip, his stance and his tone of voice all equally firm.

'Hello' he said equably, 'I'm her husband.'

'Eh?' Blinking, Morgan gaped up at him: he was seated and Jake was standing. Faintly, Ciara registered an awful sinking feeling, something freezing in her stomach; she'd only meant Jake to see Morgan, not to meet him. Oh, God!

Still smiling thinly, letting Morgan's surprise settle on the air, Jake nodded at them both. 'What's that you're drinking – Guinness, and white wine? Let me get you another round. Enjoy your evening!'

With which he vanished, to be replaced almost instantly by a bar boy come to take their order, and while Morgan stammered at him Ciara watched Jake return to Roisin, seating himself beside her with an aura of utter nonchalance, as if Morgan had not, after all, plunged a dagger into the very core of his being.

But then, she reminded herself, Jake's a pilot. Pilots are trained to stay calm in emergencies. Trained to show no emotion, to handle everything with total panache. No matter how great his shock, how acute his pain or deep his devastation, he would never show it.

Not now. Not in front of Roisin, or Morgan. Forgetting Morgan beside her, she watched him, thinking: later. Later on tonight, when I get home and he gets back to his rented apartment, he will call me, and he will be crushed.

Utterly, utterly crushed, pleading with me to reconsider, to drop Morgan, to please give him another chance on any terms or conditions I care to name. He will come running back, begging.

'Ciara? Are you listening to me? I said, what's with this husband business? That guy says he's your *husband*, for chrissakes!'

Turning, she saw with surprise that Morgan was looking both disconcerted and incensed, distinctly upset. Far more upset than Jake had looked.

'Oh' she said, patting his hand, 'don't mind him. We're separated. He – he was way too old for me.'

Frowning, biting his lip, Morgan grappled with this. And then, to her astonishment, he stood up, ignoring Jake's arriving round of drinks, grasped her wrist and hauled her to her feet.

'We're leaving' he announced, 'we're not staying here under the same roof as any man who thinks he has any claim on you or any right to mess around with me. Husband – hah! We'll see about that. Husband, my ass. I saw that guy before, in a photo on your dresser. You said he was your uncle.'

Dear Lee,

This is a nightmare. I am totally losing the plot here. You won't believe what's happened. It's all your fault for pushing me into this toyboy trap, so you'd better figure a way out!

I worked out a way for Jake to get an eyeful of Morgan. Took Morgan to that pub where Jake sometimes goes with that Harte girl and, eureka, there he was! With her . . . but anyway, he saw us, and I made it very clear we were together. An item. Cosied up to Morgan like we were Siamese twins, joined at the hip, making sure Jake got the picture. Well, he did seem to get it. But then – horror – he got up and came over to us and introduced himself and informed Morgan he was my husband!

And now, instead of Jake being all jealous like I'd planned, *Morgan* is the one who's going mad. Positively eaten up with envy. Hasn't stopped interrogating me ever since, demanding to know why I never mentioned I was married. Wants to know when I plan to divorce Jake, says he's in *love* with me and he won't *stand* for my being involved with anyone else . . . he's been hounding me round the clock, never takes his eyes off me at work, insists on spending every night with me instead of just one or two a week like it was before. I am worn *out*!

And now he's even talking about our 'future', about maybe setting up his own restaurant – he'd cook and I'd run it for him, he says! What am I going to *do*? I can't get rid of him, the more I try to brush him off the more he persists, he's starting to stick like glue . . . last night he even mentioned something about us maybe having a *baby* some day! A *family* – as if I hadn't already got two grown teenagers, I need this like I need the plague! How am I going to shake him off? He's gone all passionate and moody, almost reminds me of Tara the way he's pouting and sulking, and so clingy, I'm suffocating. Is it just him, or do all guys in their twenties carry on like this? I'd forgotten if they do, can't imagine Jake behaving like that – on the contrary, he was cool as a cucumber when he met Morgan. So civilised, so *adult*. The whole episode never took a feather out of him.

Or if it did, you could have fooled me. I was so sure he'd go mad, explode, call me right away to know what was going on, to discuss getting rid of Morgan and getting back together. But he hasn't. Not a word. Nothing.

Lee, please, *do* something! Why haven't you written, where are you? You have to write back the moment you get this with some idea how to sort out this dreadful, horrible mess. I've told Morgan I don't see any future for us – in fact, now that he's served his purpose I'm kinda bored with him – but it only seems to make him worse, he keeps saying how 'ideal' I am, how 'perfect', how he can just see me running his home and his business and his whole life . . . I think it's a mother he wants, not a wife!

Does he somehow sense that I *am* a mother? Am I giving off some kind of maternal vibe? Even when I said I was giving up abseiling (the great love of his life) after I fractured my wrist, he said that was okay, he'd sit it out with me, do something else on Sundays. I can't get rid of him, there's no escape!

And there's no Jake, either. Lee, you have to help me out here. Please. You *must*. Everything is going so horribly wrong. I've saved up nearly enough money now to get my nose done, but all of a sudden it's the last thing on my mind, all I want is peace and quiet and my husband back and . . . how could he not care, Lee? He *must* care, when he sees me with another man!

Mustn't he? What do you think? Send me some bright
ideas immediately.

Oh, and I hope you're having fun in Vietnam, whatever
the hell you're up to. Whatever it is, at least it can't be as
complicated as what's happening here. I'd give anything to
just wave a magic wand and have everything back the way
it was before.

Love, Ciara

14

Dear Ciara,

Sorry, I know it's been a while, but things here are so
distracting, everything seems to move in slow-mo, never
any rush about anything. I'm living in a little cabin near a
beach and when I wake up each morning I just lie listening
to the waves, to the breeze in the leaves, watching these
gorgeous opal clouds floating on the palest blue sky. Not
true blue as we know it in Europe or America, but a kind
of peacock blue, tinged with silver . . . all kinds of beautiful
birds sing in the trees, like a choir conducted by some
invisible god, sometimes I lie and listen for nearly an hour
before I can bring myself to even get up, go for a swim,
chop some pineapple for breakfast . . .

Huh? What was this? Was Lee taking leave of her senses, what
was all this barmy nature stuff? Get to the point, Ciara
shouted silently, tell me what to do about Jake, about Morgan,
about my entire chaotic life! This young fella wants me to
have his blessed *baby* and all you can do is witter on about the
bloody birds? What's wrong with you, Lee, where's my crisp
American friend, the one with all the brisk answers?

I may stay on here for quite a long time. So I wonder
would you mind, Ciara, putting my house with a rental

agency? I have zero desire to go back at the moment and an income from it would sustain me here. Not that it's costing much to live or that Vietnam is expensive. It's cheap and simple and offers the most wonderful quality of life for anyone seeking peace. Yet there's plenty of mental stimulus – I am meditating and studying the principles of Reiki massage – without any of the frenzy we're so used to in the West.

Meditating? Reiki? Rent out her house? But she's gone mad!

However, I'll save all the details of that for another time. Right now, I know you want some advice about your marriage and your new man. Ciara, I'm not an oracle, I can't tell you how to live! All I can offer is my view, such as it's worth, which you must then accept or reject as you choose. Think it over, ponder it and then throw it out if you find it's not for you.

Dynamic, sensible Lee? But she sounds totally different. Sounds kind of doolally, drifting along on some vague tide – Lee, you're supposed to snap your fingers and give orders, not tell me to 'ponder' your 'view'!

The way I see it from here is that you still basically love Jake. Still respect him and cherish your joint history. Still want to spend time with him and keep him in your life in some shape or form. You love him enough to want to make him jealous – or is that mere ego?

The reason I wonder is that you don't seem to love him enough to read those books he gave you.

So, what does this tell us?

I think it tells us that you and he have diverging agendas at this point in your lives. Have reached a crossroads and are not at all sure about taking the same turning, travelling any further in the same direction. If you really wanted to stay with him, you'd do anything he asked . . . so, do you want to stay with him? Stay together, for the rest of your lives?

And even if you do, does he? I have to honestly say it doesn't sound as if he does. Whatever he's going through sounds like more than some little mid-life crisis, more than mere infatuation with a young girl. You need to sit down with him, not as an injured wife, but as a grown adult, and talk to him as such. Try to find out what's happening in his mind and heart, draw him out, listen to everything he says, take it away with you and think about it.

Yes, Ciara, think! I know it's not your favourite hobby, but you did ask my opinion. As for Morgan . . . I feel sorry for him, if you have somehow emotionally enslaved him, played with him as if he were a toy. To set him free would be a kindness, and the quickest, easiest way to do it would be to tell the truth – that you're a forty-year-old wife and mother who has absolutely no intention of starting a second family at such an advanced age. If that doesn't scare him off, introduce him to Mike and Tara! Lose the sexy outfits, start wearing sensible shoes and specs, tell him you can't go clubbing because *Gardeners' World* is on television. Just act your age! That's all you have to do if you really want to get rid of the poor man.

That should be easier, at any rate, than getting Jake back. If getting him back is what you really want. If he's the same Jake he was before. But is he?

You have to ask him, and listen to his answer, and work out whether you think you two still really fit together. You've changed too, you know, you're not the same Ciara as six months ago.

If you can't honestly say you do still fit with Jake, don't worry. We each have a destiny and there's no law says we all have to reach the same one at the same time with the same person we started out with years before. We are very small creatures on this planet and the passage of centuries is but a moment.

Lots of love,
Lee

Well! Baffled and annoyed in equal measure, Ciara sat staring at Lee's e-mail, bits of it jumping off the screen at her: 'If he's the same Jake he was before' . . . 'act your age' . . . 'if getting him back is what you really want . . .'

Well, she thought furiously, of course I want him back! Naturally! He's my husband, I love him, he loves me, we love each other!

Don't we?

And marriage is for life.

Isn't it?

Amused. That was how Jake had looked, Ciara thought, the night he met her with Morgan. Just very faintly amused, as if he knew she'd set the whole scene up for his benefit, like a child throwing a tantrum for attention. Far from throwing any tantrum himself, he had been a model of decorum, almost – what was that word Mike often used? – ironic. Ironic, as if he were watching some comedy that didn't concern him, enacted by people deliberately playing to the gallery.

Had she looked silly? Made a fool of herself? Well, the fractured wrist had been unfortunate: he'd noticed it and merely smiled sympathetically, without comment. Almost as if he guessed she'd been engaging in some activity too strenuous for her. And – well, yes, admittedly Morgan had looked a bit dorky in that desperately trendy, hideously ugly hat.

And yet – Jake must have felt something, surely? Some tiny tweak of jealousy, at the very least? He couldn't possibly just hand over his wife of twenty years to another man with a cheerful wave over his shoulder, could he, *arrivederci*, it's been great, thanks and goodbye?

No. Whatever Jake might have done, he'd never been shallow. In fact he'd been going just the other way in recent times, getting increasingly serious, listening to that dreary music, starting to act so very middle-aged.

Well, he was middle-aged. With something of a shock Ciara caught herself detecting something almost attractive in that phrase. It sounded so easy, so relaxed. And Jake was still physically attractive. Not quite as much fun as once he'd been, though, there was getting to be something about him . . . ?

Gravitas. That was what. She'd seen the word in a magazine: Daniel Day-Lewis had 'gravitas' and George Clooney didn't. Same age, different pace, different attitude. Jake, this past year, had been evolving into someone extremely grown-up.

Duh! Did people have to do that, just because they'd hit forty? Go all *heavy*? Personally she much preferred to go just the other way, to aim for as light and bright as possible . . . could Lee possibly be right, about 'diverging agendas'?

Maybe she could. Maybe Jake and Ciara Lunny were, after all, 'travelling in different directions'? If I didn't still love him, she thought, I'd loathe him sometimes.

All right, Lee! All right, I'll do it! I'll talk to him and I'll listen to him and I'll think about whatever he says. Okay? Don't nag me! I don't know how anyone can possibly nag all the way from Vietnam, but somehow you're doing it, somehow I keep hearing you over and over in my head, giving me no peace until I do what you reckon I should do. I don't want to do this, don't want any kind of showdown with Jake, but if you're sure . . . Yes, I know you said to ignore your opinion if I wanted. But how can I, when it keeps buzzing round in my head like a wasp, driving me mad?

God, this is a huge risk. This is going to be terrifying. Way scarier than any amount of surgery. This time I'm the surgeon, slicing open my marriage, and somehow I don't think it's going to be a pretty sight.

I wouldn't dream of doing it, if there were any alternative, any way out.

Monday, noon. At home. No pub, no distracting music, no crowd to melt into: just Jake and Ciara, meeting at her request, for a civilised conversation between basically amicable adults. Adults who liked each other enough to at least listen to what the other had to say, and would not end up walloping each other with the nearest golf iron.

That's the deal, Ciara reminded herself as she dressed with studied restraint – nothing slashed, nothing scarlet, nothing slinky – and I am going to stick to it. No accusing, no fighting, no crying or pleading or anything, uh, undignified. We can work this out. We must. We will. We are Mr and Mrs Lunny, parents of Mike and Tara Lunny, who deserve a bit of consideration here. Who'd better be considered, if we're ever going to see them again . . . we've driven them away, with our behaviour. Mike is furious with Jake and Tara is furious with me and they're ashamed of their parents. That's why they've been avoiding us both. Lee could be right about maybe doing a little bit of growing up. Even if I don't want to look any older than Tara, I *am* older. I hate that thought, but I do have some duty to my daughter. I'll try to remember that today.

At noon precisely, Jake arrived, driving up in his old grey Jaguar, getting out, striding up the gravel drive in a way that had once been so familiar, and now echoed painfully. Like his wife he was soberly dressed in a suit, polite to a fault, raising a small smile as he pecked her on the cheek.

'Ciara. How are you?'

How am I? How do you bloody think I am, you idiot, after all you've put me through?

'Fine, thank you.'

In careful silence they made their way through to the living room, decided against drinks, and sat down facing each other on opposite sofas. Briefly, Ciara glanced down at her wedding ring, biting her lip. Now that he was here, she didn't know where to start, what to say, the sight of him unsettling her. I have to get the truth out of him, she reminded herself, without alienating him or getting into an argument. Or letting him persuade me that his behaviour is only 'temporary', because I can't stand any more of it.

Anxiously, they looked at each other, and then spoke simultaneously, in a rush.

'Jake –'

'Ciara –'

'Ladies first' he said courteously, and she thought of Morgan, who did not believe in 'ladies first', if he'd ever even

197

heard of it. Morgan who, now that she thought about it, should be the one dating Roisin Harte.

But let's not start down that track. Recrimination is the last thing we need here.

'Okay. Thank you. What I want to say is – I asked you here because –'

He was looking at her intently, his eyes searching hers in a way that momentarily silenced her; he'd looked at her in exactly the same hypnotic way the night he'd asked her to marry him. A way that made it impossible to say no, to refuse anything he might ask. Something in his face was so very irresistible.

Oh, Christ. I can't do this.

Yes, you can.

'Because I want to know whether we're getting back together or breaking up for good. I want to know what your problem is, once and for all, right now, this minute.'

The words came babbling out, sounding so peremptory she was astonished when he smiled faintly, and reached for her hand.

'Yes. You have a right to know. I'd hoped you might work it out for yourself, but . . . since you haven't . . .'

'No I haven't. I'm not a mind reader. Or a shrink. So you're going to have to tell me.' Removing her hand from his reach, she gripped the arm of the sofa. He would not charm or disarm her, he would *not*. She would stay calm, hear him out and reflect, later, on all he said. Lie face down on the floor and howl, if need be. But not now.

Seeming to sense her mood, he nodded, grimaced and took a deep breath, as if he too were braced for this encounter. Not battle, exactly: but confrontation, definitely.

'My problem, as you call it – Ciara, my problem is you. At

198

first, for months, I thought it was me. Thought I must just be overworked, or going through some kind of moody patch that was making me restless, confused. And then I met Roisin Harte one day about a year ago, through Mike, and we somehow got into a very long, absolutely riveting conversation about the pyramids.'

The pyramids? In Egypt? Had something to do with Jake and Ciara Lunny's marriage? In silence, she waited.

'We talked about their design, their engineering, their location, their history, their cultural significance, their impact on tourism and the environment, their symbolism . . . everything and anything to do with them. Talked for hours, until Mike dragged me away, and all I could think about for the next week was that conversation. I wanted to dig deeper into it, excavate more as if I were Howard Carter excavating King Tut's tomb.'

'But – but why?' Baffled, she tried to think what secrets the pyramids might yield. This was utterly mystifying.

'Because it was the first interesting – *fascinating* – conversation I'd had with a woman in years. The more I dug into it, the more I got out of it, and the more I wanted to see Roisin Harte again. She was like a soulmate, a kindred spirit. Not because I fancied her – contrary to what you may think – but because she engaged my attention. Stimulated my mind, knew her stuff, was so articulate and so philosophical. I wanted to tell you about it, but I couldn't, because . . .'

'Because?' Her voice tinkled like a glass bell.

'Because I knew you wouldn't be interested. Because the only things we'd ever talked about, for *years*, were domestic subjects. The house, the children, the next dinner party, the water bill, the Thompsons' new car, black outfit or blue? And suddenly it hit me – boredom was the problem. Mine, and yours. I was bored with the whole silly set-up, with the frivolous *tone* of our marriage – just as you'd have been bored, wouldn't you, by the pyramids? Bored stiff, if I'd started talking about Khufu or Giza or the King's Chamber? Menes, or the thirty dynasties or the fifty-one-degree angle, or any of it?'

He paused for breath, and she nodded slightly, lost already. What were Khufu and Menes and Giza and . . . what did it matter? This stuff all happened thousands of years ago, what had it to do with anyone today? Who cared about fifty-one-degree angles or any others?

'Jake, I – I'm not following this. The pyramids are in Egypt, people visit them and – and then forget them! You don't make them the focus of your life! Our life is here with our children and friends in our own home –'

Sitting back, he thought about it, his gaze meeting hers in a way that somehow made her want to duck. 'No, Ciara. Not any more. It isn't here, at all. The children, whether you like it or not, have grown up and flown the coop. And I, to my surprise, also seem to be growing up and flying the coop.

'I want to spread my wings and try all sorts of new things, visit new places, new people . . . I'm a pilot, I love to travel! Only now, I don't just want to travel physically. I want to travel mentally, spiritually as well, want to explore anything and everything. Did you know that the tombs at Newgrange, not fifty miles from here, are even older than the pyramids? No? Well, they are. And we've never even been there . . . don't ask me why, but suddenly I very much want to visit Newgrange, and Macchu Picchu and any number of other amazing places. Could you stand that, do you think? Would you be willing to give up your sun-and-sangria holidays to slog up Macchu Picchu with me?'

Good grief. He was having a breakdown.

'No? Well, I can't say I blame you. We married very young and maybe I was too fixated on your pretty face, didn't think enough about long-term compatibility? Maybe I should have thought about it the day we married in church – you'd already chosen your religion, were settled in it and had no further curiosity, no apparent need to question any further. Whereas I didn't believe one word that priest said, I was merely paying lip service the way you do when you're young . . . now, I wonder how any particular religion can possibly be the only "right" one. Don't know enough about the others to decide – but I want to find out. Want to examine them all. Hindu, Amish, Buddhist, Tao, Shinto, Methodist, Muslim . . . want to examine all kinds of ideas and lifestyles. Would you want to come with me, on that quest?'

Good God. No. She certainly would not. Apart from having apparently lost his mind, Jake was talking way out of line here, insulting their marriage vows.

'Ciara, look, I have tried. You might not think I have, but it's true. I gave you those books to give you some clue where I was going. I wanted you to read them because they demand a certain input and effort, mental agility and maturity, they're books about *growing* – Ciara, for crying out loud, you're forty, you can't play Barbie for ever!'

Abruptly, his voice rose on a note of exasperation, and she recoiled, flinching away from it.

'But you refused to read them, refused to meet me halfway. You were too busy with your facelift and your quest for eternal youth – a narcissistic, pointless quest I simply do not understand. What is *wrong* with the natural process of maturing? D'you think I want to stay married to a virtual child? D'you think your looks should matter as much, to either of us, as they did twenty years ago? Because if that's the case, you're stuck, Ciara, hopelessly stalled in the past. I want a grown woman, a partner to grow with, not a doll to play with!'

Quivering, she clung to her dignity, sitting bolt upright, refusing to let him see how much this was hurting. Barbie? Was that really how he saw her?

'Well, Jake, if that's the case I can't see what you're doing with a girl half your age.'

With a sigh, he leaned back. 'Ciara, I am not "with" Roisin Harte. We simply get on well as friends, as people do when they have interests in common. We meet for a drink and a chat once or twice a month in that little pub, which we both enjoy enormously because our talks stretch our minds. But I'm married, wouldn't dream of taking things any further – Jesus, I'm not a babysnatcher, and Mike is a friend of her brother's! Besides, she has a boyfriend, for your information. Some guy called Eddie who is twenty-four years of age and works in a library. They met on a summer work camp in Sicily and are mad about each other. I swear to you, I have never slept with her nor have any desire to do so – physically, you're way more attractive!'

'Am I?' Miserably, dubiously, she looked at him, wondering whether he still considered that an advantage.

'Yes. You are. Plus, you're the mother of my children, and I'm still very fond of you in some weird off-beat way. But . . . but not in the same way as before. If you're determined to have the truth, I don't think we're suited as domestic partners any more. I need something more profound, more engaging, these days, and I think it would be a very stupid mistake for us to stay married.'

Wham. Had he hurled a brick at her, she could not have

been more wounded. There was a long, dazed silence.

'But' he continued eventually, plucking absently at a trouser leg, 'that doesn't mean . . . we don't need to divorce or anything. Not unless you're fed up with me, and want to?'

'Jake, I'm Catholic. You married me as such. You know divorce doesn't come into the picture. Airhead as I might be, I'm not actually one of those supermarket Catholics who only buy the bits that suit them.'

No response, for a moment. Instead he sat thinking this over, apparently groping for words.

'Well, then. You see. That's how far apart we've grown. I regard divorce as a civilised necessity to personal growth. You regard it as a fixed rule that can never be broken. Ciara, we're miles apart. Miles and miles, light years, further than the Druids from the Incas.'

Druids? Incas? Was this all some kind of insane joke?

'So, what are you saying to me, then? That you don't want to stay married but don't quite want to split up either? Jake, this can't go on, I can't live in this limbo! I want to know whether you're in my life or out of it!'

Another long, ponderous silence. One in which she could almost hear their minds and hearts whirling, conflicting, fighting for – what?

'Well' he exhaled eventually, 'that depends on – on whether you see things the way I see them, or to what extent.'

Listen to him. That was what Lee had said: listen.

'Go on, then. Tell me how you see them.'

'How I see them is . . . is . . . some kind of friendship? Maybe even a – a sexual friendship? Something open, relaxed, that would give us both breathing space? Some kind of cheerful arrangement where we could maybe spend some nights together, some time with the kids whenever they're around, the odd evening with our mutual friends, without getting locked *in*? I do still like you very much, Ciara, still love you in many ways, you are good fun and relaxing company—'

'Undemanding? Is that what you mean, Jake? A bit of a laugh, bit of a birdbrain, when you're exhausted by Roisin Harte and your mystic studies?' She said it tartly, and was very surprised when he laughed.

'Yes! You're a fluffy little thing and there are times when fluffy is good, fluffy is fun! I'm not planning to become a monk or anything, nor do I want a physical or emotional relationship with anyone else. All I want is . . . is to be friends with you, and be let get on with my own personal development, wherever it may lead me. I already know it won't lead you to the same place, and therefore have no wish to bore you with it, but I would be delighted if we could somehow stay in touch, in tune . . . unless you just married me for my money, thought I was a good catch?'

It came flying out of nowhere, so suddenly she gasped. 'A – I – what?'

'A good catch, as pilots are generally reckoned to be. I wondered, when I told you about our stock market portfolio taking a dive, whether . . . how that shortfall might affect things. I must say, Ciara, you've been more stoic about money than I expected. I was very impressed when you didn't complain, took that job instead. Which is what leads me to believe that maybe you might just still love me a little bit, for more than merely pragmatic reasons?'

Something in the way he said it caught at her, some unexpectedly vulnerable note, almost shy, as if he thought she had only married him for what he could bring and buy. If she were to be horribly honest, she had to admit to a niggling grain of truth in it – and yet she wanted to shout at him. Yes, of course

I love you, you stupid exasperating man! Of course I didn't *just* marry you because you were handsome and had a glamorous, high-income career! Okay, maybe those were reasons, but they weren't the only ones! I also married you because you were nice and kind and good parent material and – and – then we grew closer and –

'At any rate, you needn't worry about money. We might not be as rich as we were, but you're still my wife and I still intend to support you, as well as the children for as long as they need me to. But we have lost a lot of money, we have to accept that and adjust to it . . . if you still insist on more of this ridiculous plastic surgery, you'll have to earn the funds yourself. I can't afford it and frankly, I don't even like the results. You used to have a such lovely smile, whereas now it looks painted on, as if it might snap or crack like varnish. I wish you'd forget the whole silly business.'

'But – but Jake, I got that facelift for you! You married me for my looks, they're as important to my job as a wife as – as a model's or actress's are to her job!'

Her candour seemed to spring from nowhere, as if in retaliation for his: you married me for my money, you married *me* for my looks!

Burying his face in his hands, he seemed to sag momentarily. 'Oh, God, Ciara . . . they're not. Not any more. By our stage of life, people are supposed to have developed some *inner* beauty, something that stems from a deeper source, from strength of character and generosity of spirit and – and that's what I'm talking about really, I suppose. Generosity of spirit. Wondering whether we have enough of that, between us, to build some kind of new relationship? Do you think we possibly could have, or am I wasting my breath and your time? Would you rather we just called it a day? We can if you like, I'll go off and explore my new horizons all on my own? Because I am going to explore them, with or without your approval, will never again be the same man you married. The best I can come up with, in the circumstances, is that we aim for some new kind of communion, not the marriage we have clearly outgrown but some kind of warmth, energy, mutual support without living in each other's pockets . . . ?'

He looked so genuinely eager, she was forced to think about it, just for a moment. Until another thought intervened.

'Maybe. Or maybe not. I just don't know, Jake. Can't decide right this minute, will have to consider – I mean, what if I met someone else? Someone who loved the way I look –?' But even as she said it, she thought of Morgan, and hastily changed tack. 'Someone who did believe in commitment, in marriage?'

'Yes. I suppose that's a risk I'd have to run. But Ciara – that'd be adultery, you know? In fact, I'd like to know whether adultery has already been committed, with that Morgan guy.'

He looked very hard at her, but some tiny twitch of his lips made her wonder . . . he couldn't possibly be *teasing* her, could he? Surely not about something so – with a horrible jolt she realised that yes, it had. Adultery had been committed, with Morgan Richards. Which did not do much, she had to concede, for her staunchly Catholic stance.

'I – well – it was all your fault. You're the one who went off, left your wife – I was upset and confused and –'

He laughed. Actually had the nerve to laugh, loud and long. 'And you know what, Ciara?'

She frowned. 'What?'

'Of all the fashion accessories, nothing ages a woman more than a toyboy. Facelift or no facelift, you looked every day of your age, beside that youngster!'

206

More laughter, hearty and, she thought, quite heartless. How could he say such a thing, be such a total brute? Indignantly, drawing herself up, she composed her hands in her lap.

'Well, actually, he's dynamite in bed, if you want the truth.' There now, buster, put that in your pipe and smoke it.

It scored a direct hit, she saw him flinch. Very briefly, before he faced her with a look that was almost paternal. 'Ciara, nearly all men of his age are. It's just hormones, nothing special. But still, maybe that's a lesson for me. Maybe I could sharpen up a bit, maybe I'd been taking you for granted – maybe we could, er, work on our game a bit. If I'm still on your team?'

Was he? Ah. That was the question. The question she couldn't answer just like that, snap, with a click of her fingers. What he was proposing here, she saw with dawning uncertainty, was a whole new ball game, something far less secure – albeit maybe more exciting? – than what they'd had before. Could that possibly work? And even if it did, could she handle it long term? Could she learn to love the new Jake Lunny, mysterious mess as he seemed to be? Let go of the old Jake? Wander off in some new direction without so much as a map?

'I don't know, Jake. I simply do not know the answer to that question at this precise moment. I'm going to have to think about it – maybe for quite a while – before I can tell you anything more. You've behaved like a pig and I'm still hurting and – and – frankly, I think you're barking mad. Think all this stuff about Druids and pyramids and Macchu Picchu and Mozart is completely bonkers.'

Cheerfully, outrageously, he grinned. 'Yeah. It may well be. Which, after a lifetime of dinner parties and the price of designer accessories, would be quite a relief. Besides, Ciara, it's better than nothing. If we don't have any way back, at least we might have some kind of way forward.'

'I will never' she said firmly, 'read those bloody books or listen to that miserable music.'

'Okay. That's fair. In fact I'm glad to find you're not so easily corrupted! Look, let's see if we can cut a deal. Why don't I try to accept what you're not, if you'll try to accept what I am?'

15

Dear Lee,

I did what you said. I tackled Jake. And here's what happened.

He said our marriage is clapped out. Says I'm just a little Barbie doll and he's bored with Barbie. Says he doesn't want a divorce but does want something more 'stimulating' and 'engaging'. A new me, but not a new look. Apparently it's my mind that needs work, not my face. Can you believe that, after all that outrageous surgery I went through, for his bloody benefit?! Now it turns out I should have been reading *War And Peace* or somesuch, instead of spending a fortune on a facelift. Is it my imagination or are men simply impossible, is there no pleasing them? There doesn't seem to be any pleasing him, anyway.

It also turns out that I was mistaken about Roisin Harte. She's not my rival after all. My rival is a guy called Menes, who lived in Egypt five thousand years ago. This is what Jake is into now – ancient history. Apparently Roisin knows all about it, whereas I'm just a birdbrain whose idea of history is last week's *Hello!* magazine. That's why he gave me all those books, to improve my tiny mind.

He said all this even while admitting he'd married me for my looks! Can you believe it? And then suggested that I'd married him for his money . . . okay, maybe there was a tiny grain of truth in both of those things, but still, I was horrified. Next, he rubbished our marriage vows, said he didn't share my beliefs and wants to 'explore' lots of other religions – Lee, I'm married to a heathen! A raving pagan! How can I possibly stay married to the likes of that?

The worst of it is, I want to. Even while he was spouting all this nonsense, I was sitting there looking at him feeling all these mixed emotions with *love* spinning round somewhere in the middle of them. He still attracts me like a magnet, there's still something so basically good about him, and kinda funny too, at times I hardly knew whether to laugh or cry. You'll be pleased to hear I didn't do either one, I was very composed just like you said, didn't shout or get hysterical about anything. Not even when he said Morgan 'aged' me, that I looked like his granny! I wanted to punch him for that, but I just sat there all ladylike, letting him rant on. Thinking what a disaster my cosmetic surgery turned out to be. Jake hates it – says my smile looks as if it might snap – whereas Morgan thinks I'm gorgeous. So gorgeous that I can't get rid of him.

Anyway, Jake thinks we need to 'restructure our relationship'. Wants us to stay friends, doesn't want anyone else, plans to still support me and the children which is a relief at least, I couldn't bear a court case or any horrible fighting. But he seems to want me to become someone I'm not. Wants me to 'travel with him' which apparently involves swopping our lovely sun holidays for vile treks to all kinds of awful places. I said I'd have to think about it, and said I definitely couldn't read any of those boring old books or listen to that heavy music he's got into. He said that was okay but that he wants me to 'make an effort' to at least accept that it's what he's into now.

Lee, I'm no brainbox! You know I'm not. Yet I still love Jake, even though he's veered way off course – some pilot he turns out to be! Still, I do want to find some way for us to stay together. But how? Can you see any way? Please don't suggest that I start reading ancient history or do an Open University course or anything – I barely passed my Leaving Cert! The mere idea of study bores me rigid, and as for all that homework, at my age . . . I'd go mad.

Even though I'd have time for it, because as he flatly stated, the children have now grown up and 'flown the coop'. I suppose I know in my heart that that's true, but it's so hard to accept! I hate the idea of letting my babies go. But he insists I'll have to. That's going to blow a huge hole in my life. A hole which I suppose will have to be filled with something . . . I must admit, working at East Meets West has been a help. You don't have so much time to brood when you're busy. Still . . . I miss Mike and Tara. I want to see them. I wish I could talk to them about all this. Maybe they'd have some ideas? I just don't know what to do, need to think it all over.

So, just when I've nearly saved enough to get the next bit of surgery done, there's no point. A waste of time, Jake says. I'm 'perfectly attractive' as I am. Dim, but attractive!

Still loves me 'in many ways' and hopes we can work things out. I don't know whether to be relieved, or angry, or what. Even though we seem to have so little in common right now, have such contradictory views of our future, somehow there's this underlying affection between us, I could feel it the whole time we were talking. Even when I wanted to smash something over his head, I could still feel it. After twenty years he's like a second skin, I feel somehow connected to him even when I haven't a clue what he's talking about.

Please tell me what you make of all this? I can't seem to get it into focus. It's like he's emptied out our entire marriage onto the floor and now we have to sort it out, try to decide what to keep and what to bin . . . is there a couple in the world who can ever agree on what stays and what goes, even when they're only talking about shoes and shirts?

Meanwhile, Morgan is sticking like glue. Can't accept that it's over. Which is really awkward when we're working together. He's haunting me round the restaurant, calling me constantly at home, blitzing me with texts (which I don't know how to get rid of), won't take no for an answer. I suppose I have only myself to blame. But I wish he'd go away and give me some peace. I can't keep up with his pace of life and I have no interest in his plans for a future that's already my past! I helped Jake build up his career because I loved Jake, for the sake of our family, but I'm certainly not about to do it again for Morgan. If I did what you suggest, told him I'm a forty-year-old mother of two teenagers, he surely would run a mile – only then, I'd feel such a fool. A nitwit and a fake. Worse, he might tell

Robin at the restaurant. Would I lose my job then, d'you reckon, for lying about my age? This is such an awful muddle, I wish I'd never got into it. Wish I'd never gone near that wretched surgeon, my whole life is turned inside out and upside down.

Help! I can't wait to hear your news, and views. I've contacted a rental agency by the way, they say renting out your house should be no problem. I'm going over with the keys tomorrow so they can measure up – are you sure you want to do this? What's the big deal in Vietnam? I wish you'd get sense and come back here. Who are you with, what are you doing?

Write a.s.a.p. Lots of love,
Ciara

It took ages to organise, but at last Ciara got her way: Mike and Tara finally agreed on a weekend on which they would both be free to visit Huxley Wood. A family dinner, with Jake, but first Ciara badly wanted both children to herself. Wanted a full afternoon with them, to find out whether they were settled into college, happy in their studies and social lives – and still remotely interested in their parents? Often on the phone they sounded as if they'd moved mental miles away, were far more interested in their own friends, activities and relationships.

Which, she was forced to concede, was only normal. Their parents, from now on, would become like her own parents, nice people whose company was occasionally enjoyable. But no longer essential. She had fulfilled her role as a mother, was somehow going to have to now let other people share her space in Mike and Tara's lives. People who – what a horrible, painful thought – would become more important.

Mike arrived first, beaming genially, bringing flowers; he had always been generous and gracious. Cheerful and hard-working too, wide awake to the rewards work could offer. Since Christmas he'd had a part-time job as a barman, and something in his brisk step as he walked into the house suggested future prosperity, future success. No question of Mike Lunny ever being unemployed, or failing at anything: he would sail through life, get a good job, marry a girl who – who'd maybe marry him for his money, for that very aura of success, the same one that had attracted her to Jake? The thought hit Ciara like a hammer. Barely was Mike seated at the kitchen table than she was quizzing him about his American girlfriend, silently praying that she didn't see in him only what his mother had once seen in his father.

'So, how's Jessica? Will you be going to America over Easter, or will she be coming here?'

Sleekly, Mike grinned. 'Oh, Jessica's grand. The only small problem is . . . er . . . Linda's grand too!'

Oh, praise the Lord. He'd met someone else. Closer to home. Someone who might not whip him off to live three thousand miles away.

'Linda?' Carefully, she kept her tone light, neutral.

'Yeah. Met her at a party a few weeks ago. Not quite as . . . um . . . deep as Jessica, maybe, but a real stunner to look at. We've been out on a few dates, she knocks all the guys side-ways, I'm the envy of them all.'

Gripping a cup of tea tight in her hand, Ciara smiled at him, silently weighing it up. A 'deep' girlfriend, or a 'real stunner' – which would Mike go for? Which would she want him to go for? It was like looking in a mirror, at the reflected Jake of two decades ago – and the Jake of today, who felt he'd maybe made the wrong decision.

'Well, I'm glad you're having fun, Mike! You're young and single, you can have two girls on the go if you like – just make sure you pick the right one whenever you have to choose.'

Almost idly, he nodded. 'Yeah. That's what I reckon. So what's your news, Mum? Work going well? Any word of – er – I mean – yourself and, uh –?'

Yourself and Dad. That was what he meant, naturally; she had never breathed a word about Morgan Richards. Suddenly, she was flushing furiously, excruciatingly embarrassed by the mere thought of Morgan Richards. How could she ever, ever have presented him to Mike, explained what she saw in him, or what he saw in her? Just a pretty face: that was all Morgan saw. And maybe someone to help him scramble a few rungs up the career ladder, before ditching her for someone more appropriate?

'Your father and I are . . . talking. Negotiating. It's not easy but it is getting somewhere. Just don't ask me exactly where!'

Looking relieved, Mike nodded. 'Good. Because I'm really not very happy about the situation, you know? I think Dad's behaved pretty badly, can't imagine what he – he's thinking of.'

'Can't imagine what he sees in Roisin Harte.' That was what Mike was discreetly trying not to say. Neither parent had ever mentioned Roisin to him, but his friend Fiach must have, she supposed; after all Fiach was Roisin's brother. Mike knew more than he was pretending to.

'Well . . . your father and I married very young, maybe we didn't know each other very well – didn't even know ourselves very well, for that matter?'

Only as she said it did Ciara realise the truth of it, and

215

wondered where it had come from. What on earth had put that into her head? All sorts of odd thoughts seemed to be floating into it lately.

A whoosh of air, a rustle of skirts distracted them both as Tara arrived, breathless and windblown, her hair wild, her Gothic look quite at odds with Mike's trim appearance. His clothes verged on the businesslike: hers were jumbled, mismatched, a taffeta skirt tangled with an army jacket and Victorian bootees, stabbed with bits of lace and jewellery in odd places.

'Hi, Mum. Hi, Mike. So, what's the party in aid of?' Already, Tara's tone suggested that she'd been dragged here against her will.

'No party, just dinner with your dad and me! We haven't seen either of you for ages.'

'Yeah. Well, have you seen each other?' Confrontationally, Tara took out a pack of cigarettes, lit one and blew smoke over their heads. For just one fleeting moment, Ciara felt disloyal relief that Tara was hardly ever at home any more. She was so touchy, there was almost something to be said for the idea of her growing up and moving on.

Except that she was so exasperatingly vulnerable, too, under all that violet eyeshadow and those naval tattoos . . . a work in progress, Ciara thought, not quite finished yet. An exhausting work. I don't envy whatever poor lad ever ends up with her on his lap. And yet . . . there's something so fragile about her, sometimes, something that just tugs at my heart.

'Yes, we've seen each other. And we'll all be seeing each other this evening, as a family.'

'Right.' Tara exhaled a sigh that conveyed scepticism.

'So, before Jake gets here, why don't you tell me what

216

you've been doing? How you're getting on, who you're hanging out with?'

Pouring tea, Ciara smiled benignly, and Tara pulled on her cigarette.

'Why don't you tell us how *you're* getting on? You and Dad? Who *you're* hanging round with?'

Jesus, Ciara thought in horror, does she know about Morgan? Or Roisin? Or both? Has someone somehow told her something – and maybe got it muddled, too? After all, I got it muddled myself.

'We're getting on fine' she said evenly, at length. 'Not hanging out with anyone, except each other, sometimes.'

'Oh, *really*?' Tara's tone was so sardonic, her look so challenging that Ciara stared at her, seeing something devastating, something that struck her dumb with shock: my daughter, she thought, is ripped apart with pain. This spiky behaviour is all an act, a couldn't-care-less act, to disguise the fact that our child cannot handle the idea of her parents fighting. Mike can just barely handle it, and Tara can't handle it at all. It's like when she was five, if we ever so much as raised our voices over a broken vase, she'd clap her hands over her ears and screech at us to stop. She'll never admit it, not now at nineteen, but she is *screaming* for Jake and me to get back together.

Oh, Tara! You're too old for me to scoop you up in a hug, tell you everything's going to be all right . . . I honestly don't know whether it is going to be or not. Your parents can't make that decision on the basis of children who are no longer children.

But I want it to be what you want. Want you and Mike to be happy, if that turns out to be the same thing as Jake and me being happy. If we can only somehow figure out how. He

217

wants me to become a different person, you know. Wants me to act and look my age, he says. Wants me to grow up.

Do I want to do that? Any more than I want my children to grow up? Wouldn't it be wonderful if we could all be flash-frozen, stay as we were only a year ago!

But we can't. If there's one thing I've learned this year, it's that nothing ever stays the same. Not my husband, not my children, not even me. No amount of surgery can stitch us into place for ever.

Well, they had done their best. For their children, Jake and Ciara Lunny had given sterling performances in their roles of almost-happy parents. Parents who, if they weren't actually living together or indeed properly married at the moment, could at least be civil and get through dinner without arguing. Get through a whole evening without a shot being fired. For Tara's sake Ciara dressed down, wearing her nearest-to-mumsy outfit, forsaking anything that might suggest youthful competiton. Stubbornly, Tara said nothing: it was Mike who remarked that she looked well, and she thought she sensed some kind of relief in him.

A truce. Was that something? Well, it had to be. Everyone stayed overnight, even Jake in the spare room, and left next day with, Ciara thought, some degree of encouragement. Some vague hope of things maybe eventually working out somehow.

But how? After they'd all left Ciara found the house resoundingly quiet, began to pace around it racking her brains, trying to figure out how she could ever become the kind of wife Jake wanted, even if that was what she wanted.

Was it? Somehow 'Mrs Jake Lunny' no longer held quite

the heart-stopping allure it had held twenty years ago. After all Jake was ageing now, going grey, and had never been promoted to captain, and had lost quite a chunk of money on the stock market, and had developed some distinctly bizarre new tastes. He was no longer such a trophy, nor even a husband who could be said to be going exactly according to plan. If we stay together, she began to realise, it will be for different reasons than before. Reasons I can't quite pinpoint, but different.

And I'm different now, too. I have a job, a new schedule, my own money. Have a toyboy who worships me, if that's what I want. Have weeded out all my dead-end friends, traded them in for just Lee, who isn't even here.

Oh, I wish she was here! Wish she'd tell me what she's at, what she thinks . . . is there any e-mail from her, I wonder? She scarcely seems to manage to write more than once or twice a month any more. If she wasn't so sensible, I'd wonder whether she's got in with some kind of oddballs . . . who is she with, exactly?

Let's see if there's any mail from her.

Click.

Dear Ciara,

So, our trip to London was in vain, huh? It was brain surgery Jake wanted you to have, not cosmetic? Oh, well, look on the bright side – now you're only twenty-five, you can go out and disco till dawn!

Or could, if you wanted. If the gloss didn't seem to be wearing off your eternal youth already. Do I get the impression that it is wearing off? Too exhausting, too *déjà-vu*, too much like hard work? Plus, it's not reeling the wayward husband back in, after all? Well, if Jake had wanted a dolly bird, I guess he probably would have had a fling with one of the trolley dollies, joined the mile-high club. So it must be something else he wants. A brighter, better Ciara, only not necessarily younger?!

Maybe he doesn't want to look like your dad alongside you? Or doesn't want to share the demanding life of a youngster? Or – could it be this simple? – just liked you the way you were before? Maybe all you really had to do to keep him happy was read the odd copy of *Time* and go on the odd trip to Egypt. And listen to the occasional bit of music composed for rusty fork and nail file.

Maybe that's still all you have to do. I mean, he hardly expects you to do a PhD in ancient history, does he? You've already rolled back the clock fifteen years, that should be enough!

Sorry. Just kidding. Tell you what. If you want to get away from the encroaching Morgan – who sounds like a horribly contagious dose of measles – and you have a bit of money saved up (well, no point in blowing that on the nose now, is there?) why not come out here and visit me?

It's a different world. It'd get you well away from Morgan. And might help you think from a new angle. Plus it's sunny, you could work on your tan. Of course tans are not trendy any more, but still, a girl's gotta look golden, huh? You probably spend more on fake tan in a month than I live on!

Anyway. Come visit. It is very peaceful, very pretty. You will have a choice of sleeping accommodation and lots of distracting activities. Very diet-conscious food. Excellent exercise regime. No Jake, no Morgan, no kids, no worries.

Love, Lee

16

Yes, Robin conceded reluctantly, Ciara could have a few weeks off work. Was she planning to go somewhere nice?

'Vietnam' she said, and they gazed at each other, equally shocked at the prospect of such a radical destination.

'Really? . . . well, bring back any good recipes you find' he said finally, dubiously, looking at her in a way that suggested she must be mad. A way that marked her as a Marbella girl, Club Med, miles out of her depth on such an exotic voyage. Already, she felt out of it, discovering how far away Vietnam was, that vaccinations were necessary, all sorts of paperwork she'd never needed before. Why couldn't Lee have gone to Capri or Cannes or somewhere simple?!

Still, she thought, I do need to get away. Far enough away to see things in some kind of perspective, from some kind of different angle. I'm too close to Jake here, can't see the wood for the trees. Besides, this is a step in the right direction. He'll be surprised to hear I'm going somewhere off the beaten track!

He was very surprised, when she informed him, spluttering with laughter in a way that made her indignant. 'I'm not a complete idiot, you know, I can make my way from – from one side of the world to the other!'

Looking unconvinced, struggling to keep a straight face, he nodded solemnly. 'Well, Lee will look after you I suppose, I'll try to get you upgraded on the flight . . . bring your mobile and call me if you . . . er . . .'

'If I get stuck? Is that what you mean? If it's all too foreign and complicated for me?'

'Yes. That's what I mean. You've never gone anywhere alone before, Ciara, never mind somewhere so way off beam!'

Had he always been so patronising, as if she were a child? Or was he just concerned? Either way, she found herself resolving to manage alone, not call him under any circumstances, show him she wasn't a total airhead. Show Mike and Tara too, who hooted when they heard her plans. Everyone seemed to think she was absolutely hopeless, could never possibly reach the Far East intact and would, as Mike grinned, 'probably be abducted into white slavery'.

Is that so, she fumed, is that so, now? Well, just you wait and see. I can do this, I'm not just a dumb blonde!

Am I? Is that really what they all think?

That's what I used to want everyone to think. Being a dumb blonde was fun. But now, it's getting to be kind of annoying. Right, then. Let's hit Ho Chi Minh City – what a silly name! – and see what happens.

Ho Chi Minh City, several weeks later, was hideous. The noisiest, dustiest, most chaotic city Ciara had ever seen in her life. Messy, milling with mobs of people, it felt somehow out of control, unsettling almost to the point of scary. Certain that the taxi driver had ripped her off on the trip from the airport, she checked into a hotel recommended by Lee, which while adequate was a far cry from any she had ever encountered before. Weary, jetlagged and unnerved, she decided she absolutely hated travelling alone, hated watching her budget, hated herself for embarking on this insane venture. Holidays were supposed to be relaxing, enjoyable, soothing; this was sweltering, mayhem, madness.

Robin's frown, Jake's smile, both swam into her mind, and now she saw things the way they must have seen them: a woman in completely unsuitable clothes hefting her Vuitton suitcase into this surging city shrieking with unrecognisable languages, steaming and simmering, almost stampeding her in its dizzy rush to wherever it was racing *en masse*. Even getting from the taxi into the hotel left her flustered, breathless, nursing a bruise inflicted by someone who'd almost knocked her to the pavement as he bolted by.

Oh, God, she thought as she attempted to check in, I miss you, Jake Lunny, where are you when I need you! I feel so – so unprotected, without you! You always took care of me, took care of everything. I never even had to figure out what was the French for 'booking'! What is the French for it, and why is this useless receptionist speaking French anyway? France is nowhere near Vietnam, I don't get it. The desk clerks always spoke English anywhere we ever went.

This city feels so big, and is making me feel so small. Like I could get swallowed up and vanish without trace. Nobody would notice, it might be weeks before anyone missed me . . . God, I'm shattered. And scared, if the truth be known. Which it won't be, because I'm not going to panic. Not yet, anyway, not until I have to. I'll be damned if I'll give Jake Lunny the satisfaction of saying 'There, see, of course you can't manage, you never went further than the golf club on your own before.'

Okay. Maybe I didn't. Maybe I should have started with something easier, a weekend at Champney's or something. I'd kill for a massage, this very minute, a jacuzzi and a nice civilised meal in a proper restaurant! This hotel looks so bare, so basic – and heaven only knows what the beds are like. I'm going to strangle Lee for sending me here, if I ever find her amongst all these zillions of people. She says she's only a train trip away . . . but how am I even going to find the train station? I couldn't be more lost if I was on the moon.

Getting muddled, missing the train that would take her to Lee's village 'a few hours' up the coast – had it left ahead of schedule, or never existed? – Ciara sat on her suitcase for six hours at the station waiting for the next train, afraid to budge in case it should suddenly materialise and leave without her. When it appeared it was immediately mobbed, and she had to fight her way on board, dragging the luggage Jake had always handled before, scrambling for a seat amongst masses of squealing, excitable people.

Was this normal, did they all live like this all the time? Hefting her suitcase aboard, clutching her handbag against pickpockets – why hadn't she thought of a moneybelt! – she squeezed into the midst of a large group loosely resembling a family, which was toting provisions for what looked like weeks. Fruit, rice, chunks of meat, vegetables, all kinds of food emerged from a series of bamboo boxes, passed around from hand to hand, sociably offered to her on its way amongst the dozen people sharing it. Friendly enough, they smiled at her, and she forced herself to smile back, suppressing a shudder – uh, all this unwrapped food, all these grasping hands, how unhygienic!

Four hours later, she had changed her mind. Four hours later she was starving, because the train did not have a dining car and she, apparently, was the only person who had not brought a picnic. The screaming emptiness of her stomach was surpassed only by the aching stiffness of her bones as she shifted uncomfortably on the hard seat on which she was wedged, catching occasional glimpses of startlingly steep mountains and vividly lush valleys between the jostling heads of her companions. Engaged in some kind of dice game, they were laughing, shouting and sweating, and she thought with longing of previous holidays: she'd be settled by the pool now, cocktail in hand, leafing through *Hello!* while Jake saw about renting an air-conditioned car. I would sell Jake, she thought, for air-conditioning on this bloody train. I have never been so hot, so grubby, so hungry, so deafened or so squashed in my life. Lee must be out of her mind – what on earth was that she said about Vietnam being peaceful? It's about as peaceful as the first day of the summer sales, you'd think all these people were scrabbling to get a diamond bracelet for a tenner. And what did she mean by 'a few hours' – Jesus, have I missed the stop, is this train taking me off into the jungle or China or where?!

Squinting desperately at every sign at every station, panic gradually mushrooming in her mind, she was virtually in-coherent with terror by the time the train finally chugged into somewhere that vaguely matched the name on her ticket – or did it? Vietnamese was impossible to read, much less pronounce, all she had to go on was what Lee had written out on a postcard – in a flurry she leaped up, grabbed her bag and hurled herself off the train, which trundled away ditching her in the middle of nowhere, heart hammering. No sign of Lee, who'd promised to meet her . . . only not off this train, because she should have been on the first one, six hours earlier. Now what? Collapsing onto a bench, she hugged herself in sheer horror, contemplating the beauty queen's first option in moments of trauma: bursting into tears.

★

'But for heaven's sake, you surely didn't expect me to hang round here for six hours?!'

'I didn't know what to think. It wasn't my fault I missed the first train, your directions were all wrong . . . I thought you were never coming, that I must be in the wrong place – thought I was abandoned here for ever!'

Lee debated whether to laugh at Ciara or smack her. Huddled on her suitcase, pouty and accusing, she looked like a child whose mother had forgotten to pick her up from school.

A child wearing the silliest wedge-heeled shoes she'd ever seen, tottering upright, wobbling a few steps as if her Chinese feet had been bound at birth. First off, Lee thought, we're going to have to get her some normal walking shoes. And a hat, before she fries.

Slapping at a mosquito – had she even brought any repellent? – Ciara looked around sulkily. 'So, where's the taxi rank? I can't wait for a shower and a proper meal.'

Stifling a grin, Lee took her suitcase in one hand, her arm in the other, steering her out of the deserted station in the direction of the dirtiest, most decrepit car Ciara had ever seen. The only one in sight. Staring at it, Ciara gasped, unable to even ascertain what colour it was.

'But – that can't be yours, surely?'

'No. It belongs to a guy called Rory, who lent it to me so I could fetch you. Taxis are, um, scarce out here.' Ironically, she nodded at the hazy hills and fields all around, in which no sign of human life was visible.

'But – how do you get around, usually?'

'By bike. Bought one for twenty bucks! Anyway, get in – here, give me a hand with your bag – and off we go. It's only a two-hour trip.'

Another *two hours*? Appalled, Ciara squeaked. 'But I'm

starving! Is there no restaurant anywhere near, could we not get a burger or something first?'

Starting the ancient car, Lee eyed her sidelong. 'Honey, look around you. D'you see any golden arches, any Ronald McDonald?'

No. Ciara saw no sign of anything, no trace of civilisation whatsoever. Nothing but a dusty road leading into the middle of miles of fields filled with some tall grass or crops or something, into which they appeared to be heading.

'Lee, I'll be dead of hunger in two hours.'

'Dieting is good for your figure! Oh, well, if you insist – there might be a banana in the back. Have a look.'

Turning to rummage under a pile of miscellaneous junk, Ciara eventually found one, peeled it and ate it almost at a gulp. Overripe, it tasted sticky and starchy, but . . . 'Better than nothing, I suppose. Now, where are we going?'

'To the village where I . . . well, it's not exactly a village, as such. Just a bunch of huts and tents where—'

'Huts and *tents*?! But – it has a hotel, surely? Lee, tell me it does!'

Laughing, fixing a scarf over the lower half of her face against rising dust, Lee shrugged nonchalantly. 'Don't worry. You'll have a comfy berth, and a shower. And a nice meal tonight.'

Phew. At least that was something. There must be an inn or guesthouse of some description – okay, maybe not luxury standard, but comfortable at any rate. With a sigh, settling as best she could into the rattling, bumping car, Ciara suddenly found herself exhausted, her head starting to loll a little as Lee drove, for reasons unclear, down a narrow track into the extremely hot middle of nowhere.

★

229

'Lee, you cannot be serious. Nobody in their right mind could possibly live *here*.' Aghast, Ciara waved a horrified hand at what Lee apparently considered 'home' these days: a virtual gypsy encampment of perhaps twenty thatched huts, half a dozen semi-permanent-type tents, and three ramshackle camper vans, all set in a clearing a few hundred yards back from a beach. She couldn't yet see the beach, but there was the sound and smell of ocean. And some other smells, too. The whole setting reminded her of some prisoner-of-war movie she'd once seen with Jake.

'Honey, I'm not sure whether I could ever live anywhere else again. Now, this is my hut' – hauling the Vuitton suitcase up some timber steps, Lee pushed open a wooden door – 'you have a choice whether to sleep inside, on a roll-up mattress, or outside in a hammock.'

'W-what?'

'The shower's over there, under those trees. Just buckets of water from the river – there's one nearby, in that forest – but really cool and clean. Go easy on the shower gel, we don't want to pollute. Would you like a shower right now?'

Ciara thought she'd like a jet plane right now, to scream overhead and swoop her up, away from this nightmare. 'Uh – maybe – in a minute – Lee, what exactly *is* all this?'

Apparently considering the question, Lee ditched the suit-case, sat down on an upturned chunk of raw tree and gestured to another, on which Ciara was evidently invited to sit. Then, reaching into a pocket of her loose, faded pink dungarees – where were the black trousers and crisp white shirts? – she retrieved a pack of tobacco and another of Rizla papers, with which she proceeded to roll herself a cigarette. Open-mouthed, Ciara thought it must be twenty years since she'd last seen an American smoking.

'I guess you could call it a kind of colony. Of sorts. Composed of about fifty people of all ages, all nationalities, some transient, some long-term, who've wended their way here for all sorts of reasons. Broken hearts, collapsed businesses, plain curiosity, sense of adventure, drop-out attitude, whatever. Everything from eco-warriors to an accountant and a biologist. It's not a proper village as such, we don't have running water or electricity or even a permanent building, but it is a community, in which we all muddle along, swop skills and stories, sing and talk and laugh. Have a lot of fun.'

Fun. Fun, she said? Ciara thought she'd never in her life seen anything so hellish. Thought she'd pay a hundred euros for one fresh, sparkling gin and tonic with ice and a spritz of lime. Two hundred, three if it came with canapés. Clearly, poor Lee was having a tragic breakdown. Jake's must have been contagious. And what else might be contagious, in this mosquito-infested mirage? Grimacing, she scratched her shoulder.

'Lee, is this even legal? Are people allowed to camp out like this? I mean, what does the local council –?'

'Ciara, in case you haven't noticed, this is Vietnam. We are sixty miles from the nearest village, a hundred from town, we are in a totally remote, semi-inaccessible jungle clearing facing out into the South China Sea. The local councillors don't, uh, visit very often.'

'You must be mad. Completely raving. I wouldn't have dreamed of coming to such an awful place, had no idea you'd lost your marbles – why on earth didn't you tell me, warn me?'

Not answering, smiling vaguely, Lee merely puffed on her cigarette, crossing her insect-nibbled ankles, thoughtfully contemplating a thin spiral of blue smoke twirling slowly up into the turquoise sky.

So, all right, the beach was beautiful, a full mile of powdery, silvery sand shaded by palms from the glittering sun. Yes, a swim was wonderfully refreshing in the warm, translucent sea. And a fish kebab, plus a platter of fresh fruit, did make Ciara feel distinctly better even if she had to eat with her hands like a savage.

'Lee, this is frankly not my idea of a holiday. If I'd known this place was so primitive or so remote I wouldn't have come in a fit. My idea of a holiday involves shops and jet-skis and waiter service. Clubs and casinos at night, places to glam up for! What on earth do you lot do here at night?'

'Oh . . . we talk. Play cards, or a guitar, some of us might do a little yoga or meditate for a while.'

'Well, count me out of all that. Are you and the rest of these people out of your minds or what?'

Serenely, Lee smiled. 'I guess that would depend on how you define out of your mind . . . oh look, there's Rory. Hey, Rory, come say hello to my friend Ciara!'

Animatedly, Lee sat up on the sand waving to a tanned, ponytailed blond man as he came onto the beach, carrying some kind of net on a stick, wearing only khaki shorts, a beard and a smile. Sauntering over, he bent down and surprised Ciara by kissing Lee's cheek before raising a hand in greeting.

'Hi, Ciara. I remember you. You visited Lee's house the night we were planning this trip.'

Huh? He must have some memory. Distantly Ciara recalled her distraught arrival at Lee's house on the night of her birthday, the fatal forty, to find some unexpected dinner guests all huddled over a map. But they were a blur, she certainly didn't remember anyone who'd looked remotely like this man. Was that really only six months ago? It felt like a million years. Nodding, she said hello to Rory.

'So, Lee finally persuaded you to come visit, huh? I hope you're going to enjoy Ba Chan, will you be staying for a while?'

He sounded pleasant and civilised, looked so friendly that Ciara was unable to retort that no, actually, she'd only be staying twenty-four hours after all. Or however long it might take her to persuade Lee to take her back to the train station, a four-hour round trip away.

'Uh, maybe a day or two.' Max, she thought, absolute maximum. After coming such a distance, this has been the most awful mistake. How soon can I decently leave?

'Good. Lee's told me quite a bit about you, been looking forward to seeing you. Now you're here, would you like to try a bit of fishing?'

What? Ciara thought she'd rather try parachuting from ten thousand feet. Blinking, she looked quizzically at him.

'See, all you have to do is trawl this net through the water, there are thousands of tiny fish in the shallows . . . c'mon, I'll show you how.'

Extending a hand, Rory waited for her to take it, leaving her no option but to let him haul her reluctantly to her feet. Lee, she thought, say something, put a stop to this!

But Lee merely watched, smiling remotely as Rory led Ciara into the shallows, showed her how to use the net and then, appearing to lose interest, left her holding it, absurdly sweeping it back and forth as if she might catch some fish. Hey, she thought, lesson over, you can have it back now!

But Rory was walking back across the sand to where Lee waited, sitting down beside her and . . . and putting his arm around her shoulder, quite casually, as if such familiarity were not only permitted but encouraged. Open-mouthed, Ciara watched as Lee turned to him, smiling absently, kissed his cheek and took his hand as it rested on her collarbone.

What? But –?! Lee hadn't mentioned anything about this man before, never hinted at any kind of relationship in any of her e-mails, and Ciara was as surprised as she was bemused until an even more startling thought struck her – were they hippies, all of them, into free love, drifting from one to the next as this net was drifting, idly, in the water?

Hastily, turning her back lest Lee think she was staring at her, Ciara swivelled to face out to sea, her mind filling with a whole raft of thoughts, one worse than the next. I'm trapped, she thought, marooned with a bunch of nutters in the middle of nowhere – Jake, help!

How am I even going to call you? How do I charge my mobile, if there's no electricity? Where's the nearest landline? What in God's name am I doing standing here in this water with this net – oh dear God, there's a fish in it! Flapping and – waaahh!

Dropping it as if it were on fire, she ran squealing back to Lee, and Rory, who was laughing already, getting up to come to her rescue. 'Don't worry' he called, 'it won't eat you! You'll eat it, if it hasn't got away!'

Praying that it had – uhhh! – Ciara flopped back down on the sand while he dealt with the wriggling creature, her whole body trembling with shock. Never in her entire life had she come closer to a live fish than a packet of Bird's Eye or something in sauce. Turning to Lee for sympathy, she was outraged to find her laughing.

'Lee' she said as soon as she could speak, 'I don't know what the hell attracted you to this wretched place, but it is definitely not my scene. And I think you should explain what's going on with this Rory guy and – and –'

And apologise for dragging me to this dreadful dump, she felt like adding. But, looking as contented as a cat in the sun, Lee simply stretched on the sand, folding her arms under her head into a kind of pillow.

'Ah' she murmured, 'you know how it is, Ciara. One thing leads to another, things simply happen . . . if you're not going to fish then why don't you just relax for the moment, have a little nap if you like?'

A nap? Here on the beach, did she mean, or in that shack of hers? I'll never be able to sleep in it, Ciara thought, on that wooden floor – and what about this Rory, suppose he shows up overnight?!

'Lee' she muttered between gritted teeth, 'I'm sorry if it disappoints you, but I have to tell you, I'd appreciate a lift back to the train station just as soon as you can face the drive. Maybe tomorrow?'

Eyes closed, Lee exhaled a small sigh. 'Sure, Ciara. Whatever you like. Maybe tomorrow.'

What? Was that all? No protest, no argument or even token attempt to make her stay? Nothing about Rory, either, no explanation? Feeling somehow dismissed, and extremely put out, and nervous of that fish as it was carried flapping across the sand, Ciara thought of home, of heavenly Huxley Wood, and wanted to howl aloud.

17

Ciara did not sleep a wink on Lee's roll-out mattress. She slept for twelve hours, almost comatose after the trauma of arrival, to wake next day aching in every bone, oddly light-headed after a deep sleep spattered with strange dreams.

'Another swim' was Lee's suggestion, 'and maybe a massage later.'

Massage? Such luxury was available? Oooh, bliss. Ciara beamed, before remembering that she was leaving today, and wouldn't have time for one. What a pain, to have to pack up and trek all the way back home, after the hassle of getting here! But nobody in their right mind could possibly stay. I suppose I do at least owe Lee a long chat, she conceded, but after that I'll be on my way. Even if it does mean having to endure more Morgan . . . oh, God, which is worse, him or here? Could I possibly look as ghastly as I feel?

'Lee? Is there a mirror somewhere? My little compact isn't big enough to see whether I look as bad as I think I do, and put on some make-up.'

'There's a small one somewhere . . . but who's looking at you? Give your skin a break!'

Lee seemed completely unconcerned, wearing no make-up herself as she put together a breakfast of sorts before heading, nonchalantly, back to the beach on which she appeared to spend most of her time. At least the weather is great, Ciara conceded. I suppose if I slather myself in sunblock an hour or two wouldn't hurt. Before we leave.

Three hours later, after an unexpected doze on the sand followed by a long, undeniably divine swim in the warm water, she lay on the sand idly trickling grains through her fingers, listening to the story of Rory. Yes, Lee confessed, there was a 'thing going on' between the two of them.

'But you said – never again! Said Freddie was the first and last man you'd ever marry!'

'Yes. I did. And he was. Rory and I are . . . mmm . . . simply enjoying each other. He's a bright, articulate, athletic guy and that's as much as I want, now or ever. Sympatico. Day-to-day. Nothing more.'

Day-to-day? Musing on that, Ciara thought of herself and Jake, exchanging vows 'until death do us part'. Vows that hadn't, apparently, been inviolable after all. Not even where children were involved – or not after they'd grown up, anyway. At least Jake had had the decency to wait that long. But how could a couple just lurch along from day to day, without any idea where they were going? Was that possible, or would the uncertainty of it ruin the whole thing?

Or was the uncertainty of it part of the fun? Lee certainly didn't look as if she were pining for permanence. Some people, she supposed, might get some kind of kick from living on the edge. Masochists.

'Where are the rest of your friends?' Surely they couldn't all have stayed in this wilderness.

'Gone back home. Rory and I actually made it as far as the airport with them before changing our minds. They were horrified. We ran off, he bought that old car in Ho Chi and we wandered around for a while before meeting an Australian couple who told us about this place. They'd stayed a year here and said it was great, so we decided to try it. So far, so good.'

'You make it sound so simple!'

'Honey, it is simple, really. Life can be quite uncomplicated if you're prepared to drop all the baggage you've accumulated. We pared ours down to a minimum. Rory was going through hell that first night you met him, his girlfriend had left him after he was made redundant . . . now he's just living on his little bit of redundancy money and reckons he had a narrow escape from her. I'm living on the rental money from my house and have entirely stopped worrying about the stock market. Losing Freddie's money enabled me to finally lose *him*. To forget all about him, and move on.'

Yes. Well. Lee smiled vaguely, complacently, quite dazzling in her indifference. How could anyone stop caring about money? Ciara was hypnotised. But she had to admit that Lee did seem to have moved on, in every sense.

'But what do you *do* all day?'

Contentedly, Lee yawned a little. 'I live my life as the good Lord grants it. I swim and walk and cycle, read whatever I can lay my hands on, talk to the others when the mood takes me, join them for yoga or dance sessions on the beach, sometimes eat with some of them. We don't live in each other's pockets. But when we do get together it's because we want to, and usually quite rewarding. I'm learning a lot about all sorts of things.'

'Such as?'

'Such as kadampa buddhism, and ashtanga yoga, and how to chop a log without losing my fingers, and what an awful misery Gustave Flaubert was, and a dynamite recipe for banana curry.'

Ciara couldn't see how any of that mattered. Had no idea

who Gustave Whatsit was. 'What about your jewellery? Surely you haven't let your career slide? Not after making me go out and get a job!?'

Lee had the grace to grin. 'You needed a job. Not to earn money for surgery but to keep you sane. Bet you haven't much time to brood at work, huh?'

'Well – no. Especially not with Morgan Richards chasing me round the restaurant. Boy, was he a mistake.'

Lee laughed. 'So toyboys are hard work, huh? At least now you know. And you did have some fun, learned a few new tricks – nothing's ever wasted.'

Ciara flushed. 'You still haven't told me about your jewellery.'

'Oh, I still make a few pieces, out of whatever's available. But I won't bother trying to sell them until I have to . . . it costs so little to live this way, out here. If the shops lose interest in me, if I eventually have to find new outlets, what the hell. The world is full of shops.'

'H'mm.' Ciara couldn't deny that. 'And Rory? What's his career plan?'

'I'm not sure. At this moment, I hope it involves cooking our lunch. After that, I'll introduce you to Judy, who gives the best massages this side of Mars. When she's in the mood. We all only ever do things we're in the mood to do, which means they get done really well.'

Ciara blinked. Such laziness, such indulgence! Where would the world be if surgeons only ever operated when they were in the mood, or pilots didn't feel like flying planes, or hairdressers washed their hands of their customers? The entire planet would slam to a standstill. Even if Lee Warner didn't seem to see it that way.

Sitting up, Ciara looked around her, noting the few other

people on the beach, all of them scruffy-looking, some vaguely arty, presumably part of this crazy community in some shape or form. So far she had spoken to none of them, and they did not appear to be very interested in her. Thus far, there had been nothing more than a languid nod or wave directed at Lee from a distance. Piqued equally by curiosity and hunger, she sniffed the air, detecting a faint odour of woodsmoke and grilling fish. For a change. All hope of fillet steak fast receding, she reached for some kind of sarong thing Lee had loaned her, and tied it over her swimsuit. For a woman in love, Lee didn't seem to be exactly rushing to spend every waking moment with the man of her dreams.

Nor even to discuss him, dissect every detail the way the women did when they met a new guy in *Sex In The City* or on *Friends*. You'd get more chat out of a tree.

And yet, Ciara conceded bemused, she looks happy. She does look well, and calm, and happy. Carefree, and rested.

She looks *younger*.

Judy, a petite brunette from Yorkshire, was an affable lady, but not very talkative. Merely smiling at Ciara, she instructed her to stretch out on the sand, closed her eyes, flexed her fingers and embarked on an incredibly slow, thorough, bone-deep massage. Trying to be sociable at first, Ciara attempted to talk to her, but got such minimal response that she gave up, drifting off instead into a silent haze, scented with some kind of oil Judy was using . . . eucalyptus, sandalwood?

Next thing, it was late afternoon, and as she sat up Ciara realised, almost woozily, that there was no chance of being taken back to the train station today. Lee had vanished, leaving her alone with Judy, who merely shrugged on hearing of her thwarted plan to depart.

'Never mind. You can leave tomorrow, or whenever . . . what's the rush?'

Such was the soporific effect of the massage, Ciara couldn't quite recall what the rush was. Today was already half gone, she could struggle on somehow through the rest of it. Belatedly, it occurred to her to ask Judy what she charged for massages.

'Nothing. We don't use money, between ourselves, we just trade services. If there's something you're good at maybe you'll do it for me some time . . . what do you do best?'

What *did* she do best? Mulling on it, Ciara wondered; somehow 'looking after my family' or 'giving dinner parties' didn't sound quite right. Or 'looking good' – even if it was her speciality, it was hardly the kind of thing you could put on your CV. Not out here, anyway. Right now she had no idea how she looked, but was surprised to find herself feeling very good. Judy had the touch of an angel with just the right amount of sumo wrestler, all her bones felt looser, rearranged in some much better design.

'You're such a great masseuse, you should go professional' she enthused, and Judy smiled as she stoppered her little bottle of fragrant oil.

'I am professional. Or was. Had my own beauty salon back home. Ran it for twelve years, until I woke up one morning sick to the teeth of running a business. Loved the work, but hated the administration. All those endless forms to fill, staff to recruit . . . someone was always cancelling an appointment or calling in sick or having childcare problems. It was soul destroying, in the end. Just couldn't take it any more. So I sold the salon and took off on the proceeds. Ended up here, and haven't got round to leaving yet. Can't see any reason to, really.'

'But – what about your friends? Your family?'

'Oh, we keep in touch.' Nonchalantly, Judy knelt back on her heels, wiping her palms, gazing out over the slowly silvering horizon. What time was it? Instead of retrieving her watch, which Judy had made her remove, Ciara found herself squinting at the sun instead, which while still hot was cooling and lowering a little. Maybe around four? Five?

'So – what kind of services do you people swop?' Intrigued, Ciara hestitated, half wondering whether the answer might reveal some colony of sexual deviants or criminals. Half of these odd-bods might well be on the run from the police, for all she knew. Escaped from asylums, hunted by Interpol.

'Well, let's see. I do massages. Lee drives to town with Anita to do all our shopping and e-mailing. Rory fishes and cooks. Sam is our doctor. Johnny, for reasons beyond me, likes doing laundry. Giorgio can chop wood for hours at a time. Aurélie adores sewing – she made the sails for our boat, which was built by Jim and Francesco. Gerhard teaches karate, Dara teaches yoga, Kim's a mechanic . . . really we're quite self sufficient, between one thing and another. Plus quite a few people can sing or play a guitar, Hannah has the most beautiful voice. When she's in the mood. There's no pressure on anyone to do anything if they're not, unless it's an emergency. All the basic jobs, like cooking for instance, can be shared as need arises.'

Trying not to look as bemused as she felt, Ciara nodded. What was going to happen to all these people's careers, back in civilisation? Their spouses and children? Were any of them even worrying about any of that? Where would this jungle fever eventually end?

'So' said Judy, standing up, 'glad you enjoyed your massage, Ciara. See you round.' Strolling off the beach with

243

a little wave, she vanished into the shady clearing without, apparently, much further interest in conversation. Left sitting on the sand, Ciara wondered where Lee had got to, and what she was supposed to do until she reappeared.

Nothing, seemed to be the answer. Just sit here and watch the sunset, doing sweet sod all. An exquisite sunset as it happened, streaked with rose and apricot and gorgeous, glowing gold, slowly melting under the horizon. The first sunset, Ciara realised in surprise, she had ever watched on her own. Ever watched for more than six seconds, without dashing off to change for cocktails.

Two days? Three, four? How long did it take, Ciara wondered later, to abandon hope of leaving? To lose interest in leaving? To somehow slip into this silken pool and simply drift with the tide? Nobody tried to make her stay, nobody expressed the faintest interest in whether she came or went; the subject seemed to evaporate with each morning's dew. By the end of a week, she was beginning to feel like some other person, floating in some other world.

'This' she said to Lee, 'is the strangest holiday I've ever had in my life.'

'Are you enjoying it?'

Was she? 'Well . . . it's different. I thought I'd go mad at first, with nothing to do, no shops, no jet-skis or nightclubs or anything, but now it seems to sort of fit me in some crazy way. I just wish there was a hairdresser to do my streaks.'

'Ken is a hairdresser. He'll cut it if you want. But no streaks – even if he had the facilities, we try not to pollute the place with chemicals.'

Saying nothing, Ciara wondered whether to be glad or sorry. Getting her hair done always made her feel so good –

but what could she offer here, in return? So far, all she had contributed was a bit of cooking and cleaning, and she got the feeling that everyone was politely avoiding mention of her lack of skills, undoubtedly because she was Lee's friend, only visiting. But it made her feel awkward.

'Lee, I'm hopeless. I never realised before just how little I can do, how few skills I have.'

Carelessly, Lee smiled at her over a piece of fabric she was painting, sitting crosslegged on the floor of her rudimentary verandah. 'Don't worry about it. The lilies of the field and all that.'

'Huh?'

'They neither toil nor spin, they're lazy as hell, but lovely to look at – it's in the bible. Beauty is a contribution of sorts.'

No doubt she meant it well, but the effect of the remark was to make Ciara feel exceedingly silly. Rather than impressing anyone, looking pretty in this exotically gorgeous place seemed somehow pointless. Far more important, she sensed, were the respect and esteem people managed to attract. So far, she felt she'd scored a perfect zero. Which gave her the uneasy feeling of being invisible.

'But I can't hang round all day every day doing nothing!'

'Then let's get you into some activities. Esther's dance group, maybe? Or Pete's poetry workshop? Sometimes Olaf holds political seminars—'

'Er, dance would be good' she said hastily, before catching the merriment in Lee's eyes. 'You're winding me up!'

'Me? Not a bit of it. The dance is great. You'll enjoy it.'

And so, to her surprise, Ciara did, when she joined Lee and half a dozen other people on the beach early next morning, barefoot in just a swimsuit and sarong. Esther, a young dance teacher from the Bronx, took no prisoners, and the unaccustomed movements were gruelling under the hot sun, but even as Ciara's limbs began to stretch and ache her mind began to stretch and flex, floating free of her body, rising like a butterfly on the pearly air.

Flutterbyes. That's what Tara used to call butterflies, she thought, raising her arms, smiling at the memory, wondering how Tara was at this moment. And then, out of nowhere, a thought hit her.

Tara doesn't want a mother who looks or acts like a sister. If I want to continue to have some role in her life, *that's the way to keep her.* Not by trying to look young or act young, which makes her feel as if I'm competing and drives her away. I can stay much closer to her by growing up and acting my age. By giving in gracefully, and letting nature take its course.

'And up – and back – and one – two – three – four –'

Everyone was stretching skywards, the group moving as one, and somewhere deep inside her she began to feel a slow wave of contentment welling up, a sense of belonging, of keeping in step, of sharing the enjoyment of this warm, lovely morning, moving in rhythm with the other dancers until they were like a single being, swaying in harmony.

It was never like this at the gym. My God, this is so different! At the gym everyone pumped away furiously, counting calories, checking out each other's leotards, heaving and grunting . . . whereas this is so quiet, by comparison, so calm. Nobody's competing with anyone, we're just dancing, there isn't even any music and yet everyone's in step . . . it's every bit as strenuous as the gym, only without the pressure. I'm not doing this so I can fit into a size ten, I'm doing it because I'm enjoying it. Enjoying it no end in fact, far more than I ever enjoyed exercise before. Lee's done me a real favour, getting me into this.

Lee is wonderful. I owe her for lots of things. Yet she never makes me feel like I owe her anything.

Rory, Ciara decided, was a nice man. Not her type at all, but very easy company, a giving kind of guy who was, visibly, warming Lee's soul. Never had she seen such a relaxed relationship, and wondered at the precariousness of it, but if it suited Lee . . . well, maybe not everyone craved a wedding ring and a 4x4 in the cobble-lock drive? Maybe there were various kinds of relationships after all, as Jake had hinted . . . how was Jake, why was she not worrying about him? After she had spent nearly a year doing little else? Now, she found his image blurring very slightly in her mind, couldn't summon the energy to care whether he was reciting passionate poetry to Roisin Harte or not, couldn't seem to concentrate on the question of why he hadn't got promoted to captain. For years she had pushed him towards that goal; now, she merely wondered whether the extra responsibility might put further strain on his overworked mind.

Actually, a few weeks in a place like this might do him a lot of good. Would he come, I wonder? He said so much about wanting to travel new paths, do something different . . . this is different. I'm starting to feel quite different, myself. It must be the sun, or all this fresh fruit, fresh fish, fresh air, a whole new cocktail I never tasted before.

'Ciara?'

Looking up, she found both Lee and Rory watching her quizzically; apparently her mind had been wandering. 'Sorry, I must have been daydreaming – what did you say?'

'We said that Kim and Hannah and a few of the others are going to eat with us this evening, we're going to build a campfire on the beach – would you like to join us, are you in the mood for company?'

247

Was she? Until now Ciara had steered well clear of the other members of this loose community, because somehow she felt inadequate amongst them – why? Nobody had ever said a hostile word, been at all unfriendly. In fact the atmosphere was decidedly more pleasant than ever it had been at the golf club, peopled as that was with Sara Thompson and those other fickle, neurotic bitches. Thinking of Sara, with her puffed-up pride in her puffed-up boutique – and her puffed-up prices – Ciara found herself laughing. Losing Sara's friendship had not been a blow, after all; it had been a merciful release from a stuffy society that seemed, now, like some kind of mad mirage. As if a golfer's handicap could really be improved by wearing Ellesse shorts! Was the game more enjoyable if you wore expensive labels? I must have been out of my mind, she thought, to ever imagine such nonsense, much less partake in it. Nobody here's wearing any designer clothes, but what difference is it making? None, that I can see. In fact it's a nice break not to have to think about what to wear.

'Yes. Yes I am, Lee, thanks, I'd love company tonight, love to join your friends!'

'Good. Then go get some vegetables and start chopping with Rory. He needs a hand, there'll be about ten or twelve of us. I'm heading off in the car to see if I can liberate some beer somewhere.'

Cheerily, Lee departed with a wave over her shoulder, leaving Ciara to work alongside Rory and talk to him, finding out more about him as they went along. In some small ways, she was surprised to find, he slightly resembled Morgan Richards, seemed interested in politics and other things that had been discussed at that awful dinner party they'd attended. But there was one major difference: whereas Morgan had glowed with the fire of youth, Rory was cynical, wryly amused by life and very – what?

Mature, was what. Listening to him talk, obliged to respond, Ciara had the unnerving sensation of being treated like an adult, feeling as if she'd grown six inches in the eyes of the grown-ups. In her bare feet, without even a wedge heel to stand on.

Nine or ten people gradually gathered around the campfire in the milky dusk, each bringing a little gift: a handful of wild flowers, a paperback book, half a dozen precious teabags. Fascinated, Ciara thought of dinner parties at home; you might as well not go as arrive without the wine of the month wrapped in its magazine review. You certainly wouldn't go in tatty shorts or sandals, no matter how hot the weather. But then you wouldn't be eating freshly slaughtered chicken with your fingers at home, as was the case here. Watching Rory turn kebabs over the flames, she thought how relaxed he looked, what a contrast to Morgan swearing and sweltering over his high-tech hob. East Meets West, indeed! And now, would this bunch of flakes all start yakking about things she knew nothing about, had she been rash to join this little party? Might she be bored, or socially sidelined, or out of her depth yet again? Rory hadn't treated her like a bimbo, but . . . ?

She needn't have worried. Nobody started in on anything difficult, chatting instead about a local festival, a great boat trip someone had taken, somebody's brother who'd announced he was gay. If Mike had ever announced he was gay Ciara would have hit the roof, but amongst these people it sounded almost mainstream, as if the brother was no more barmy than anyone else. They are all barmy, she reminded herself, and they're smoking cannabis too – if Tara did that, I'd have a fit. Please don't let anyone offer me any.

When someone did, she waved it away, feeling prim. 'Thanks, but I don't smoke.' Whereupon the joint continued on its way without comment from anyone, leaving her wondering if she'd made a bit of a mountain out of a mole-hill. Evidently nobody cared what she did or didn't do – which again was not how things worked back home, where you did whatever was trendy and swore off whatever wasn't. Which, given how often trends changed, got to be kind of confusing at times. Where, she wondered, did Lee get this beer? Whatever is in it is making me feel kinda weightless.

After they'd eaten, sharing simple food without any mention of celebrity chefs, Lee sat on the sand propped against Rory, glancing hopefully at a burly, unshaven Texan called Glenn, who looked as if he normally rustled cattle for a living. Catching her eye, without saying a word, Glenn suddenly sat back, drawing a deep breath that worked like some kind of magic wand, wafting silence down upon the whole group as they settled in the sand, pulling on sweaters, snuggling closer to one another. Closing his eyes, gripping the belt of his denims, he began to sing.

'Down by the Salley Gardens, my love and I did meet . . .'

What – but I know that song, Ciara thought, we used to sing it at school! Leaning up against Lee, she listened as much surprised by its familiarity as by Glenn's unexpectedly beau-tiful baritone, accompanied only by the wash of the wavelets and the slow chirp of some distant bird. What a lovely voice! Rich and resonant, fruity as Christmas pudding, it seemed to be entrancing everyone, even without any music to go with it. Someone's guitar lay nearby, but Ciara grasped why it was not being played; there was no need.

In the absolute hush, Glenn's voice rose and fell, swooping and soaring, so lovely that tears gleamed in Lee's eyes and Ciara, mortified, felt something seize her throat. Something searing: could this possibly be what Jake meant by 'real music'? Was this how Mozart made him feel? Every nerve in her body was starting to tingle, Glenn's plaintive voice reaching out to her, spiriting her into the heart of the song. But how could this beefy, rough-looking guy have such an effect, silencing her completely, making her vision blur, her head swim with emotion?

She couldn't imagine how. All she knew, as the song faded to its grieving, lilting end, was that she would never forget this moment. Around her, the others were humming, murmuring in delight, but she sat as if punched, feeling stricken.

Is this what it's all about? Aching, fleeting moments like this? Moments you can never grasp, never hold in your hand? Moments that, like youth, can never be recaptured? This song reminds me of my youth – and that I can never be young again. Could this be why Jake makes such a fuss about music, is it a way of visiting somewhere in his soul? It's certainly touching a chord somewhere in mine . . . some memory buried dark and deep as that Egyptian king he talked about. Someplace I'd forgotten existed, in the land of my childhood, where I really was young, and so innocent. I wish this Glenn guy would go on and on, keep singing all night, I could listen to this for ever.

But other people began to sing other songs, including Rory who made an almost equally memorable job of 'Joe Hill'. Ciara had never heard of the song, but its haunting lyrics made her skin prickle, unnerving her as if Joe's militant ghost were about to march in on the moonlight. This, she shivered, is eerie. Music never made me feel like this before.

It was nearly midnight, the fire's embers dying down before Kim, the Malaysian mechanic, gazed rather moodily into the ashes, as if seeing shapes in them. A sallow, good-looking guy in his thirties, he seemed distracted; and then without warning he quietly began to recite in a low tone, little more than a murmur.

'I will arise and go now, and go to Innisfree . . .'

Again, astonished, Ciara was wafted back to her school-days, remembering a poem that had been drummed into her as into all the children, a part of what their teacher had called their 'heritage'. But she couldn't remember the lines, or who wrote it. Only something about glades and honey-bees and lake water lapping . . .

'Yeats' chirped Lee, so suddenly she jumped, and Lee laughed. 'You looked as if you were wondering! This was one of Yeats's first poems. Kim loves it, it's his party piece.'

Oh. Yes, well, foreigners always seemed to rave about that bloody poet – the same one Lee had overheard Jake so eagerly discussing with Roisin Harte in the pub. But this was the first time Ciara had ever connected the name with the work, actually listened to the words of a poem, finding them unexpectedly simple and sweet. Not replying, she sat listening, dimly beginning to make sense of something, connecting hazy things in her mind as if she were stringing opals on a necklace.

Could this be what Jake means about poetry, is this what draws him to it? This – this feeling of making away into another world? I always thought poetry was pointless, and complicated too, but there's nothing very tricky about this. I can make sense of it. I like it. It's so soothing, like that scented massage Judy gave me. Making me feel sleepy, like a child's bedtime story . . .

As if they were reading her thoughts, the others began to yawn, slowly getting up and dispersing in little clusters, blowing kisses as they went. Lee grinned at their receding shapes.

'Isn't it great not to have to worry about a designated driver! Olaf must have had at least five or six beers, and I'd say Aurélie wasn't far behind.'

Yes. No doubt it was great. But Ciara found that she didn't want to be jolted back to reality, didn't care if anyone had had fifty beers. All she wanted was to fall asleep under the stars, in that hammock strung between the trees, to dream of Jake. Jake and that lovely music, that haunting poetry, that made her wonder if she'd ever really known her husband before, ever properly seen or heard the man she'd been married to for twenty years.

18

Four weeks? Five, six? How long did it take to melt, finally, into this new country, new context, new community? Ciara couldn't say. Time seemed to move so lazily under the hot sun, as if her body clock were ticking in slow motion.

'I mustn't be well' she told Lee, 'not myself at all.'

'You look very well to me' Lee replied, 'and not yourself at all! Jake would scarcely recognise you.'

That was for sure. Jake had said goodbye to a pale blonde, elegantly dressed as fashion dictated; now his wife was a bare-foot brunette, her skin freckling, clothes makeshift, hair chopped short because of the heat and sea water. Instead of driving an urban jeep she was riding a bike, instead of playing golf she was reading poetry, and instead of attending church she was discussing philosophy.

That was what Lee called it, anyway, when Ciara slowly, hesitantly started asking questions about this new world she found herself in, about what had drawn all these people together, about the purpose and point of it all. She couldn't remember what had set her off on this track, only that she'd been learning yoga, gazing for long periods of time into space, letting her mind float free of everything that normally anchored it to reality. At first this had seemed absurd; but then her thoughts began to rise like balloons into the air, spiralling into infinity, leaving her trying to follow them as far as her mind's eye could see. And then she'd got mixed up in some talk with Rory about religion, which he said caused wars and was the root of all evil. Whereupon some Israeli girl got all excited about being Jewish and someone else got revved up about Hinduism and Rory had said, see, there we are, nearly coming to blows already. Saying little, Ciara had listened to everyone arguing, hearing new viewpoints, beginning to see her own half-baked ideas as small bits of some vast jigsaw, some kind of global quiz. Not everyone seemed to share her beliefs about the permanence of marriage . . . maybe Jake was not alone in his doubts, after all? Maybe it would do no harm to hear some other opinions, and think them over a bit?

It was very hard not to think, when everyone else seemed to be doing such a lot of it, when there was no reality television, no children to ferry around or golf to play or a sale to ransack at Benetton. When someone would look up at the moon and wonder 'how did it get there, why is it there, will it always be there . . . ?' and then start talking about the way it affected tides and hormones and what they called 'the rhythm of life'. When people seemed able to raise these strange subjects without feeling in the least silly, or conspicuous.

'Only curious' Lee said. 'That's all. We're only curious. It's perfectly normal to wonder about life on this planet and whether there's life on any other, what's the source of that life or reason for it . . . it's *not* wondering that seems weird to me. How people can get through their whole lives only ever wondering what's for dinner or what's on TV. That's the real mystery, the one that beats me.'

Ciara didn't get involved in that. But she did find her mind wandering, more and more as she got to know the others better, feeling increasingly free to chat with them, less afraid of sounding dumb. At home, nobody had ever taken her very seriously; here, people seemed to listen when she spoke, not interrupt wanting to know where their socks were or what she'd be wearing to the Taylors' party. Instead, incredibly, they seemed keen to discuss what she said, without verbally patting her on the head as if she were a cute but slow-witted child. Even her own children had done that, scarcely seeming to hear a word she said. Not that she could remember ever having said anything very important to them. Or things that seemed important now, at any rate.

'Here' said Kim the mechanic one day, 'thought maybe you'd like this.' And he slipped a little book into her hand: *Painless Poetry*. Well, it would be churlish not to read something that sounded so easy! And so she did read it, dipping in and out, discovering that poetry could be not only pretty but funny too, sometimes smart, sometimes sad . . . all sorts of things, that could affect your mood, leave you sitting in perfectly peaceful silence – why, she wondered, did I so resist those books Jake gave me, absolutely refuse point-blank to read them?

Was he hurt, when I did? It never crossed my mind that he might be hurt, or feel rejected. I just felt that he was forcing them down my throat, suffocating me.

'Oh, he's a guy' Lee grinned lazily, 'if he was wounded, he'll get over it.'

But Ciara was beginning to suspect that what Lee said about men wasn't quite the same as what she felt; she just had this way of putting things that made her sound tougher than she was. Which was only natural, maybe, after what she'd been through with Freddie. But sometimes Ciara glimpsed Lee looking at Rory and thought she looked very different now to the brisk American of a year ago, softer and somehow warmer, still not sentimental but distinctly happier. No surgeon, she thought, could ever have put that sparkle in Lee's eyes, that glow on her face.

Did I sparkle like that, when I first met Jake? And if I did, what sagged since, how did I end up in London having a facelift?

Something must have got lost, somewhere along the way. Something that Jake could see, but I never could, no matter how much I looked in the mirror.

'Not that I could live this way for ever, Lee! Sooner or later, I'm going to have to go home and – and figure out where I go from there.'

'Yes. You are. Nobody stays here for more than a year or so, Ciara. People come, people go as they feel the need. Rory and I have only been here six months, but we're already starting to think about moving on.'

'Oh!' Unexpectedly Ciara felt a prickle, as if a bee had stung her. 'Are you? Together, both of you? To where?'

She hoped Lee might simply say 'home', meaning Huxley Wood. But somehow she sensed she was wrong, that Huxley Wood was no longer home to Lee, not a place in which she could ever settle permanently. Increasingly, she was wondering how she was going to settle back into it herself.

'Oh, we thought we might just take the car and start driving on a bit. I've always wanted to visit Cambodia, and Rory would like to see Laos, Thailand . . . who knows where we'll end up. But I guess we'll recognise the right place when we reach it.'

Serenely, Lee smiled, and Ciara marvelled at her ease, her

amazingly relaxed way of looking at things. Was this what smoking cannabis did for you? Or was it what love did for you? All she could see for sure was a new Lee, refreshed and rejuvenated. Which is funny, she thought, when I'm the one who paid a fortune to be rejuvenated.

'I hope you will, Lee. I hope you and Rory are going to travel a long way together, and be very happy.'

'So do I! At least I'm willing now to take the chance, and so is he, we're ready to move on from our previous mistakes. Losing Freddie's money was so liberating, in the end. I feel like I've shaken off all the shackles that still tied me to him even after I'd left him. Now I can move on with Rory, in every sense. But what about you, Ciara? Have you any plans, any idea what you want to do?'

No. Nothing definite. Not yet. Somehow Ciara couldn't yet imagine herself back in Huxley Wood. It seemed so far away, another life, another world. One she couldn't just jump back into, overnight. And yet – Jake was so far away too, when she was starting to miss him in a whole new way, to want him near and close. Closer than he'd ever been before. There was so much to talk about, so many things she was seeing differently from her new vantage point here in this eastern wilderness, as if looking down the other end of a tele-scope. Thus far, she had only sent him and the children a few postcards, assuring them she was safe and well. Would they want to hear about what she'd been doing, would Jake think she'd gone mad if he knew she'd been cycling and dancing on the sand and discussing Buddhism and floating in the sea, gazing up at the stars and . . . and even reading? Someone had slipped her a book called *Men Are From Mars, Women Are From Venus*, and to her own amazement she was devouring it. Would he be delighted to hear she'd belatedly

259

begun to discover music, too, and poetry – or would he say, too bad, too late, I'm fed up waiting for you to grow up, to meet me halfway? I've changed my mind, I'm not coming back, let's just call it a day?

I want him back, she thought with sudden yearning. The old Jake, and the new one too. I feel ready now to tackle whatever new way of living he has in mind, even to contribute a few ideas of my own. I want him to see how I'm growing, to know he's not the only one, we can all change and – and develop. I'll never be any Einstein, but I'll never refuse to read a book again either, nor listen to music that's new or eat food that's unfamiliar or . . . or do anything that's different. I'd even go to Egypt with him. It'd be like five-star luxury after what I've coped with here. I seem to need so little now, feel stripped of so many things that maybe I never really needed in the first place. I'm being dismantled, and rebuilt. Sometimes I can almost feel my mind opening out, blooming like a flower under the sun.

But I still want Jake. If he still wants me. Do I dare find out whether he does or not?

'Lee?'

'Mmm?'

'D'you think maybe we could drive into town some day soon? I know it's a long way, but—'

'Let me guess. You need a manicure?'

'Well – yes! But what I really want is to find a phone and call Jake. I need to talk to him. We badly, urgently need to talk.'

No, said Jake, sounding startled and somewhat wary, of course he couldn't just drop everything to fly to Vietnam. He'd had no word from Ciara for weeks, what was this all about? Was she not planning to come home, could they not see each other then?

'Oh, Jake' she implored, 'do come. Please. I want you to – to see things from my point of view! It's so different, out here, everything is a different colour, a different shape – even me! Can you not get a bit of time off?'

'You've taken too much yourself. You've overstayed your leave and you'll lose your job. Which is a pity – I thought you liked it.'

'Yes. I do like it.' And I'm going back to it, she thought, even if that does mean dealing with Morgan Richards. 'I'm going to call Robin and ask him if it's still open. Look, if you'll come here to me, then I'll go back there with you. How's that?'

Eventually, somewhat grudgingly, he agreed. 'Only it won't be overnight, Ciara. I'll have to put in a special request.' Hanging up on that unsatisfactory note, saying she would call him back in a few days, Ciara turned to Lee, feeling deflated.

'He doesn't seem in any mad rush to see me, Lee. He sounded so unenthusiastic, I wonder if we – if we're not further apart than ever.'

Sagely, Lee studied a huge bunch of bananas piled in her arms. 'Chill out, honey. Men hate surprises, is all. He'll come, you'll see. Probably just needs a few days to get his head around it.'

Mmm. Maybe. Or maybe not? Despondently, Ciara trudged with Lee through the dust to the car, wondering how much longer it would be before Lee decamped with Rory, leaving her high and dry. If that happened, she would have to go too, home alone, because the idea of surviving here solo was simply out of the question. Even if I'm growing up a lot, she thought, I haven't got that far yet, I could never be totally independent.

I'd be scared, here on my own without Lee. I'd go mad. How would I even *get* home, if she wasn't around to take me as far as the train? Please don't let her leave yet. Please let Jake arrive before she goes. Please let him come, and not faint when he sees the state of me. I can't get back to blonde, I'm out of cosmetics, my clothes are in tatters and I don't think I could get into high heels again at gunpoint. No way am I his glamour girl any more. Yet I want him to see me as I am now, the – the way nature intended. He's never seen me like that before in his life, and it's risky to let him. But I have to. It's time we found out whether our relationship goes more than skin deep.

A week. That was all Jake could offer, finally, but Ciara seized it with a whoop, pinning him down instantly – what day, what flight, what time? Somehow she would persuade Lee to take her to Ho Chi Minh City, all the way to the airport to meet him, he couldn't possibly endure that awful train journey.

'Don't be silly. I'll rent a car.'

'Uh – we're kinda out in the wilds, Jake –'

'A jeep, then. Put Lee on, so she can give me directions.'

Glumly, Ciara got the message. He thought her incapable of giving them herself. And worse, he was right. Putting Lee on the line, she stood back with that recurrent childlike feeling, while the adults talked over her head. There are so many things, she conceded, I still can't do. It must be a pain for other people to have to do them for me. But I'm going to learn, going to get a much better grip on my life in future. From here on in, I'm not going to be just a pretty face. It causes too much work for everyone else.

'Okay' said Lee, hanging up, 'all sorted. He's going to drive down here from the airport – brave man! He must be mad about you, to come all this way for a week.'

'Oh – I hadn't thought of it like that. It is a long way, isn't it.'

'Ciara. There are men who wouldn't cross the street for their wives, never mind hack their way down here to the back of beyond for them. I just hope it's going to be worth his while, is all.'

Cheerfully, Lee laughed; but Ciara bit her lip, wondering whether it was or not. For this amount of inconvenience, Jake was surely entitled to expect a substantial reward. A whole new take on their marriage. But then, wasn't that what marriage was supposed to be about: a lot of give and take, on both sides?

'Oh by the way' Lee added nonchalantly, 'Rory and I have decided we need a little fix of home comforts. We're going to check into a civilised hotel in town and leave you two love-birds to mind the hut for us.'

Scruffy, sweaty and visibly disgruntled, Jake arrived some days later in a cloud of dust. Cutting the engine of his rented jeep, he sat at the steering wheel, taking in the encampment as if surveying the aftermath of nuclear war. Trembling with nerves, Ciara stood on the splintering verandah of Lee's tiny abode, unable to speak or move, waiting for him to spot her. Waiting for any reaction at all; but nothing happened. Continuing to sit in shock, Jake seemed to be staring right through her.

He's horrified, she saw. He's exhausted and bewildered and – and he doesn't recognise me. He thinks he's come to the wrong place, made some dreadful mistake.

I hope he hasn't. I really hope he hasn't. Hope I haven't, either.

'Jake?' Eventually, summoning strength, she raised her hand, waving to him, hearing the strange pitch of her voice as a whole slew of emotions flooded through her, nailing her to the spot. She couldn't move if a tiger were to leap from the trees.

Frowning, he squinted over the wheel of the car, gaped, and then opened the door, getting out slowly, cautiously, as if the ground might melt from under him. For a moment they stood facing each other, and she saw all the disbelief in his eyes as he tried to match his wife to the vision that stood before him.

'Ciara?'

'Yes! Yes!' Suddenly, her voice was working. 'It's me – oh, Jake, it's so good to see you! I'm so happy you're here!' And her feet were flying over the bare earth to him, her arms hauling him into a hug. 'I've missed you – are you all right – I – you – oh!'

Hurling herself at him, she clutched him fiercely, every pore in her skin absorbing both his familiarity and his strangeness. How long had it been, since she'd wanted him like this – wanted him solely for himself, to herself? Looking up into his face, she smiled hugely; and only then did he suddenly smile in return, looking down into her eyes with something that made her legs quiver.

'Hello, lady. Nice to meet you. I'm looking for my wife, Mrs Lunny. Would you happen to know where she is?'

Half laughing, half crying, she thumped his chest. 'Jake, you fool, stop it! I know I must look different, but –'

Standing back, putting a hand on her shoulder, he peered into her face and whistled. 'Different? But you can't be Ciara. You're not my wife. Don't believe a word of it. Has she been kidnapped, what have you done with her? Hand her over immediately.'

'Oh, *Jake*! Do I look as bad as all that?'

Another long stare. And then, to her consternation, he exploded laughing. 'No, you don't look bad! You just look like you've been miscast in *South Pacific* . . . Ciara, you cannot seriously be wearing a sarong, cannot seriously be here in this – this –!' Words failing him, he tried again. 'And since when has Ciara Lunny been a brunette?'

'Uh . . . since the day she was born, actually. Sorry. I'll get back to blonde as soon as I can.'

'Right. And who knows, maybe you'll even rediscover a taste for shoes some day too?'

Looking down at her bare feet, she thought of her shoes. More than sixty pairs, neatly racked in the closet at home. Yes, she had had a taste for shoes.

'I'm sure I will. Maybe not quite as avid as before, but . . . Jake, are you tired, are you hungry? You must be shattered. It's so good of you, to come all this way . . . there's some pineapple . . . the river water is really clear and fresh . . .'

Apprehension was making her babble, and he was looking at her in that old Jake way, as if she were one of the children, breathless when they were little, sweet and amusing. But not to be trusted with anything serious.

'I'm fine, Ciara. Just getting my head around the shock, is all. I had no idea you were living in such – such primitive conditions! What on earth is all this?'

Wide-eyed, he gazed around from one timber hovel to the next, taking in the tents, the makeshift laundry lines, the heat haze hanging like gauze between the trees. 'Have you lost your mind? And where's Lee?'

'Lee has gone off with her new man. Left me here while she

265

checks into a hotel a hundred miles away – uh, that's the nearest one there is. Said she wanted a blast of air conditioning and cool sheets and a very long bubble bath. We can have her house to ourselves.'

'*House?* You mean that *hovel?*' Appalled, he squinted at it, and she tugged at his bare forearm, slick with sweat.

'It's okay, really, you'll get used to it – if I did, anyone can! Come and sit down, have a drink.'

'Okay. I could use one. But first, let me get my stuff. And yours.' Freeing himself from her grasp, he turned back to the jeep, rummaged in it and extracted two bags, his suitcase plus one of her own, the same Samsonite she'd taken to London with Lee. It looked wildly cosmopolitan, and seemed to weigh a ton.

'Here' he said, trundling it up to the palm-thatched shack, 'I thought you might want a change of clothes by now.' And boy, his tone conveyed, was I ever right.

Once, she would have hurled herself on it, shrieking with joy. Now, she simply kissed his cheek, clicked it open and smiled. 'My black linen dress! And my Donna Karan shirt! And make-up, perfume, nail polish . . . oh, Jake, thank you. How good of you to think of all this.'

There was a thoughtful pause, in which he looked at her speculatively. 'Well – I never knew *you* to think of much else.'

Whoo! But it didn't sound accusatory; more a statement of fact. One that might, she conceded, be justified?

'Maybe I didn't ever think of much else. But Jake, that was my job. Looking good, looking like a proper pilot's wife. Glamorous, successful. I was only doing my best, you know? For you, for us both.'

Thoughtfully, he nodded. 'Yes. I've had a bit of time to think about all that, Ciara, since you've been gone . . .

266

maybe you were only doing your best.' Plunging his hands into his pockets, he stood looking at her, as if debating whether to confess something, get it off his chest. Something he'd had time to think over on the long journey – or even for weeks, since she'd been gone? His stance was somehow intent.

'Maybe I should have appreciated that more, and expected less of – you – in – in other ways. Maybe I was asking too much of you, that day I piled you with all those books when you'd never even read the basics. Maybe I had a bit of a nerve, actually, to demand so much of you, all because I was having a mid-life crisis and – and . . .'

Abruptly, his voice trailed off, and he stood looking at her bemused, running his hand through his hair, curling damply in the heat.

'And what?'

No answer. Instead he continued to stand in silence, breathing deep lungfuls of the warm air, turning to contemplate the tall fronds of greenery concealing the beach and ocean beyond. Not pushing him further, she waited, letting him work through whatever was happening in his head.

'Ciara. I have to tell you, this is the very last place in the world I want to be. It's hot and sticky and bloody awful, it's messing up my work, it has taken for ever to get here and I am exhausted, but I had to do it. I had to come to see you, to talk to you –'

She nodded. 'I need to talk to you, too, Jake.'

'To talk about . . . something . . . Roisin said.'

Roisin? She felt as if he'd produced a blade and slashed her with it.

'Roisin Harte? Oh, no, oh, Jake – you've only just arrived! Do we have to start in on her already?' Just one day, she thought; I so much wanted to have just this one day at least with him, without that little witch coming between us. Could she not even leave us that much to ourselves?

'No' he said, sounding suddenly weary. 'No, we don't, Ciara. We don't have to say anything more about her until I've had a very long sleep and recovered from the total disorientation I am feeling. Is there – uh – is there anywhere to sleep?'

He looked so doubtful, and so tired too, she abandoned her suitcase full of goodies, hastening to his side. 'Yes. Of course there is. Just a mattress on the floor, but there are pillows and a mosquito net, it's much more comfortable than it looks. Come on, let's get you to it.'

As she led him into the hut she felt a frisson, and wondered: did he want to fall fast asleep alone, or . . . what? From nearly a year ago, a memory welled up, of the day he'd come home from a long flight and she'd run him a bath, only to find him deep asleep by the time it was ready. That same night they'd gone to dinner with the Hartes, and she'd found out about Roisin. Since then, they had never again slept together.

But as they made their way inside Lee's cabin he slid his arm around her waist, and kissed her sunburned cheek.

'Thanks, Ciara. Thanks for being so patient, for putting up with me. For putting up with so much, for so long.'

And they sank down together onto the mattress, and he was out like a light. But his arm wrapped tight around her, pinning her to his side, as if he had been missing her for a very long time.

'So much, Jake. I've discovered so much, learned so much, changed so much . . . it's really strange. We've been on so

268

many holidays over the years, but this is the first time I feel like I'm actually travelling.'

In the pearly morning, fresh from a swim, he was sitting propped against a tree trunk, wearing only shorts and an enigmatic look. Crosslegged beside him, Ciara sat holding his hand, feeling his wedding ring dig into her finger. Even if he'd questioned the worth of their wedding ceremony, at least he'd never thrown that away.

Thoughtfully, he looked at her. 'What makes you feel that way?'

She reflected. 'Well, this place is so very far away from home. It feels so foreign, so fresh, and there are absolutely no distractions at all. I only intended to stay long enough to see Lee, but then . . . I can't explain what happened. I just seemed to get sucked in, get talking, and thinking, get interested in all sorts of new ideas. In a way, it's kind of like a health farm! Only not just for the body – for the soul, too.'

'Dear God. This is worse than I thought. I had no idea you had a soul.'

He grinned, and ruefully she grinned with him. 'Neither did I! But I must have, because something has been happening to it, I can feel it stretching and flexing as if it were doing exercises, it reminds me of the babies kicking when I was pregnant – how are they, Jake? Have you seen Mike lately, or Tara?'

He smiled. 'Yes. I've seen Tara. She and I spent Easter together at home. Just talking, hanging out. We went bowling, to the movies, played a bit of tennis, ate pizza and drank wine . . . Ciara, I think she misses you very badly.'

Her eyes widening, she felt something flinch inside her. 'Do you? Does she? I thought she was sick of me, hated my – my quest for eternal youth! Which, I hope she'll be happy to hear, is over.'

269

'What?! You can't be serious. Ciara Lunny is trading in her plastic surgeon for her pension book? Barbie is joining the *Golden Girls*?'

'Nooo! Barbie will soon be back to blonde and getting her nails fixed. But meanwhile she's been thinking a bit. I heard the most lovely song here one night, and then a guy read a poem that – that did something to me. Touched some chord, opened up something in my head, gave me a glimpse of what might be going on in yours. Maybe I needed to come all this way to get a proper view, to see you clearly, see things from your point of view? I'm not the only one who's changing, Jake. You are, too. You've been working your butt off for years to support us all and – and you need a bit of support, now, if you're going through a difficult patch. As does Tara. She needs to be let enjoy her youth without her mother trying to steal it from her, trying to hog the limelight. I feel I should listen more to her, and to you . . . I don't know the first thing about Egypt, but I'll go there with you if you like. Maybe we could take Tara, too. I'll even try to read those damn books you gave me.'

He squeezed her hand. 'It's okay. You don't have to. I was trying to mould you, to do my own little bit of cosmetic surgery on you. Trying to turn you into another Roisin instead of letting you be yourself. You've been a wonderful wife in so many other ways, Ciara, maybe it was greedy of me to want more. I'm sorry if it was.'

Looking into his eyes, she saw he was sincere. But so was she, determined not to let this precious time together go to waste, the first peaceful, uninterrupted time they'd had for years.

'No. It's time there was something more, to me! I've been learning yoga, meditating, accepting that I'm halfway

270

through my life and, try as I might, there can't be any replay of the first act, it wasn't a rehearsal. I have to move on, can't ride the bike backwards. It can only go forwards. I'd like to go somewhere beautiful, somewhere worth the effort . . . and I'd like to go there with you. If you still want me to?'

It was a risky question, one she hadn't meant to ask so suddenly or bluntly, and she shuddered inwardly. But he smiled.

'You mean, on a tandem? Pedal together? Ha! You only ever rode an exercise bike before, at the gym, going nowhere.'

'Well, I've been riding a real one here, and doing a lot of other things too, that you wouldn't believe. Been attending a kind of masterclass, as Lee says. Nobody made me, I just got drawn into it. But it's time I went home, if – if anyone would like me to, if anyone still needs me?'

Silence. A long, speculative silence, in which he dropped her hand, plucked absently at a blade of grass and began to fritter at it, peeling it intently into long, curling fronds.

'Well, Tara still needs you. She may be nearly twenty, but she's young for her age, far less mature than Mike and more – more vulnerable. As for me . . . Ciara, I know you don't want to hear about Roisin, but I have to tell you what she said. About you.'

'Me? You've been discussing me with her?'

'No. She's been discussing you with me. I'd never talk about you, but it was she who raised the subject. Apparently Mike told her brother you'd come on this trip, and he told her, and she – she told me I'd better watch my step.'

'What?'

'Mmm. She wondered whether you might have wanted to get away from me, might have had enough of my mid-life crisis. Which is what it is, Ciara. A crisis. You're not the only one who's been thinking. I have, too. And it has struck me quite forcibly that I might not be quite the husband you wanted me to be. That I might never be that man, ever.'

Frowning, she could hardly look at him, wondering at the oddly tentative note in his voice. Not crisp, clear, soon-to-be-Captain Lunny, at all.

'Jake, I – I'm not sure what you mean?'

'I mean I'm forty-three years of age, and let's face it, if I haven't got promoted by now then maybe I never will. I know you always wanted me to go as far up the career ladder as I could, but younger guys than me have got further, faster . . . don't ask me why, Ciara, but my promotion prospects do not seem to be exactly sizzling. Plus, there's the money I lost on the stock market. I guess that's the risk you take, when you gamble. I gambled because I had two children doing expensive college courses and a high-maintenance wife. But it didn't pay off. Which leaves you stuck with a husband who is not quite the shiny trophy of your dreams. One who can still support you, yes, but not keep you in the luxury to which you aspire. One whose career can't be played like an ace at dinner parties, to trump all the competition.'

Oh. Oh . . . so that was what Roisin Harte had meant, was it? She'd been trying to tell Jake that he had no future? That his vain, flighty wife wouldn't want him back if he wasn't coming with lots of money and status?

Stunned, Ciara sat contemplating it, turning it over in her mind, conceding that yes, maybe her expectations of Jake had always been very high. Too high?

And what bloody business was that of Roisin Harte's?! Suddenly she was furious, rage rushing through every vein in her body. How dare Roisin Harte, how dare that smart-ass little whippersnapper say, or even think, such things! Things that had damn all to do with her, things she knew even less about, at twenty-one bloody years of age!

Time elapsed, between them; time in which neither of them spoke, knowing they were assessing their marriage, that it was crunch time. Ciara O'Kane had married a high-flyer with a fast-track career: could she be happy, now, with this middle-aged, middle-income man, his prospects receding, his mind wandering, his eyes betraying disappointment in himself?

Could *he* be happy with her? He'd married a young, sexy, elegant girl, pretty as a picture; today she was forty, with little or no substance to her, only the vaguest new inkling that there might be more to life than shopping and spending and cutting a dash. With a toyboy yapping at her heels, and a pretty poor track record, all things considered.

And yet, not entirely without hope. After a long interval, gazing out over the sea, she touched his hand.

'Jake. I've been living here almost literally on fresh air, for weeks now. I've learned to do without nearly all the things that used to seem essential. I've scarcely even looked in a mirror, haven't given one single thought to our house or possessions or social life. Normality, when I get back to it, will be utter luxury by comparison. I had no notion, before, of the comfort in which we live! Plus, I have a job to go back to. Not a career – I'd never have the brains for one of those – but a job I like, that does actually pay a bit of money. Yes, it is a shame we've lost so much on the stock market, but it's not the end of the world. We can cope. Maybe nobody will be getting a new Mercedes or a Dior wardrobe, but nobody will starve either. So why don't we just write off our losses and start over? I wish you'd stop worrying about it, Jake. I really wish you would. Money doesn't matter as much as it used to, whereas you matter a lot more. Please let's just forget whatever is behind us.'

What went through his face? Some mixture of surprise, and emotion, something she couldn't quite read. Resolutely, she ploughed on.

'And as for your promotion – yes, that is a shame. I don't deny that I did want to be married to Captain Lunny. Now, it doesn't look as if I am going to be. But instead, I might be going to be married to a man who has less responsibility, more time to spend with his wife if he still wants to spend it with her. I'd rather be your wife than your widow – my God, Jake, how many men's careers kill them, how many have heart attacks from all the stress! If you're not going any further up the ladder, maybe it's a blessing in disguise. And no, I wouldn't have seen it that way a year ago. But that's the way I see it now. I love you and I'd far rather have a healthy, happy husband than a frazzled, exhausted wreck. Even if I don't always understand you, I do still love you.'

Weight lifting. Once, she'd only done it at the gym; now she saw with astonishment that she was doing it for real, taking some huge weight off his shoulders, setting it down and rolling it away. Not saying a word, he sat looking at her; looking for a very long time, examining her face. Her bare face, ungilded, with the eyelids not smoothed out, the nose not tilted, the chin not sculpted. Unblinking, she let him look.

Whatever shows in it in the future, she thought, will be all my own work, and nature's; not the work of any surgeon. The problem with plastic surgery is that it's plastic. The stuff Barbie's made of. I'm a grown woman. A living, breathing human being. Not plastic, not a doll, any more.

Is that enough for Jake Lunny? Are we going to go on

together, or – what? I so much want to go on with him. Despite his confusion, despite Roisin Harte, despite all his problems. Or maybe even because of them. I do love this man, and I do want to stay with him. But there's one more thing I have to tell him.

'Jake?'

'Yes?'

'You know, I – I sometimes get really angry with you. There are times I could hit you over the head. Until now, I've tried not to let you know that, because I was supposed to be the perfect wife and – and anger is not a pretty picture. But I can't pretend any more. There are times when you make me mad as hell.'

'Really?'

'Yes, really. Especially when you treat me like a child, talk down to me as if I were totally dumb – I'm not, you know! In this past year alone I've got a new job and learned to use a computer and survived two months in this godforsaken gypsy encampment and – and if you ever try to pat me on the head again it will be entirely at your own risk.'

Indignantly, she paused for breath, and he laughed. 'All right! I'll try to remember that. You can wallop me if I get out of line – and you'll be sorry in turn, if you get out of line.'

'Me? What have I ever done?'

'You've had an affair with that young fella, is what. I did *not* sleep with Roisin Harte, but you did sleep with Morgan Richards. Didn't you?'

'Yes.' Guiltily, she nodded. 'But only because I thought . . . you . . . it's your fault, Jake, you started all this!'

'I did. And now I'm ending it, okay? If we're going to work out our relationship then we're going to have to forget about scoring points. Forget all the distractions, the external things, and concentrate far more on us. I want us to stay married, Ciara, but not because some priest said we had to twenty years ago. We're not the same people we were twenty years ago. We need to establish who we are today.'

Yes. She could see that neither one of them was the same as before. Try as they might, they could never turn back the clock. So why try? Why wear yourself out attempting the impossible? It would be so much easier to go forward than back. Go with the flow, as Lee would say.

Sitting on the sand, taking his hand, she raised her cheek to him and puckered her lips, flirting with her eyes. 'If you give me a kiss, I'll give you my word. We'll work on our marriage, Jake, and try to mend it. Make it stronger, make it *real*.'

Gravely, he nodded. And drew her to him, and kissed her. It was a very long, slow kiss, memorably real, and more beautiful than she'd ever dreamed a kiss could be.

Of all the romantic hotels she'd ever stayed in with Jake, Ciara thought none could or ever would compare with Lee's little timber shack. No pool, no bar, no room service, no chic restaurant to dress up for: and yet it was bliss. 'A second honeymoon' Jake said, but she shook her head.

'No. More like a first. We were only kids when we went to Puerto Banus, all I cared about was getting a tan and showing off my wedding ring, dressing up at night to go out with the good-looking guy I'd bagged. It was – it was playschool! Whereas this time it's only the two of us, there's nobody to impress, nothing to distract us. I feel as if I'm getting to know you for the first time.'

He smiled. 'If I said you had a beautiful body, would you hold it against me?'

'Ha! I would . . . but it won't always be beautiful, Jake. Some

276

day it'll be old and frail and . . . will you still want me then, d'you think?'

Circling an arm around her, he held her to him, considering the question. 'Yes. I hope I will. I'll be old and maybe frail too, but so long as our minds are active, we still have things to do and talk about, we'll muddle along. I won't mind your wrinkles if you don't mind mine – I'd much rather you looked lived in than looking like there's nobody home.'

She glimpsed what he meant. That marble look of artificial beauty, taut with tension in case anything slipped or cracked. What a relief, not to have to get new lips or eyelids every year, after all! He was giving her permission to relax, to be herself, to grow into whoever or whatever she wanted to be. Her spirit would keep him by her side, not her surgery. Snuggling up to him, she murmured in his ear.

'Jake?'

'Mmm?'

'Would you do me a little favour?'

'I would. What is it?'

'Would you drive me to a phone! I need to call Robin to find out if my job's still there. I've been away so long, I'm petrified he's given it to somebody else.'

It was an extremely long drive into town, but it was worth it: Robin sounded thrilled to hear Ciara. Expecting him to be angry at her long absence, she could hardly believe her ears.

'Oh, Ciara, thank God. I was afraid you were never coming back. We have a temp in, but she's not half as good as you. When can I expect you?'

Next week, she said, and hung up hugely relieved, elated. 'Jake! You won't believe what he said – he said he can't wait for me to come back, that the temp isn't half as good as me!'

Only a small compliment, but she was thrilled, incredulous

were leaving. Reality would involve his work and hers, with no comforting funds in the bank to fall back on, no busy social life any more because, after a friend like Lee, most of the others seemed pointless. The Hartes would have to go, the golf club gang was already gone, she would have to be more discerning and start putting quality before quantity. And then there would be Mike and Tara to work on, to convince that yes, they still had a proper family, a home worth visiting. Parents they need no longer resent, or be ashamed of.

Of the twins, Tara would be by far the more sceptical, more difficult, and yet it was Tara Ciara thought of now, suddenly longing to see her. Moody, chippy Tara, throwing tantrums, pouting, sulking and . . . and so badly in need of her mother. Of both parents, of some stability and security in her stormy life. No doubt they would have many more rows, soon she would produce some godawful boyfriend or fail her exams or do God only knew what provocative thing, but . . . but if you loved someone, you had to keep trying. That's all you can do, she thought looking at Jake beside her: keep on trying.

Tara is a gorgeous girl, so pretty in that wild way of hers. But I want her to feel as good on the inside as she looks on the outside. I want her to be happy in her skin. The next bit of surgery won't be about reconstructing lips or noses or anything else, it'll be about reconstructing our relationship. I have to let her fly free and yet I have to keep her close, too. She needs to know that we'll always be there for her – both of us, Mum and Dad. With a temperament like hers, she'll probably get through dozens of men, need a haven to come home to when things are falling apart.

And then some day she'll finally marry some poor guy, and make his life a living hell, and have babies. Some day, I will be a grandmother.

Jesus. Am I ready for that? Ready for the grey hair and babysitting and raspberry purée all down the front of my silk shirt? Baking apple pies, reading bedtime stories, staying home with Junior while Tara whirls off to parties with her hunky husband?

I don't care whether he's hunky or not. I don't even care if he loses his fortune on the stock market, like Jake Lunny. If he's good to her, if he's half as warm and kind and patient as Jake Lunny, she will be a very lucky girl. All I ever want to see in her face is happiness – so she'd better marry someone with stamina. Someone with staying power, who'll stick with her even when she's driving him mad.

I never knew I was driving Jake mad. Never realised I was such a triumph of style over substance. Even now, I can't wait to get to the hairdresser and the beauty salon and get glossed up again – oh, bliss. But from now on there'll be somebody inside the shiny wrapper, a woman with the sense to realise that getting old isn't a disaster.

It's an achievement. It's survival. It's growth and progress and why would anyone want to fend off any of those things? It says hey, look at me, I'm still here!

And Jake is still here, too. Despite everything, he's still with me. This is a long trip home, but we're getting there. I can't wait to arrive, to see my children, see whether there's any e-mail from Lee, see how things are going at work.

Those are all the things I want to see, next time I look in a mirror. The reflection of friends and family and a life going forward, being lived to the full.

And then she must have dozed off, because next thing the plane was landing, and she and Jake were decanting disorientated into the airport, and in the arrivals area somebody was shouting, wildly waving flowers.

281

'Mum! Dad! You're home!'

And there was Tara breathlessly running up, hair flying, hurling herself into their arms, engulfing Ciara on a tide of joyful tears.

'Yes, darling, at last, Dad and I are home.'

'But you look so – so different!'

'Yes. I am different. I hope I'm very different now, in ways not even visible to the naked eye.'